GUARDING
Gwen

New York Times & *USA Today* Bestselling Author

CYNTHIA
EDEN

PROLOGUE

"You keep your damn hands off her, you understand?" Simon Forrest snarled as rage pumped through him. "Gwen belongs to me."

The prick that he'd just decked slowly pushed up from the sandy beach as the waves pounded into the shore. "You sure about that?" Xavier Gray asked, swiping his hand over his bloody lower lip. "Because Gwen was sure as hell acting like she wanted me."

Gwen tried to lunge past Simon and attack the guy. "You are such a *lying—*"

Simon caught her, wrapped his arms around her stomach, and pulled her so that her back was against his chest. Putting his mouth near her ear, he whispered, "I got him, baby. I got him."

She didn't relax against him—Simon knew she was far too pissed for that—but he could feel a bit of the tension leave her.

Carefully, he moved Gwen to the side. He didn't want her getting caught in the crossfire. The fight had begun in the nearby club when that piece of crap had thought he had some kind of right to put his hands on Gwen. On Gwen's ass. Oh, hell, no.

The fight had spilled outside, and so had the crowd. At least two dozen folks formed a tight circle around them. Simon recognized some of the faces—they'd recently graduated with Gwen—but the others were just strangers in the normally quiet beach town on the Florida Coast.

"The lady isn't interested in you," Simon said, his voice ringing out loud and clear. "So don't put your hands on her again."

Xavier laughed and spat blood on the sand. "I think she likes it when my hands are on her. She's been playing this game with me for years, acting like a tease who wants me, and I'm gonna give her exactly what she—"

Simon was done. Just fucking done. He didn't waste more energy on talking, he simply attacked. He drove straight at the bastard and hit him hard and deep, exactly like he'd been trained on the football field. Simon tackled that jerk and trapped Xavier beneath him. He pulled back so that he could drive his fist at the guy. The fool barely fought back because Xavier was too used to pushing around those weaker than him. Too used to his rich daddy's money protecting him from the world.

Not this time.

Simon was pretty sure Xavier's nose broke beneath his fist.

"Simon." Gwen's voice. Soft. Her fingers curled around his arm, and his head whipped toward her.

"Stop, Simon. Let's get out of here."

For her, anything. He immediately backed away from the guy. The crowd was whispering. He barely spared those people a glance. Gwen. She was all that mattered.

His fingers locked with hers, and he walked away from the fool bleeding in the sand. The crowd retreated so that Simon could cut a clear path through them.

"*You'll be fucking sorry, Simon Forrest!*" Xavier's bellow followed him. "I'll make you *pay!*"

Simon didn't stop. What the hell could the guy do to him? Simon was shipping out tomorrow. The Navy was waiting.

His hold tightened on Gwen's hand. *I ship out, and I leave her.*

He took her to his motorcycle. He climbed on, and then Gwen slipped onto the seat behind him. Her body curled around his even as her arms wrapped around his stomach. The engine growled to life, and the ride shot them out into the night. A million stars glittered overhead, and Gwen—his Gwen held tight to him. He drove and drove until Simon got them to *their* place. A private stretch of beach that only the locals visited. He braked, killed the engine, and shoved down his kickstand.

They left their helmets behind, and he walked with Gwen down to the water's edge. They hadn't spoken during the whole ride. That was the way it was for him and Gwen. Sometimes, they didn't need to talk at all. They could just be together, and he knew that she understood him.

What the hell am I going to do without her?

Simon turned toward Gwen. The wind blew her long, dark hair over her shoulders. She stared up at him. Beautiful Gwen. *His* Gwen.

But...only his for a little while longer.

"Do you have to go?" Her voice was low, sad.

Yeah, he had to go. He'd already done all the paperwork. Set the gears in motion. He was nineteen years old, and he had to get a plan for his future. He had nothing to offer Gwen, and she—hell, she had a scholarship waiting. In a few weeks, summer would be over. She'd be going to FSU.

And he'd...

*I've always been good at fighting. Always been strong. The one thing my father used to say about me...*It was time he put his skills to use. Time to make a difference. Time to become someone better.

He used to not care about things like that. About being better. But that had been before Gwen.

His hand lifted and slid over her cheek. There was something important she needed to understand. No matter what else happened. "If you ever need me, baby, I'm there. I'd lie for you, steal, hell, I'd even kill for you."

Gwen gave a little gasp and stepped back. "I don't want that. I'd never want you to do anything like that." She lifted his right hand. "Your knuckles are all messed up."

Because he'd pounded the jerk—

"I didn't need you to fight him. What if he calls the cops on you? What if—"

"He took the first swing in that club. Everyone there saw it. I doubt even his daddy's money could buy him out of that one."

Her fingers traced over his knuckles, and then she lifted his hand to her mouth. Her lips pressed gently to the skin.

Gwen. How was he going to walk away from her? It was going to gut him to leave her.

"You don't have to go. You can stay with me. We can make things work. We can—"

I have nothing. He couldn't tell her that. A guy had to have some pride. A girl like Gwen deserved so much more. And, maybe, maybe one day, he'd have more to give her.

"We can't, Gwen." His voice was flat. Too hard.

She flinched and dropped his hand.

"You have school. I have the Navy."

Her head tipped forward. "I just want you."

God...He reached for her. Pulled her against him. Tipped back her head. He couldn't imagine ever not wanting Gwen. But it was the wrong time. So wrong. And he couldn't keep her when he had nothing.

His lips lowered to hers. He kissed her. Held her.

Loved her.

***

They were still on the beach when the sun rose. He hadn't been able to let her go, not on their last night together.

But...

The air seemed oddly cold for summer. And the waves weren't crashing quite as hard any longer. Gwen sat beside him, fitting him so perfectly, and when she looked at him with her gorgeous, golden eyes...

I have to let her go. "It was a mistake," he blurted.

Gwen frowned at him. Then hope lit her eyes. "You're not leaving? You're staying—"

God, baby, no. "This was a mistake, Gwen." This...them being locked so tight to each other. The emotions that seemed to swamp him sometimes. "We're too young." She'd just graduated that June. "I don't have anything to offer you." And it wasn't about not loving her enough, she had to get that, didn't she? She had to see—

Gwen stood and brushed the sand off her hands. "The only thing I wanted was you."

That wasn't enough.

Her lower lip trembled as she stared at him. "But I don't get that, do I?"

His heart iced as he scrambled to his feet. "Gwen—"

"Take me home, Simon."

Her home...but no one was there. Her grandmother had died that spring, and her parents hadn't been part of her life. Her dad had been gone for as long as she could remember and her mom—Gwen never talked about her mom. Another reason why she was going to FSU. So she could start fresh.

She turned away and began walking up the beach. He stared after her. He wanted to tell her that he'd be back. But...

But as he watched her walk away, he couldn't manage to say a word. And the ice in his heart seemed to spread through his whole body.

CHAPTER ONE

"I want Simon Forrest." Gwenevere Soloman sat in the leather chair, her long legs crossed in front of her, casually swinging one high-heeled foot. The shoes were Louboutin, black on top and fiery red on the bottom. They screamed money and style, just like the rest of her outfit. The pencil skirt and the designer blouse had been custom-made for her. Gwenevere—or really, just plain Gwen—knew that she looked wealthy and in control. That had been the plan, after all. To appear to have her shit together.

When in truth...she was freaking the hell out. It was a good thing that she made her living as an actress. Otherwise...

The man across the desk cleared his throat. His dark eyes studied her and his handsome face showed his curiosity. "Ah, Ms. Soloman, clients don't generally get to request specific security personnel."

"Gwen, please. We'll be working together, so let's not be formal." Her heart was racing in her chest, but her voice was perfectly calm. "I came to Wilde Protection and Securities because I was told you were the best in the business. That you handled high profile clients with the utmost discretion." *Don't show fear. Don't.*

Eric Wilde—the man who *was* Wilde—inclined his dark head toward her. "Yes, we are the best."

No modesty there.

"But you just came in from the street and you told me that you wanted my Vice President—not some regular agent—to personally handle your case." He gave her an apologetic smile. "That's not how things work here."

Okay. Not good. She slowly uncrossed her legs and leaned forward. She put one well-manicured hand on his desk. "I will pay whatever is necessary, but I need Simon Forrest."

Eric's eyes narrowed as he seemed to assess her. "Why him, in particular?"

Because they had a past. Not a good one. Actually, a rather messy and extremely painful past, but Simon Forrest was the most lethal bastard that she knew. And in this particular situation, lethal was needed.

"Money doesn't matter to me." The words were so easy. She knew he'd have no clue that, once, money had mattered. Mattered so very much. Once, she'd had nothing. She'd been so desperate that she would have done anything to survive.

But that girl...she was dead. Long gone. Gwen gave Eric another broad smile. "I need the services of Wilde, and do you really want me to leave this office and spread word to my friends that you refused *me*?" That sounded way arrogant. Unfortunate, but necessary. And it was a total bluff. She had no intention of telling anyone that she'd ever visited this high-rise office in Atlanta.

Eric weighed her words. He studied her with his head cocked. Could he tell she was bluffing? Oh, jeez, no, he couldn't. *Could not.* Or at least, he'd better not be able to tell. She'd won a freaking Academy Award last year. She could surely fool one security guy. Right?

Eric pushed a button on the phone that perched on his desk. "Dennis..."

Dennis was his assistant. The guy had tripped when he'd first seen Gwen. Cutely charming.

"Get Simon in here, would you?" Eric continued, his voice brisk. "I have a case that I need him to consult on."

Consult? No, Simon needed to *take* her case. And she wasn't leaving this office until she got him.

Eric leaned back in his chair. Crossed his arms over his chest. "Why." Not a question. More of a demanding growl.

She blinked. Looked innocent. "He was recommended to me."

Eric shook his head. "Try again."

"Excuse me?" She thought her frown of confusion was a nice touch.

"No one recommended Simon. He's a dangerous asshole that most people avoid. His people skills are...less than desirable. He growls more than he talks, and the guy lives for adrenaline."

Okay, yes, that was the Simon she'd known and loved.

No, no, I didn't love him. A teenage crush. That crush had ended long ago. And he'd sure as hell walked away from her fast enough. Walked, run. Whatever. Then he'd *stayed* away. Long after the point when he should have come back.

But that didn't matter. She'd moved on. So had he. And she would have stayed out of his life permanently, except...

Well...

Her past had come back to bite her in the ass.

"Ms. Soloman?" Eric prompted.

"I told you, call me Gwen. Everyone does." She dropped her smile. It wasn't working on the guy, anyway. What was he? Made of stone? Ice? "I know that Simon is dangerous. I heard that fact about him." She rolled one shoulder in a careless shrug. "I happen to need a little danger in my life."

If anything, his dark gaze became even more intense. "Tell me what's happening."

She glanced over her shoulder. The door was still shut. "Why not just wait for Simon? Then I only have to share the story once." And she could better keep track of her lies.

Eric exhaled on a long sigh. "You know that I can tear into your life and know every secret that you possess within about five or ten minutes? You understand that, don't you?"

Her head whipped back toward him. No, she most certainly had *not* understood that.

Eric lifted a brow. "It's kind of what I do. And a woman like you...a woman whose life is lived in the tabloids, well, it's not like you have a lot of deep, dark secrets anyway."

You'd be surprised. She'd managed to bury a whole lot of secrets. Too bad some of them had decided to crawl out of their graves.

The door opened behind her. She heard the faint squeak of the hinges.

"Where's the fire?" A deep, dark voice demanded. "I was working on a case with Julia, but Dennis said I had to drop everything and get my ass up here, pronto."

Chill bumps seemed to cover her. Gwen licked her lips and hoped like hell that her expression had remained contained. Eric's eyes were on her. He'd been studying her so carefully. He'd been—

"You know him," Eric said flatly.

Okay, Eric was good. Very good at watching people. She'd have to remember that trait for the future. But then, she'd come to Wilde because the firm was supposed to be the best. Score one for Eric.

Simon's footsteps padded closer. She hadn't looked at him yet. She should. Just get it over with. He'd probably changed in the years. Maybe he wouldn't be as handsome any longer. Maybe she could just look at him and not feel a single, solitary thing—

"Is this a new client—" Simon's words ended. Just stopped as he finally got a look at her. As he stared down at her, Gwen saw the absolute shock fill his green gaze. He shook his head, as if he couldn't quite believe what—no, *who*—he was seeing. Then... "Gwen?" He reached for her. Bent toward her and pulled her out of the chair. His hands wrapped around her shoulders, his grip tight, a little rough, and he stared at her as if—

"Uh, right. Figured as much," Eric noted dryly. "You two *do* know each other."

Simon's head had been lowering toward hers. His gaze had been on her mouth. Oh, no way. The guy hadn't thought he was going to kiss her? Not happening. She wanted his protection, his particular skill set...not his mouth.

Gwen raised her hands and pushed against his chest. His very *muscled* chest. Someone had been working out, hard. Even though he wore a fancy suit, she could feel the strength and heat of his body far too easily. "Let go."

He did, instantly. Simon stepped back and shook his head. "This isn't a dream?"

What?

"Because I swear, I've had dreams like this." But then his gaze cut toward a watchful Eric. "Only your ass is never in my dreams."

Eric's lips twisted. "Good to know."

Gwen backed away from Simon. "I'm not a dream. I'm a client." And, dammit, the years had been *kind* to Simon. More than kind. He was even more muscled than he'd been. Not a boy, but a man now. Wide shoulders. Powerful chest. Dark hair that was a little long. A square, chiseled jaw, perfect cheekbones, and a line of stubble on him that was just downright sexy.

He wore a suit, but looked rough and ready. Fierce.

Some things didn't change...

"A client?" Simon rolled back his shoulders. He shook his head. His gaze slid over her, and she could have sworn she felt the scorching heat of that look like a burn on her skin. "*Gwenevere.*"

"Gwen," she gritted out.

His gaze snapped back up to her face.

She lifted her chin. "You're in the protection business, aren't you?" She waved between him and a too-watchful Eric. "Well, I need protection. The best money can buy."

Simon's gaze went cold and hard. "Who's threatening you?"

Ah, that would be the question. "If I knew, then I would have taken care of him myself." She sat back down. Took her time about it. Crossed her legs. Swung her high-heeled foot. Noticed that Simon's gaze went straight to her legs.

And...heated.

Her heart jumped. No, no, dammit, this was going to be professional. The last thing she wanted to do was walk down that particular road with Simon Forrest again.

Her lips twisted as pain knifed into her heart. "At least it's good to know you remember me."

He leaned over her. Got all in her space as he caged her with his hands on either side of her chair. "A man doesn't forget a woman like you."

Oh, that was—

"Especially when your image is shoved at him twenty-four hours a day, on every TV set or movie screen in the area."

Had he just sounded bitter? Like he had a right to be bitter. She raked her gaze over him "If you don't like watching," she advised coldly, "turn the channel."

His features hardened.

Okay, this was *not* going as she'd planned. Maybe she hadn't planned well enough. Truth be told, she'd panicked. She'd been in Atlanta, filming a superhero flick that would not—could not—be named due to contractual issues, and when the latest threatening message had come to her, Gwen had freaked. She'd freaked and thought of the one person who could handle a mess like the one she was in.

She'd...oh, damn, it was humiliating, but she'd immediately gone running to her ex for help. An ex who hadn't spoken to her in years. An ex who apparently hated having her image "shoved at him." Her chin notched up. "Move your hands."

A muscle jerked in his jaw. That really sexy, stubble-covered, lickable jaw.

He moved his hands.

He backed up, and he took his delectable scent with him. A masculine, crisp scent.

She smoothed her perfectly smooth skirt. "This was a mistake. I shouldn't have come here. I don't think you are the right security firm to handle my...situation."

"Your situation?" Simon fired back. "What's wrong, baby? A sex tape about to hit the Internet? Want us to stop it for you?"

A sex...She laughed. Laughed at him and it actually felt good to laugh.

He didn't laugh with her. But then, he'd never really been the laughing type. *Always so serious and intense.* Intense was the keyword for Simon. Gwen tipped back her head and gazed up at him as he continued to glare. "Oh, Simon, really. A sex tape doesn't hurt anyone's career these days." She waved her hand vaguely in the air. "Sex tapes just make people *more* famous."

A snarl slipped from him.

Someone needed to relax. "But I don't need to be more famous. And I don't have a sex tape. Thanks for asking, though." She folded her hands and put them in her lap. Her gaze slid to Eric. Now that she was up-close and personal with her ex, she realized the error of her plan. Such a mistake. Why had she thought Simon could help save the day? The guy was pissed at her. *Who the hell knew why?* After all, he'd been the one to walk. But...

I don't know him. Not anymore. The old Simon would have immediately jumped to her defense. He'd always protected her, back in the day. From every threat out there. No one had hurt her, not when Simon was close.

Then he'd left, and he'd been the one to hurt her worst of all.

The past is over. Move the hell forward.

Instead of protecting her, Simon had entered the fancy office and immediately attacked.

Actually...Gwen thought about the situation for a moment. No, he'd...come in and tried to kiss her. That had been his first act.

Then he'd attacked.

And, jeez, she couldn't handle this drama. She liked to keep her drama on the movie set. "A mistake." She pushed to her feet again. Slid around him and headed for the door. "This was—"

"I've always been your mistake. We both know that."

His words stopped her cold. Gwen glanced back over her shoulder at him. Why would he say that? She'd never regretted anything they did.

His hands were fisted at his sides. His gaze burned as it held hers. "Why are you here, Gwen?"

Because I'm scared. No, terrified. Someone is watching me. All the time. Someone who knows my deepest, darkest secrets. Someone who wants to destroy me.

"I thought I could turn to an old friend for help," she said, voice halting. *Someone I could trust.* "But I see that I was wrong." She reached for the doorknob.

"*Stop.*" Eric's voice. Low but all authoritative. The guy was probably used to giving orders. She wasn't used to taking them. Not unless those orders came from a director on set. So, Gwen opened the door.

Dennis stood a few feet away, his eyes huge behind the lenses of his glasses. She started to stride past—

A warm, strong hand—with slightly callused fingertips—curled around her wrist. "Please, stop."

Simon's voice. Only it wasn't growling any longer. It was low and soft, almost tender.

A shudder slid over her body. For just a moment, she could so easily remember the way things had been. Back when she'd been eighteen and absolutely, completely obsessed with him.

Those days are long gone. You need him now for an entirely different reason. Use him and move the hell on.

Her head turned, and she found herself looking up into his eyes. His gaze practically blazed with emotion as he stared at her. And if she didn't know better, Gwen would swear...the man was staring at her as if he wanted to eat her alive.

"Uh, yes." Eric cleared his throat. "Simon, you and I need to talk privately for a moment. Gwen, why don't you sit back down in my office? I'll have Dennis bring you some coffee."

Simon's hold tightened on her.

Eric closed in. Tapped his shoulder. "Conference room," he prompted. "Let the pretty lady go. You and I are going to have an important business meeting *in the conference room.*"

Simon slowly let her go. As he freed her, his fingers slid along the inside of her wrist. Her pulse gave a fast and hard jerk. Did he feel it?

A cracking voice announced, "I'll get coffee!" Right. The assistant. Dennis.

Eric steered Simon down the hallway while Gwen returned to the office. Gwen sucked in some deep, much needed breaths, and when the assistant burst in with a giant grin on his face and a coffee mug gripped in his hand, she managed to give him a faint, grateful smile.

Even as she realized that her whole world was probably about to implode.

All of these years... and one touch from Simon could still stir desire within her. Dammit, if she was going to use him, she needed to be one hell of a lot more careful.

**

"What. In. The Hell?" Eric put his hands on his hips and glared at Simon. "Are you insane? Having some kind of breakdown that I need to know about? Because I *know* you didn't just antagonize the most famous actress in the world for shits and giggles!"

Simon winced. They were in one of the conference rooms at Wilde, and Eric was pissed. Obviously. Eric's voice wasn't loud. No, on the contrary, it was dead soft—always a bad sign. The angrier Eric got, the quieter he became. "She's not the most famous," Simon mumbled.

Eric's brows shot up. "Are you kidding me right now?"

He shrugged.

"Gwenevere Soloman is on the cover of every magazine out there, and she was in *five* movies last year. If word gets out that someone on my team is being a jackass to her...that crap will not look good for me."

Okay, yeah, he'd overstepped. He'd screwed up. But... "Since when do you care what some Hollywood celeb says about you? You've got more money than God. You don't need another client."

Eric stabbed a finger toward him. "I don't turn my back on people who need me. And *she* is scared."

Simon took a step back. He didn't like the idea of Gwen being scared. Didn't like the idea of *anything* bad ever happening to her.

Wasn't that the reason he'd stayed away from her for so long? Because he *was* the something bad. And her life was literally fairytale perfect without him. Only, if it really was perfect, then why was she at Wilde? "She has to have her own bodyguards." He scrubbed a hand over his face. His fingers sawed across the stubble on his jaw. Hell. He'd just come off one case from hell, and he knew he had to look like shit. *Of course,* Gwen would see him this way. She looked perfect, the sexiest thing he'd ever seen, while he'd probably seemed like some thug off the street.

"I think this is more than some bodyguard situation." Eric dropped his hand. "She came in and asked for you. Specifically, *for* you. She wanted *you* to take her case, and right before you stormed in and showed Ms. Soloman what a true ass you are, she had just told me that she'd be willing to pay any sum in order to get you to personally take her case."

Uh, that was odd. "She hates me."

"I can see why," Eric muttered. "Charm is not your strong suit."

He glowered at his friend. "I can be charming." Under the right circumstances. And those circumstances did not involve walking into Eric's office and coming face-to-face with Gwen. With *his* Gwen.

Holy fuck. She was even more gorgeous now. Even sexier. With that warm, golden complexion, with all of that thick, dark hair. Long and curling. Red, plump lips. High cheekbones. The faint mole near her right eye. A little mark he'd kissed so many times in the past. And her body. Damn. The woman had curves that went on for days. High, firm breasts. An hourglass figure with flaring hips. And her legs...he'd always loved her long legs. Her legs were freaking perfection, and Gwen in those fuck-me shoes...

How many times have I fantasized about seeing Gwen again?

Only this hadn't been a fantasy.

"A sex tape? Seriously?"

Oh. Eric was still talking. Simon tried to focus.

"You asked her about a sex tape?"

Simon closed his eyes. He should probably confess. "When it comes to Gwen, I'm a jealous bastard."

"You think?"

His eyes flew open. He glared.

"What is the history?" Eric demanded. "Wait, let me guess...lovers?"

"*Ancient* history."

"So ancient that you saw her and your first instinct was to try and kiss her?"

Okay, yes, guilty. The past and present had blurred for a moment. He'd messed up. Typical for when he was around Gwen.

"Gwen Soloman is important. Too important to screw with. So, can you keep your control and do the job with her?" Eric exhaled. "Or do you want me to refer her to someone else?"

If Gwen was in trouble, he would be the one helping her. Always. Fury grew within Simon as he tried to figure out just what was happening. Who could be hurting her? And why? "I want to help her." No, he *had* to help Gwen. Protecting her had always been as natural as breathing to him.

A smile came and went on Eric's lips. "Figured as much. But I also figured you needed to get some space before you jumped the woman."

Her skin had been softer than he remembered. Her eyes a deeper, darker gold. She'd smelled like sweet vanilla, and he'd been dying to pull her into his arms, to take her mouth with his, and make sure she wasn't a dream.

Instead, he'd insulted her, been an ass, and had the woman running for the door. Yep, way to reconnect with the woman who'd owned his heart when he'd been nineteen. But he wasn't a punk kid anymore. And she wasn't *his*. Not any longer.

So why do I still feel like she is?

Eric studied him with faint curiosity. "How the hell did an ex-SEAL get involved with the Hollywood 'It' girl?"

"I wasn't a SEAL back then." His words sounded too dark and rough. He cleared his throat and tried again. "And she wasn't rich and famous." She'd just been Gwen. His Gwen.

His first.

Just as he'd been hers.

If anything, Eric appeared more worried by that admission. "You gonna be able to stay professional on this one?"

Simon wasn't going to make a promise he might not be able to keep.

"Or should I convince her that another agent would be better? I mean, you're VP here. I didn't think you were going to do more field work. I thought you were more managerial now—"

But Simon gave his friend a slow smile. "What can I say? You know I like getting my hands dirty."

The more dangerous the job, the more he liked it. "And you don't need another agent. I've got Gwen." The words came out with a possessive edge.

Since Eric had his own possessive tendencies—particularly when they came to his wife, Piper—the guy just gave a nod. "Then let's not keep our new client waiting." Eric turned on his heel and led the way back to his office. When Eric swung open the door, Simon saw that Dennis was inside with Gwen.

The guy was practically fawning over her. Seriously? People should know better than to drool on clients. That shit was unprofessional.

"Want more sugar in your coffee?" Dennis asked her. "Some cream?" He inched closer to her.

Simon rolled his eyes, caught the guy's elbow, and steered him back toward the door. "She takes her coffee black."

He pushed Dennis out and shut the door— maybe a little too hard, but what the hell—before he spun back to face Gwen.

She frowned at him. "Um, I do like sugar and cream in my coffee."

He opened his mouth. Closed it. Realized that when she'd been eighteen, she *had* liked her coffee black. But she wasn't an eighteen-year-old girl any longer.

And I might not know her at all.

She put her coffee mug down on the desk. Squared her shoulders. Focused not on him, but on Eric. "Will Wilde be taking my case or do I need to look elsewhere?"

Eric opened his mouth.

"We're taking the case," Simon assured her. "Now tell us what in the hell is going on."

Because he was watching so closely, he saw the slight sag in her shoulders. The slump of relief. She'd been afraid that he wouldn't help her.

As if he'd ever been able to refuse her anything.

She should have remembered the promise he'd made her long ago...

He'd sworn then that he'd lie, he'd steal, he'd *kill* for her.

Of course, he'd also promised to love her forever.

Simon forced his hands to stay loose at his sides. "Gwen?"

Her tongue swiped across her lower lip. "I have a stalker."

Yeah, he'd suspected that. Simon wanted more details.

"He's been watching me for some time now. Wherever I go, he's there. He takes pictures. Sends them to me. He wants me to know that he's watching."

"Surely your security team is on this?" Eric asked. "I know the studios are always watching out for their talent—"

"He's been able to discover secrets about me." Her gaze fell so that she was staring at her hands. Hands she'd twisted together. "Information that if—should these particular details ever make it to the public—I'd be destroyed."

Simon strode closer to her. "Gwen?"

Her head tipped back. Her hair slid over her shoulder. Her incredibly thick lashes lifted as she gazed at him. "*Not* a sex tape," she muttered. "Something a thousand times worse."

His heart surged in his chest. "What is it?"

But her gaze cut toward Eric. "How does all of this work?" And she lifted one hand to push back her hair. "Like...do you guarantee confidentiality to your clients?"

"Everything is kept strictly confidential," Eric assured her.

She nodded. But then Gwen bit the lower lip she'd recently licked. "Even if it's something...illegal? Even if...say, in the course of the investigation...you were to discover that I'd committed a crime?"

Gwen? Commit a crime? She'd been squeaky clean back in high school, even when things had gotten bad.

"It depends on the crime." Eric's expression showed no emotion. "And if you *are* covering up a crime, you need to realize right now that the first thing we do is uncover secrets. We have to know every aspect of our clients' lives if we are going to protect them. You can't hold back. If there is something you've done..."

She was on her feet. "Thank you for your time."

What?

"I appreciate the consult today, but, um, I really should talk more with the studio." She hurried for the door. "I didn't think this through. There are other people I should see. Thank—"

Simon stepped into her path. "You're scared."

He could see the fear in her eyes.

But she just lifted her chin. "This was a mistake."

Those words...fuck, they were the same words he'd given her long ago. Right before he'd shipped out.

"This was a mistake, Gwen. We're too young. I don't have anything to offer you."

He could see the memory, right there between them. Could practically feel it in the room.

"I thought I needed you," she whispered. "I don't. My mistake."

No, no, but...

She skirted around him. Walked out of the office. The door closed behind her with just the softest of clicks.

He'd been the one to walk away before. When he'd left her, he hadn't glanced back, though he'd wanted to. He'd wanted to turn back, wanted to run to her, wanted to hold her and never let go. He hadn't. He'd lost her.

Was he really supposed to just let her go this time?

"She doesn't want us to know what she's hiding." Eric's tone was quiet. Thoughtful.

Tension burned in Simon's gut. "She's scared." And that shit just wasn't going to work—not on his watch. "Fuck what she said. We're *taking* the case."

"Uh, our would-be client just walked out the door. I think that means that there is no case."

Simon marched for said door. "We're taking the case."

Gwen wasn't going to slip from his life, not again.

No fucking way.

CHAPTER TWO

"I can tell when you're scared."

His voice was low and deep and dark, and the jerk was *in* her dressing room.

Gwen froze, her hand on the knob of her dressing room door. She was on set—freaking *on set*—and the guy had gotten into her personal space. "How in the hell did you get in here?"

He leaned forward and turned on the nearby lamp. Illumination spilled onto Simon as he lounged in *her* chair. "I spoke to the security agents in charge of the production. I let them know that *I* would be taking over your protection detail."

She crossed the threshold and shut the door behind her. "And what? They just let you waltz into my room? Did they even ask for ID?"

"Security sucks here," Simon agreed as he unrolled his body and stood to his full, towering height. Simon was close to six-foot-three, and she'd forgotten just how big he truly was. He winked at her. "It's a good thing you hired me."

Her mouth opened. Closed. Then... "I didn't hire you! I walked away, remember?"

He seemed to consider her words. "You actually ran. Very fast. So fast that I didn't get to stop you before you left the building." He shrugged. "And I was going to stop you. You came to Wilde looking for me. You wanted my help." A pause. "So, you've got it."

"Simon..."

"Don't you remember my promise, Gwen?"

She sucked in a hard breath. Yes, she remembered. It was the reason she'd sought him out. Even as he'd freaking broke her heart and said that being with her was a mistake...he'd told her...

"If you ever need me, baby, I'm there. I'd lie for you, steal, hell, I'd even kill for you."

He gave her a grim smile, and Gwen knew he was remembering that long-ago promise, too.

Her arms wrapped around her stomach.

"So, sweetheart," Simon finally drawled, "who is it that you want me to kill?"

She flinched. "I don't need you to kill anyone." She shouldered around him, and when her body brushed against his, an electric current of heat shot through her. It had always been that way. They touched, and bam, they wanted. In the past, they hadn't held back. Hadn't fought the white-hot desire. They'd just given in to the need.

Until they'd both gone down in flames. The fire was always so beautiful, from a distance. Until you felt the pain of the burn on your skin.

She looked around. She could use a drink. But she had a rule about never drinking on set. The last thing she wanted was to ever appear to be some drunk prima donna who couldn't handle a professional gig. She'd worked too hard to lose everything she'd gained.

"You have a stalker." His voice was flat. No emotion. "You want me to get rid of him for you?"

"Yes." She wanted the bastard to disappear.

"How long has he been contacting you?"

"About six months." Six long, nightmare-filled months.

Gwen found Simon's gaze locked on her. His stare...She swallowed. He'd been the first man to look at her with such heavy desire in his eyes.

"Six months. What did he do that got your notice?"

How much could she reveal to him without destroying herself? "Roses." A rough laugh slipped from her. "At first, I thought they were from the guy I was dating. Then I read the card. It just—it was off. Scary off."

He waited.

"The card said, *'I've missed you.'* There was no signature, and when I tried to track down the roses to see who'd sent them to me, none of the local florists had a record of the order. The roses were delivered to my doorstep. Someone snuck onto my property in California, got past my security cameras, and left the roses there for me."

"The note doesn't seem threatening."

Did he think she was being dramatic? The actress, looking for attention? That *wasn't* who she was. "Shortly after that, the pictures started coming. Pictures of me...on set. Walking in the city. Going to the damn grocery store. And...other pictures."

He waited. The tension in the dressing room seemed to thicken. The air felt warmer against her skin.

"Pictures of me at my pool. Pictures of me with...with the man I was dating at the time." A former co-star. They weren't together any longer. She'd cut him out of her life. She'd had to do it. She couldn't let anyone get too close, not then.

"Did you go to the cops?" Again, there wasn't any emotion in Simon's voice.

He used to run hot and fierce. And the way he'd first reacted to her...well, she'd thought that Simon hadn't changed. Yet now, he seemed to be made of ice. Only his eyes burned, but everything else was locked down tight.

Maybe he had changed.

Only fair, she'd certainly changed, too. Changed so much. She'd had to change in order to survive.

Anger spiked in her. Anger directed at him. At the past. At everything she'd lost. "I've never been tight with the cops. They don't have a history of believing me."

She saw the understanding sink into his eyes. Gwen rolled back her shoulders. "I get creepy letters all the time. Fans who go a step too far. They see me on the screen, and they think they know me. Sometimes, they can't see the difference between fantasy and reality." She blew out a breath. "I have an assistant who usually keeps track of the more...creepier contacts. He makes sure my bodyguards know who to watch out for when I'm at premieres or public events."

"But this isn't something you want your assistant handling?"

Okay, she had to be careful here. She closed the distance between them and lifted her hand. Her fingers curled around his arm. The jolt of awareness shoved hard through her.

She'd never reacted to anyone the way she did to Simon. Not that she'd tell him that particular truth. She had plenty of secrets that she needed to keep from him. "The stalker is blackmailing me."

His eyes narrowed. Went all cold and lethal instead of hot and fiery.

And she paused because...what did she really know about Simon? About who he was, now? She remembered the boy he'd been. The boy who'd swept her off her feet only to vanish from her life. The boy who'd protected her so fiercely, putting himself as a shield between her and the world.

Then he'd gone off to save the world.

"What's he using to blackmail you?"

She turned away from him. Made her way to the small vanity near the right wall. Gwen slid down onto the plush seat and stared at her reflection in the mirror. The mirror was surrounded by soft lights, putting off a gentle glow and illuminating her skin. She stared into the mirror, stared at the woman there, and wondered...

Who in the hell are you?

He closed the space between them. Stood behind her. All tall and dark and dangerous-looking. His hand rose and curled around her shoulder, and his touch was ever so careful. "What's he using to blackmail you?"

Proceed with caution. "Do you remember Xavier Gray?"

His hold tightened, just a little bit. "Yeah, I remember him." His gaze met hers in the mirror. "I kicked the shit out of the asshole right before I had to leave for enlistment. He got handsy with you at that club back in town."

Back in town...he meant back in Pensacola, Florida, because that was where they'd both grown up. Right in that beautiful, quiet beach town. They'd been the poor kids who worked all the summer jobs while Xavier—his parents had been the ones with the multi-million-dollar beach house. And Xavier had thought that he could buy just about anything.

Even her.

She released a slow breath. "Did you know that Xavier disappeared?"

"Yeah." His brow furrowed. "But I didn't exactly make a point of keeping track of the guy."

No, of course not. "You joined the Navy. Set sail. Didn't look back."

"I looked back." Right then, he was looking at her in the mirror.

And seeing a woman she didn't even recognize.

"Gwen?"

"He disappeared shortly after you left. Never was heard from again. He's presumed dead." She released a slow breath. "He took his boat out, and he didn't come back." She pushed her hands against the top of her thighs. "Everyone says he's dead. And the bastard blackmailing me? He thinks I killed Xavier. He says he has proof."

"What. The. Fuck?"

She laughed, and it was a desperate sound. "So, no, this isn't about a sex tape." Gwen rose and turned to face him. "This is about life and death. It's about the sins from the past coming back to bite me in my ass. It's about murder. It's about *hell*. And I need help. Help so very badly, and you're the only person that I could think of who might be able to fix this mess and keep it quiet for me."

Simon shook his head, as if he couldn't quite believe what he was hearing. "This isn't possible."

"I wish. He says he has proof. He keeps wanting me to do things. Keeps asking for things. And he says if I don't do exactly what he wants, then he'll make sure the whole world knows I'm a killer." There. Her secret. One of them, anyway. "The night that you fought with Xavier—when you fought with him because of *me*—this guy has pictures of that night. He sent them to me."

"Show me. Now."

She shook her head. "They aren't here." What? Did he think she'd just be hauling them around for everyone to see? Um, no. "They're at the hotel I'm using. Locked up tight in the safe in my room."

Simon's frown deepened.

Did he think she was lying? "Jeez, you think I like having to tell you this? You think I *liked* having to drag myself to your door after all of this time?"

He shook his head. "You didn't drag yourself anywhere."

"I thought about keeping you out of this but...God, you're in the photos, too. You're the one hitting Xavier, and I'm grabbing your arm, trying to pull you back." Gwen shoved away the memory. "You're involved so that...it should give you incentive, shouldn't it? You don't want your name pulled through the mud, not now that you're some big-time VP at Wilde Protection and Securities. You'll want to stop this mess, too."

He didn't speak.

She held her breath. *Say something!* What did he want? For her to beg for his help? She was so freaking desperate and scared. "I'm at the point where I will do just about anything to stop this mess." She had so much to lose. And she wasn't just talking about her career. Her very life. Her freedom was on the line. "What do you want? Name your price, okay? Just do it. I can pay *anything*." The girl who'd had nothing—who'd grown up in thrift store clothes and in the smallest house on the street—now she had the world at her feet.

But everything could come crashing down if she wasn't careful.

"I don't fucking care about my name getting dirty." His words were rough and deep.

And they scared her. He *had* to care. He had to help her. "Then what do you care about?" The words tore from her. "What do you want?"

His gaze was locked on hers. So much heat in his stare. Anger. No, rage and...

Need?

"The same thing I always fucking wanted."

"Simon?"

"You." His head lowered. His lips pressed to hers in a hot, rough kiss. A kiss that reminded of the past. A kiss that ignited an explosive desire inside of her. A kiss that told her—going to Simon for help might have been a terrible, horrible mistake.

But, oh, God, she still wanted him.

She still needed him.

His hands locked around her waist as he hauled her closer to him.

The same thing I always fucking wanted.

CHAPTER THREE

A rap sounded at the door. A female voice called out, "Ms. Soloman? They're ready for you on set."

Simon felt Gwen stiffen in his arms. Stiffen— and then pull back. She stared up at him with her incredible, golden eyes, seeming to see straight into his rather battered soul.

She didn't say a word. His gaze dropped to her mouth. Lips that were red and swollen from his kiss.

Holy shit, had he really just kissed her? He hadn't planned to do that. Okay, yes, he'd wanted to kiss her. He'd been desperate to taste her once again, to see if the fantasy of Gwen really lived up to the reality, but he hadn't meant to—

"Ms. Soloman?" The woman rapped again. "Everything okay?"

Gwen licked her lips. Her pupils expanded a bit. "Everything is fine." She cleared her throat, but when she spoke again, her voice was still husky as hell and ever-so-sexy. "I'll be right out. Tell everyone I'm on my way."

Footsteps rushed away. And Gwen retreated, putting space between her body and Simon. "Is that the price? Is that really what you're saying?"

"Price?" He wasn't sure what she was talking about. When he kissed Gwen, his mind tended to get a little foggy. It had happened when he was a nineteen-year-old kid, and it happened now. Dammit.

"The price for helping me. For finding the bastard who is trying to ruin me. You want me to sleep with you? Is that it?"

Oh, hell, no. "I kissed you because I wanted to taste your mouth. Because for a minute, I looked at you and got lost in the past." *Get your act together, man. Now. Don't fuck this up.* "And I don't trade sex for services rendered. Jesus, Gwen, you *know* me. You really think I'm a piece of slime like that?"

"I don't know you." Her expression never wavered. "I knew the boy you were. I have no idea what kind of man you are."

His hands curled into fists at his sides. "And yet you still came to me."

"You were involved in this mess. You were in the pictures." A shrug of one delicate shoulder. "And when I looked you up on the Internet, I realized you worked for the biggest security company on the East Coast. A company with a base in Atlanta—the town I happen to be living in, temporarily, while I'm shooting." She lifted her hand to her lips. Pressed her fingers against them a moment and then...her hand dropped. "It seemed like a good idea—at the time—to go to you. Trust me, I keep rethinking the plan." She turned away. "And I keep realizing it was probably a major mistake."

"*Don't.*"

Gwen glanced over her shoulder at him.

"I am taking your case. I'm helping you."

Her gaze searched his. "Because you want me to sleep with you."

The woman must really think he was a piece of shit. So much for picking up where they'd left off. He should bury that particular fantasy. "Sweetheart..." Simon drawled out the endearment.

She tensed.

"What kind of guys *have* you been hanging out with? Hmmm? Because it sounds like they may need to be taught some life lessons. Lesson one, you don't barter sex with a woman."

Her gaze sharpened on him. "No sex? That's what you're saying?"

He took a step toward her and caught her delectable scent. "I'm saying sex between us isn't about any kind of deal. Sex between us is only about desire. About primal need. About wanting to rip each other's clothes off and fuck for hours just because the need is so savage and raw."

Because he was watching her so closely, Simon saw the faint flicker of her eyelashes. The flaring of her delicate nostrils.

He smiled. "You didn't stop the kiss. Not until the lady was knocking at your door."

"Everyone likes a walk down memory lane sometimes."

Is that what he was to her? A walk? "You still want me."

"Do I?" Now she laughed. "Simon, I'm an actress. Guess what that means?" Her eyes widened expectantly.

He didn't guess.

"It means I can act. I can kiss a man and have him thinking that I want him more than I've ever wanted anyone before."

Bullshit. Her desire had been real. Hadn't it?

"Don't believe me?" She batted her lashes at him. "Then maybe you should watch what happens next." She strode toward the door.

"We aren't finished, Gwen. We need to talk about your case—"

"We were finished years ago. When you walked away." She didn't look at him. "And I'm needed on set. I don't leave the cast and crew waiting. Not ever. I do my job." Her voice was vibrating with emotion. Emotion that he couldn't figure out. "But I do want to talk to you about the case. About a *real* payment for the case, but it has to be after I'm done."

"Fine." His hands were still fisted, mostly because he wanted to reach out and grab her. To pull her against him. How long had he thought about being with her again? About kissing her? Tasting her? Seeing if the desire would still be there between them?

He wasn't a freaking saint. There had been other women since Gwen. But he'd never wanted them the same way. And when he closed his eyes...shit, it was humiliating to admit but...

It's always you, Gwen.

She'd already left the room. Hell. He hurried to keep up with her. Until he found out all the specifics on this case...

He caught her arm. Pulled her close. "You're not getting out of my sight."

She turned her head. Gave him a slow smile. One that he remembered too well. The smile that had always wrecked him. "Going to watch me work?" Gwen asked him.

"I'm going to watch every single move you make, sweetheart."

Her smile flickered.

"I'm sticking to you until you tell me everything about this case. If you're in danger, then I'm going to help you."

He thought she'd give him one of her sassy, smart-ass replies. She didn't. She simply said, "Thank you," and Simon realized just how scared Gwen must be.

He followed her to the set. He didn't gawk when he saw the other actors even though he was a fan of one guy in particular. Damn, but he'd enjoyed the shit out of that fellow's spy movies. There were cameras and cables and bright lights all over the place and—

"Closed set, buddy." A man shoved his hand against Simon's chest. "You're gonna want to turn around and get the hell out."

Simon glanced down at the hand, then back up at the asshole who'd just shoved the hand into the middle of Simon's chest. The fellow had bright, blond hair—hair that appeared mussed but Simon was willing to bet the jerk had spent too much time carefully styling it that morning.

The guy was a few inches shorter than Simon. Fit, but on the lanky side.

And his hand was still pushing against Simon's chest. "You're gonna want to move that hand," Simon advised him flatly.

"And you're gonna want to back out of here. *Closed* set means—"

"He's with me." Gwen's shoulder brushed against Simon's arm. "Thanks, Van, but Simon is here because I want him to be."

Simon didn't smirk at the guy, but he thought about it.

Van dropped his hand. "New boyfriend?"

Sure, that was one option.

"Bodyguard," Gwen fired back immediately.

Van blinked. "But...I hire your security."

Oh, did he? Now Simon looked at the man with interest. "Not this time, you don't," he murmured.

Van frowned, his features not looking so perfect now.

Someone called for Gwen. She shot a quick glance at Simon. "Don't cause trouble."

As if he were the trouble-causing type.

She skirted away from him and hurried past the crew. She took up her position on set. Someone else called for total quiet and then...

Well, shit, then they started filming the scene. He'd never been on a movie set before. Never seen the magic behind the curtain, so to speak. Simon crossed his arms over his chest and got ready to enjoy the show. Back in high school, Gwen had always been the star of all the plays. He'd thought she was freaking fabulous, of course. Not that he'd told her. He hadn't even approached her until after his graduation. Even then, he'd known the woman was far too good for him.

But he'd gotten tired of admiring her from afar. He'd finally wanted to put his hands on her and—

And her co-star had his hands on her. Right the hell then.

Simon's eyes narrowed.

The co-star—a tall, tanned, too-good-looking guy—pulled Gwen in close. His head bent toward her. And he kissed her. Fucking kissed her right in front of Simon.

Oh, no, this was *not* cool.

Gwen gave a little moan. Her hands curled around her co-star's shoulders. She pulled him against her, seeming to be greedy and aroused. Completely into the bastard.

The same way she'd seemed to be completely into Simon just moments before.

Seeing her in that jerk's arms, seeing her body pressed to the other man's...

Sure, there might be guys out there who were into the thrill of watching a woman with someone else. Someone who liked the voyeuristic rush. That someone sure as hell wasn't Simon. He didn't like seeing Gwen with anyone else. He and Gwen weren't together any longer. They'd stopped being an item long ago but...

But he'd been kissing her in her dressing room.

And it took all of Simon's self-control not to stalk out there and drive his fist into the pretty-boy actor's face.

"Simon, I'm an actress." Gwen's words played through his mind again. *"I can act. I can kiss a man and have him thinking that I want him more than I've ever wanted anyone before."*

Yeah, fine, he got it now. Lesson freaking learned. Gwen had been playing him. Shit. *Shit.*

Someone yelled, "Cut!"

Gwen immediately pulled away from her co-star. She laughed. Brushed her fingers down his arm, then turned and looked straight at Simon. She lifted one brow.

Message received. She was an actress. The kiss in the dressing room had meant nothing to her. She just wanted his help.

Too bad the kiss had meant everything to Simon.

"She is phenomenal," Van gushed. "The best actress I've ever seen."

One hell of an actress, all right. "Yeah. She's something else."

Van frowned at him.

"What the hell are you to her?" Simon demanded.

Van's frown became deeper.

Hell, Simon was always being told by the other agents at Wilde that he needed to work on his tact. But as a former SEAL, tact wasn't big on his list of attributes. He was more of a get-shit-done kind of guy.

Van straightened his shoulders. "I'm Gwen's personal assistant."

Gwen was heading for them. The co-star was behind her. Following her like a happy puppy, eager for more affection.

Not happening, buddy. Not on my watch. The co-star could have her while the cameras were rolling, but when filming stopped...

Gwen. Is. Mine.

Gwen paused right in front of Simon. "I'll probably have to do that scene ten more times today. At least."

"Good for you." Jealousy was like bile in his throat. He had no claim on her. But...*dammit.* "Point received. You're one hell of an actress."

Her delicate brow furrowed. "Thank you."

Van was watching them. Listening too carefully.

"I want to try this from a different angle!" After making that announcement, a woman waved her hands toward the set. She stood near one of the cameras, a ball cap on her head. "Gwen, let's discuss..."

Gwen nodded to Simon. "You don't have to stay. This will take a while."

Staying and watching her kiss her prick of a co-star? Not the way he'd planned for his hours to go, but...when he stared deeply into her eyes, Simon could have sworn that he saw fear in those golden depths. "I'm not going anywhere."

A smile came and went on her lips.

He would start his recon work right then and there. He'd talk to the crew, and he'd see who was paying too much attention to Gwen. He'd figure out the dynamics at play. Too often in stalking cases, the predator was someone who liked to insert himself into his prey's life.

But this wasn't a typical stalking case. Blackmail was involved.

Gwen hurried to the woman in the cap—the director, Simon figured.

And while Gwen chatted, her co-star made his way to a long table that was stuffed with food. Simon narrowed his eyes on the guy. Then he stalked toward the former spy movie hero turned—well, what-the-hell-ever he was supposed to be in this movie.

The guy—Austin Quest—turned toward Simon. He even gave a faint grin. "Hey, mate." The guy's Australian accent was strong, though Simon knew the fellow could easily lose the accent when the filming started.

Simon just looked him up and down. So much for the spy movies being a favorite. "You're dead to me now."

Austin cocked his head. "Come again?"

But Simon smiled. A very cold, very evil smile.

Austin backed away.

CHAPTER FOUR

"I'm taking you home."

Gwen glanced up, frowning, as Simon closed in on her. She'd been in three-inch heels all evening, it was nearing nine o-clock, and she'd had to make out with Austin so many times that her eyes had nearly rolled back into her head. Austin was a gorgeous guy, sure, but kissing him was like kissing a fish. A fish who enjoyed really garlicky food.

Asshole. She was pretty sure the garlic had been deliberate. She'd seen him diving into the food that had been provided by a local Italian restaurant for the cast and crew. Would it have killed Austin to grab a mint?

Oh, yes, she was sure the garlic had been deliberate. The man liked to think he was a comedian. She'd pay him back next time. Maybe with some sour cream and onion dip before the cameras rolled.

"You're done, aren't you?" Simon asked.

She glanced around her dressing room. "Uh, yeah, but I can drive myself home." She snagged her keys. Her fingers curled around them and she hurried for the door.

He shadowed her steps, but he didn't touch her. Didn't so much as let his body brush against her.

"You don't have a driver?"

"No, I like driving myself. I'm not helpless." She liked the freedom of her own wheels. What was wrong with that?

They headed for the designated crew parking area. A security guard waved to her. Her BMW waited a few feet away.

And Simon was still tailing her. She stopped and glanced over her shoulder at him.

"My team needs to check out your car, Gwen. Standard in these situations. Make sure there is no tracking tech on it."

A little shiver slid over her. "Tracking tech?"

"Yes, if someone is watching you, it's an easy enough way to keep tabs on you. I should have gotten a team over earlier, but I was busy talking to the film crew."

She'd seen him making the rounds. It had appeared as if he was just casually talking to everyone, but she'd suspected the truth. The guy had grilled them all.

His jaw hardened. "I'd prefer to drive you until we can be sure the car is clear."

"I think you just want to take me home." Her words were flippant.

But he nodded. "Sure, of course, I do. What straight man in America doesn't want to take you home?"

Uh, what? "Plenty of them," Gwen assured him. Irresistible, she was not. Hell, right then, she was wearing some old, faded jeans and a t-shirt.

She'd swiped all the makeup off her face when filming was done, and she was pretty much weaving on her feet from exhaustion.

Behind him, she saw Van hurrying past the guard.

Simon stepped closer to her. "If I'm in charge of your security," his voice was for her alone, "then that means you have to follow my orders. You're scared, and I can see it. Let me help you." A pause. "That is why you came to me, isn't it? Because you wanted my help?"

Yes.

"Because you thought I could handle the danger around you?" Simon pushed.

She looked into his eyes. Darkness surrounded them, the only illumination coming from the light posts on the edges of the parking lot. "Yes." She figured he could handle any danger. Wasn't that really his thing?

"Great job tonight!" Van called, slightly out of breath as he rushed toward Gwen. "Fabulous, as always." He nodded briskly and seemed to ignore Simon. "You're supposed to be on set at six p.m. tomorrow, don't forget. If you need me to pick you up—"

"I don't." Her hold tightened on the keys. "But I do need you to...um, can you get the guard to secure my car for tonight? I'm leaving it here."

Van's head jerked between her and Simon. "Leaving it...oh, you're going with...*him?*"

Simon reached for Gwen's fingers. She tried not to flinch at his touch. His hand was warm and strong and those slightly rough calluses on his fingertips....Jeez, why did they turn her on? What was up with that?

"Yes, the lady is going home with me." Simon pulled the keys from her fingers and handed them to Van. "Let's get her car moved to a more secure location. I don't want it out in the open like this."

Van frowned down at the keys. "Yeah, yeah, I can move it." He pressed a button on the fob, and the vehicle growled to life. Remote activation. One of the perks the guy at the rental place had been so excited about when he'd convinced her to take the ride. "Anything for Gwen. I'll move it now—"

An explosion ripped through the night. There was a deep, booming *roar*, and Gwen swore she heard screams. She heard the screams even as a ball of fire seemed to hit her from behind. She was picked up and hurtled through the air.

Hard arms grabbed her and pulled her against a strong, rough body even as she pitched toward the ground. Gwen didn't hit the pavement, though. She hit *him*. She sprawled on top of Simon, and his arms held her tightly against him. A ringing filled her ears, then the rush of what sounded like waves pounding against a beach. When she stared down at Simon's face, utterly terrified, she saw that his lips were moving, but Gwen couldn't make out a single word that he said.

She shook her head, and the ringing faded a bit even as her heart thundered in her chest and—

"...baby, are you all right? Dammit, *tell*—"

"I'm okay." Her voice seemed distorted, as if it came from a far-off distance. She sucked in a breath and tasted smoke.

"Ms. Soloman! Ms. Soloman!"

Her head whipped up. The security guard was running toward her.

She looked behind her and saw the flames raging from what *had* been her car. "OhmyGod." She shoved away from Simon. Stumbled to her feet. Her gaze went from the blaze to the lot, frantic. "Van!"

Coughing.

She whirled and saw Van on the ground. He was pushing himself up, and blood trickled down his forehead.

"Gwen?" Van mumbled her name, looking absolutely as confused as she felt.

She ran to him. Gwen slid her arm under his shoulder to help steady him as he rose to his feet.

"What...happened?"

"My car exploded." The flames were hot around them. Smoke billowed into the air. The blaze was so bright. She could hear other voices rising and falling—others on the set were rushing to the scene. A siren screamed in the distance.

She'd almost gotten in that car and driven to her hotel. If Simon hadn't been there, if he hadn't stopped her...

Van had the keys. He could have been inside. "You could've died," she whispered.

Van coughed. Then he swiped at the blood dripping in his eyes.

Simon was there in the next instant, pulling Van from her, quickly checking the guy out and barking questions at him. She barely heard Simon. Gwen wrapped her arms around her stomach and stared at the blaze. Someone had just tried to kill her. Someone had *almost* killed her assistant.

The sonofabitch stalker wasn't playing any longer. He'd meant his threats. He'd warned her that if she told anyone about him...

"I'll make you pay." Those had been his words. Words she'd ignored because she'd been so desperate to get to Simon.

Only now, she'd just brought Simon into her nightmare.

Lights flashed. A quick pulse of illumination. Squinting, she turned. Men and women with cameras were there. Not just regular people with fancy phones, but the actual paparazzi. How had they gotten to the lot? They were gaping and filming and firing questions. Sure, reporters often hung out near the filming locations but this...to be there while her car burned, while she could barely stand upright...

"Get the hell back!" Simon shouted.

She hadn't even realized how much they were closing in on her. Not until Simon was there. He pulled her against him, shielding her from the throng.

But the cameras were watching. Seeing everything.

And there was no place to hide.

***

The firefighters put out the blaze. Her car was nothing more than a blackened shell. Uniformed cops patrolled the scene, they stopped to bark a few questions here and there, and Gwen just watched them. Her body felt numb.

She had scratches on her hands and knees. The knees of her jeans had ripped when she'd been tossed through the air and slammed into the ground. Or, rather, into Simon and the ground. She'd been straddling him when she landed, and her knees had thudded into the concrete. Luckily, though, she didn't have any other injuries. Simon had protected her.

Her head turned. He was talking to the cops. His hands were on his hips and his face—under the illumination of a parking lot light—clearly showed his rage.

Van had been taken away in an ambulance. The EMTs had assured her that he was okay, but they'd still taken him to the hospital. She wasn't quite sure why. Precaution? Precaution was good. No one dying or being seriously hurt was *good*.

The reporters had been pushed back as the crime scene had been established. Only it wasn't just reporters who gawked now. The area beyond the lot was filled with people. Young, old, men and women. All talking excitedly. Phones had joined the fancy cameras, and everyone seemed to be filming the scene.

"Isn't it wonderful?" The soft voice reached Gwen's ears. The familiar voice carried a crisp, Boston accent. "I swear, you can't buy this kind of publicity. This film is going to have so much buzz!"

Gwen blinked. Then she focused on the woman who'd been her agent for the last five years. Ever since she'd been discovered on that beach in Florida.

Eveline Jacobson smiled at her.

Gwen didn't smile back. "I was almost killed tonight."

Eveline's smile faltered. "Of course...I mean, how are you?" Concern instantly filled her voice. Eveline wore form-fitting black pants and a loose, billowing top. Her blonde hair had been pulled back in a tight twist, a style that accentuated her razor-sharp cheek bones. "I was told there were no serious injuries, but if those EMTs lied to me—"

Gwen stood up. She'd been sitting in a chair the security guard had brought for her. "My car exploded. I was less than ten feet away from it. Van was about to get *in* it. This isn't some PR dream. It's a nightmare." Her nightmare.

Eveline glanced around. "Lower your voice." Her words came out as a warning rasp. "You know those microphones can pick up everything these days."

She didn't feel like lowering her voice. She just wanted to get out of there and go to her hotel.

"You're alive. Van's alive. Those are *good* things," Eveline said.

Uh, yeah, they were.

"And you are going to be the darling of the media now. The victim who survived a savage attack. You cannot buy press like this."

Eveline wasn't a bad person. Really. "I know you have a heart," Gwen said. After all, Eveline had been the one to give Gwen a place to sleep when she'd first started her acting career. Eveline had literally taken her off the street and into her own home. She'd slept on Eveline's couch for the first six months of her acting career. Eveline was ten years older and when it came to Hollywood, the woman had been worlds wiser than Gwen. She owed Eveline for everything she had. "But you are sounding stone-cold. I'm absolutely freaking terrified, Evie, and I need a friend, not some slick agent with an eye for the prize right now."

Eveline faltered. "I...sorry?"

"I'm *scared.*" She grabbed her friend's shoulders. "I didn't know what was happening. I was flying through the air, and I could feel the heat all against my back."

Eveline blinked. "I know it was frightening. But it was just an accident. Terrible things happen sometimes. What's important is that you're okay."

Gwen shook her head. No, she didn't think it had been an accident at all. Especially not since she was pretty sure her car's ignition had started and then the BMW had erupted into flames.

"I doubt it was an accident." Simon's deep voice came from right behind Gwen.

She gave a little jump. In all the commotion, she hadn't even heard him approach.

She let go of Eveline and angled toward him. His suit coat was torn. His hair was shoved back from his face, and she was pretty sure ash was on his cheek. A line of dark ash that somehow just made him look extra rough and tough.

"I think someone targeted Gwen," Simon added in his grim and mean voice.

She shivered. It wasn't cold, but she was suddenly covered in goosebumps.

He shouldered out of his coat and put it around her. The coat swallowed her, but she liked the feel of it against her. It carried his warmth and scent.

And, well, the scent of fire, too. But she was trying not to dwell on that aspect at the moment.

"Are you a police officer?" Eveline frowned at him. "Perhaps a detective?"

"I'm private security, hired this afternoon by Gwen." He offered a hand to Eveline. "Simon Forrest with Wilde Protection and Securities."

"Eveline Jacobson. I'm Gwen's agent." She took his hand. Gave him a smile. She always had a smile for handsome men, but her gaze darted to Gwen. "You hired new security without consulting me?"

She didn't have to run everything in her life past Eveline.

"Gwen and I go back a long way. She knew that she could count on me." He let go of Eveline's hand and his arm immediately wrapped around Gwen's shoulders. "We'll be talking in depth very, very soon, Eveline. For now, though, Gwen is dead on her feet."

Dead. She didn't like that word.

"So, I'm taking her home," he finished.

Eveline nodded. Appeared uncertain. "Uh, sure, of course."

Gwen pulled his coat a little tighter around her.

"Come on, baby." His lips brushed against her ear. "Let's get out of here."

She was more than ready to ditch that scene. Gwen could feel the cameras on her every second. The way he was standing next to her, the way his arm was around her...she knew how the story would play out in the media.

By morning, every scandal site on the Internet would be claiming that Simon was her mysterious new lover. The reporters wouldn't see him as protection. Just sex appeal.

I dragged him into the limelight. And she knew he'd never been the kind of man who liked attention.

Crap.

A few moments later, she was in his SUV. The passenger door slammed shut, and then he walked around the vehicle. There was blessed silence once he climbed inside and shut his own door.

He cranked the vehicle and turned on the heat. For her, she knew. She was the only one shaking from a cold that wasn't even there.

"Shock," he said, voice almost tender. "Give yourself some time. Your body will recover soon."

That was why she was shaking apart? Shock? "I'm sorry."

He drove them out of there. Left the lights and the fire trucks and the police cars behind. Left all the reporters and the gawking crowd. "For what?"

"Going to you was a mistake." She'd been warned. She hadn't listened. God, she hadn't *listened.*

He slanted her a fast glance before focusing back on the road. "You think I'm scared of some car bomb?"

Uh, yes. Wouldn't a sane person be scared? She was terrified. "He told me not to contact anyone." Her teeth were chattering even as heat blasted from the vents in front of her. Simon had even turned on the seat to warm beneath her. Thoughtful of him. "But I did. I went to you."

Simon braked at a red light. His stare slid to her. "When you are scared, you should *always* come to me. You know I'll take care of you."

Because he was the big, bad, lethal ex-SEAL? But even he could be hurt. He'd been flying through the air with her that night and slamming into the ground. "You can die, too." And the idea of his death terrified her.

"I'm pretty hard to kill. I had to be." He drove forward when the light changed.

She just wanted to get home. Or, to her temporary home, anyway. She never stayed in one place too long these days. City to city, movie to movie. Putting down roots wasn't exactly an option for her. And— "This...isn't the way to my hotel."

"No, it's the way to my home."

She whipped toward him. The seatbelt dug into her chest. "I'm not going to your house."

His hold tightened on the steering wheel. "Someone just blew up your car. That tells me you are *definitely* being watched. You've been staying in some swanky suite at a hotel, right?"

"Yes." She winced a little. "The Presidential Suite." The studio had booked the place for her— and rooms for all the main actors in the movie.

"Anyone could get access to your suite. You lift a key from a maid and presto, you're inside."

He'd better be wrong. *Please, let him be wrong.* "The hotel has great security."

"Bullshit. Hotels can be the absolute worst. And until I have a chance to go over the place with my team, I want to make sure that no risks are taken with your safety." A pause. "*Please,* Gwen."

Wait, please? He'd just said *please?*

"I know I can be a controlling ass. It's one of my character flaws."

Well, if he wanted to list them all...

"But I know protection. And I know danger. You're in danger right now. My goal is to get you into a protected environment. Once you're safe, then we can start figuring out who this jackass is."

"And your place is safe?"

"It's got a top of the line security system. One of the perks of my job."

Okay, yes, she could see the logic. A hotel versus his fortified home. But they should be crystal clear on one point. "I'm not sleeping with you."

Silence. Then... "Thought we worked that out earlier. You were just showing me your fine acting skills, not asking for us to pick up where we left off all those years ago."

Fine acting skills, her ass. She'd been completely and totally into him. His kiss had been panty-meltingly hot, and, as usual when she was with him, she'd responded instantly. All the crap she'd said after—*that* had been her fine acting. Her way of trying to salvage a bit of pride. The man had walked away from her before. She didn't want to look all desperate and overeager to take him back.

Playing games, are you, Gwen? She ignored the nagging voice in her head.

"I can bunk on the couch," Simon told her, sounding all smooth and—yes, dammit—in control. "Don't worry about it. You can take my bed."

"Still doesn't solve the main problem, though. This guy—he *knows* I went to you. He warned me to tell no one, but I didn't listen. I thought maybe—God, I *wanted* him to be all talk. Someone that we could make vanish. He's not. He said he'd punish me if I disobeyed him, and that is exactly what he did. Now I'm scared as all hell, and I *hate* feeling this way."

Scared, like some lost kid. Like she'd been long ago. She had to blink back freaking tears. Tears of all things! She'd once vowed to only cry for the camera. To keep her guard up all the time. But...

One car bomb later...

He blew up my car. He could have killed me. He could have killed Van or Simon! Her breath heaved out. "I think...I think I should go with someone else. Another security firm." On second thought.... "No, I should just handle this on my own, and I should—"

"You need me, and you've got me. I'm not scared of this bastard, but believe me, the perp out there *will* be afraid of me before I'm done with him."

She closed her eyes. They drove in silence for a time. "Thank you." She hadn't even figured out how much the guy was going to charge her. He was putting his life on the line for her, literally, and she hadn't even given Simon a down payment on his services.

He'd walked out of her life before, and here she was, dragging him right back into her world.

But he kissed me like he didn't mind being with me again. In fact, he'd kissed her with a raw hunger that she remembered all too well.

The vehicle slowed. Turned. She opened her eyes, then frowned. It looked like they were pulling into some old warehouse. He hit a button under the rear-view mirror, and a wide garage door opened. The vehicle swept inside.

"Bought the place last year. Converted it. Thought maybe I'd turn the downstairs into a brewery one day." A shrug as he killed the engine. "Or not, fuck it. That was just an old dream of mine. Got to have dreams when you're on a battlefield, you know? Something to get you home." He turned toward her. "Even if you get back and find out that those dreams are long gone."

She licked her bottom lip. "Simon—"

"The upstairs is my home. Don't worry. You'll like it. Or at least, I sure as hell hope you will." He climbed out of the SUV and hurried to the passenger door. He opened it for her and stood back, all gallant-like. He'd always done that. Opened the doors. Waited for her.

Old school.

"This way."

She pulled his coat a bit tighter around her.

He led them to an elevator. One with a very fancy-looking keypad. He typed in a code, swiped a card, and the elevator doors opened. But before she stepped inside, he pointed to the walls behind her. "Security cameras watch the bottom floor. No one gets in without me knowing about it."

Then he motioned for her to go into the elevator first. She slipped inside. The walls were bare. The floor spotlessly clean. The elevator gave a faint hum as it ascended. She could feel his gaze on her. She could feel his heat surrounding her. She should say something to him, but instead, she just stared straight at the closed doors.

And when the doors opened again, she stepped into his home. A big, open-concept home. Gleaming windows to the left and right looked out at the city. Exposed brick lined the walls, and the place was absolutely gorgeous. A white couch. Comfortable, huge. A TV. A bookshelf overflowing with hardbacks. Security monitors to the right. A whole wall of them. A kitchen that looked like a gourmet's wet dream. Beautiful white marble.

And when she peeked in the door to the left, she caught sight of a massive, four-poster bed.

"Not what you were expecting?"

She spun. He was right behind her with one dark brow cocked.

"I had no expectations." That was the truth.

His lips twisted. "The boy who had only the clothes on his back the last time you saw him—he has more now. A lot more." He rolled back his shoulders. "Of course, so do you. I guess we both got everything we wanted, huh?"

No, not even close. A shiver slid over her.

Instantly, he frowned. "You're still cold? Shit, here, let me get you a drink. I think we could both use one." He strode toward a bar that waited against the exposed brick.

She stood there, biting her lip, wearing his coat, and a moment later, he brought her back a gleaming glass of amber liquid. She reached for it, and their fingers brushed. The shot of heat was instantaneous. Gwen knew he had to hear her quick inhale, but he didn't say anything about it.

She took the drink. Downed it fast.

"Wait, Gwen, it's—"

"I can handle my whiskey. Thanks." Whiskey, she could handle in her sleep. Crazy stalkers who blew up her car? Not so much. She put the glass down and paced around his home. "I didn't even bring clothes." She was a mess, and she probably smelled like smoke and ash. "Hell, I didn't even think to—"

"I have plenty of t-shirts you can borrow. And if you don't want to wear one of those, I'll call Wilde. I can get an agent to bring you any items you need."

She stopped pacing and stared down at the street below.

"I need to know every detail about this bastard, Gwen. That was a bomb. It could have *killed* you."

"I didn't think he wanted me dead." She wrapped her arms around her stomach. "He wanted me to-to do things. Why say I had to do all of those things and then try to kill me?"

"What things?"

"Money. Of course, he wanted money. He wanted me to send him one hundred grand. I told you, he was blackmailing me." She released a long breath and kept staring at the street below. It was so much easier to talk to him when she didn't have to stare into his eyes.

Then she saw movement on the street below. A man, hurrying down the sidewalk, and she tensed, realizing that the lights were blazing behind her, and anyone who looked up would be able to see perfectly into the—

"Relax." Simon was right behind her. She hadn't even heard him cross the room. But suddenly, she could feel the heat of his body behind her. His fingers rose and curled around her shoulders. "You can see out, but no one can see in. I like my privacy."

"So do I." Her lips pressed together. "Though it's not something I really get much of these days." She turned to face him. His hands slid away from her. "I shouldn't bitch and moan about it. I mean, I knew what I was getting myself into. Just part of the business."

"You're not bitching or moaning, and you have a right to say anything you want." His gaze held hers. "Just because you're an actress, that doesn't mean that every aspect of your life has to be put on display for the world."

She should give the man back his coat. They were inside. She wasn't cold, but she was...tense. Nervous. Her heart raced too fast. Gwen felt as if she was about to jump right out of her skin.

"What else did he want?" Simon asked.

And at that question, that low, growled rumble, she could feel herself blush. He'd mockingly asked if this whole thing was about a sex tape, in the beginning. It wasn't and yet...

Her chin lifted. "What does he want? What did he demand in return for his silence?"

Simon just watched her.

"Me."

CHAPTER FIVE

Simon wanted to destroy the sonofabitch.

"What did he demand in return for his silence?"

Fuck, fuck, fuck.

"Me."

Gwen's voice seemed to echo in his mind. He held his body perfectly still, and Simon made sure his rage didn't show on his face. Adrenaline pumped furiously through his body. She could have died that night. When the flames had erupted and the fire had lanced over his skin, he'd reached out for her. He'd been absolutely desperate to hold her, to shield her, and he'd known, in those terrible seconds, that there was nothing he could do to stop the explosion.

Nothing.

He'd also realized...

I missed her. I want her. I don't want to let her go. Not ever again.

But then, he'd realized all of that shit long ago.

"Tell me *exactly* what that means," he finally managed.

"I think you know."

He didn't *like* what he was thinking.

"Pictures. The guy wanted me to send him pics of me. Naked pictures. Naked videos." She shook her head. "Like I was going to do that?"

"Don't send him a fucking thing."

"I'm not planning to, I'm—" She broke off because her phone had just given a little ding. A text had been received.

Fear came and went on her beautiful face. She reached into the back pocket of her jeans and pulled out the phone. She read the message on the screen, and he saw her fingers tremble.

He took the phone from her and read the text.

A warning.

What the fuck?

The phone gave another ding.

I knew you weren't in the car. I could see you, precious Gwen. But you needed to understand just how serious I am.

"I've changed my number three times," she whispered. "He always gets it. Always sends me texts from numbers I can't trace."

"*I* can trace him." Simon yanked out his own phone. He called the agency. Barked orders. Told them what the hell was happening and gave them the number appearing on her screen. Then he swiped his finger over Gwen's phone, and, using her phone, he dialed the number that had just texted her.

"He won't answer," she muttered. "You think I haven't tried this? You think I didn't even bribe some local cops to try and figure out where—"

The bastard picked up. Laughed. The laughter was robotic. Grating. Simon put the call on speaker so that Gwen could hear the sonofabitch.

"I told you," the distorted voice filled the air. *"I didn't mean to kill you. I need you, Gwen. Just as you need me. But don't fuck around again, don't break my rules...or you will get hurt next time."*

Her lips parted. Before she could speak, Simon snarled, "She doesn't follow your damn rules, asshole."

Static crackled. Then... "I want Gwen."

"Too bad. I'm Gwen's bodyguard. I'm the man who will stand between her and any threat out there. You're not going to get close to her again. You're not going to touch her. You're not going to hurt her. But guess what I'm going to do? *I'm going to fucking destroy you."*

More robotic laughter. "You don't know my Gwen. You don't know her secrets."

"I know that you're a fool." All he had to do was keep the bastard talking. He'd gotten his team to put a lock on her phone and the number he'd given them. They'd be tracing the call's signal. Pinging it off towers. Finding the jerk. *So talk, you'll just hang yourself.* "You been watching her movies and you got obsessed? You think you can have her? That you can possess her? Think again. She's not for you."

"Is she for you?"

Simon stared into Gwen's eyes. *She was. And I screwed that to hell and back.* Now she was so far beyond his reach. He got that. He'd understood from the moment he came back from his first twelve months of initial SEAL training. Hell, those months had passed in a blur as he completed Basic Underwater Demolition, Parachute Jump School, SEAL BUD/S work, and then his SQT—the SEAL Qualification Training that had often left him so exhausted at night he could barely drag himself to bed. And when he'd gotten to bed, when he'd closed his eyes, she'd been there.

When he'd gotten some leave, he'd wanted to see her. And...

He had. On the pages of a glossy magazine at a check-out line. *His* Gwen.

Totally out of his reach. *Want to know how long it takes to lose everything you ever wanted?* In his case, it had taken one fucking year. One year to have every shot wiped away.

"Maybe you're the one obsessed," the voice blasted. "Can't let go of the past, *Simon?*"

"You know my name. Want me to give you a freaking cookie?"

Static.

"No? Then how about I just give you an ass whooping—"

The static ended. The line went dead.

Gwen stared at Simon with wide eyes.

He called his team. "Tell me that you got the bastard." He waited, holding his breath. And...

"We have a location," Julia Slate responded quickly. Julia was a former firefighter and a damn good Wilde agent. "You're not going to like it."

"Where the hell is the call coming from?"

"According to what I'm seeing, it's a posh hotel in Downtown Atlanta. Could be from any floor, you know I couldn't get that specific—"

"What hotel were you staying at?" Simon demanded of Gwen.

Her eyes widened as she rattled off the hotel's name. A very recognizable, five-star name. "It's on—"

"Peachtree Street," Julia said in his ear at the same time. "We've already got agents on the way now."

His gut was tight. "Tell them to start in the Presidential Suite." Because he feared that was exactly where the bastard was.

Gwen's room.

He spoke to Julia just a moment longer, making sure the team was ready to go and that they'd hit the hotel fast before he ended the call. He wanted to go to the hotel, too. He wanted to be there when they stormed in, but he also didn't want to leave Gwen alone.

For all he knew, the guy could be trying to lure him away from Gwen.

"Are you going with your team?" she asked, voice halting.

"I'm staying right here with you. Julia can run things. If she finds the bastard, she'll have the cops lock his ass up."

Gwen swallowed. "And his threats about telling everyone that I was tied to Xavier's death?"

"He set a bomb in your car. The first step is getting the bastard off the street. And I doubt the cops are going to buy that a would-be killer is spilling the truth about your past."

Her gaze cut away from him. "You didn't mention Xavier to the cops at the car bomb scene."

"No. Right then, they were more interested in making sure no victims were on the ground. I gave the uniform in charge my name and contact info. Told him that you had a stalker."

Her stare came back to him.

"The cops aren't your enemy, you know."

Her hands twisted in front of her. An old habit. He remembered that Gwen used to do that when she was nervous. When they'd first started dating, she'd twist her hands together when he picked her up. He'd had a beat-up motorcycle, and she'd stand beside it, twisting her hands, then he'd reach for her hand and he'd pull her onto the back of his bike. She'd hold him tight, and—

He reached for her hand.

And he saw the cuts on her palm. "What the hell?"

"It's nothing. Just some scratches from the fall—"

He'd thought that he'd cushioned her. "You were hurt."

"It's nothing, really. Just—"

He turned and pulled her toward the bathroom. "Where else? Where else are you hurt?"

"Um, my knees, a little. It's nothing, though. Not a big deal."

Her being hurt in any way was a big deal to him.

He flipped on the lights in his bathroom. Tugged her toward the sink. Then with as much care as he could manage, Simon carefully washed her palms, cleaning the cuts—the scratches. Rubbing his fingers carefully over her skin and then telling her, "Strip."

She laughed.

And it was a real laugh. The laugh that he remembered so well. A warm, deep, boisterous laugh.

With a smile still on her lips, Gwen told him, "I don't think so."

His heart seemed to squeeze in his chest. "You said your knees hurt. Let me see them. I mean, come on, I bet some studio has your legs insured for a like a million dollars or something. Do you really want to make a studio exec have a heart attack—"

"Because I didn't let you look at my legs?" She lifted her eyebrows. "Nice try, but I'm not stripping for you."

He was still holding her right hand. He'd turned off the faucet, and his fingers were lightly caressing her skin.

Her pupils expanded, the darkness sliding over the gold in her gaze. "You can let me go now."

"But I did that once," the words slipped from him. "I don't want to do it again."

Her breath caught. "Simon?"

Fuck. She was a client. She'd told him already that she didn't want to walk down that particular road. But here he was, damn well *driving* down it at full speed. "Sorry." He let her go. The confines of the bathroom were too tight so he got out of there. "Riding an adrenaline high. To be honest, it can make me an irritable asshole. It can also make me horny as hell." A lie. The adrenaline wasn't what caused his arousal. It was just her, pure and simple.

"An adrenaline high." She followed him. "Is that what I'm feeling? Because I'm shaky and scared, and I'm worried that bastard is in my hotel room. And I'm worried that he's not. I'm worried that when your team gets there, he'll be long gone." Her hands were at her sides. His coat swallowed her delicate frame. "Is that adrenaline? Or just fear? My heart is racing, my body is shaking, and all of that...I swear, it just gets worse when you touch me."

He locked down every muscle in his body—mostly so he wouldn't rush to her and yank her into his arms.

"How do I get rid of it?" Her voice was husky and sexy and it was driving him mad. "What are the best ways to work off an adrenaline high?"

"Sex is an option." Christ. He'd just said that. Out loud. Screw it. Why stop now? If she truly wanted to know what worked... "Rough, dirty, wild sex."

She backed up a step. "That works for you, huh? Guess being a super SEAL and all of that, you had to deal with lots of highs."

Was that *pain* in her eyes?

Her smile was brittle. "I think I'll go for door number two and just take a cold shower and head to bed. You did say I could have your bed?"

She could have any damn thing of his that she wanted. "Yes."

She marched back toward the bathroom but stopped at the door, her hand rising to curl around the white, wooden doorframe. "Your agents will call if they catch him?"

"Yeah, they will."

Gwen glanced back. "Do you think they'll catch him?"

He didn't think things were going to be that easy. But he didn't want to crush the hope he saw in her eyes. That was the thing about Gwen, he'd never wanted to crush her. He'd pretty much just wanted to make her happy.

But he'd been the one to hurt her the most in their past.

"I hope so," he finally said.

Her lashes flickered, then she headed into the bathroom. The door shut softly behind her.

***

"I assure you, no one is inside Ms. Soloman's room!" The hotel manager was sweating.

Julia Slate got it. He was in charge of the swanky place, he had clients who were all rich and famous, and the last thing he wanted was any kind of scandal knocking at his door.

Unfortunately for him, she was the scandal of the moment. Julia and the team of agents behind her.

"I can't let you inside." He drew himself up to his full height and looked down his nose at her. "That is absolutely not allowed. Only Ms. Soloman can get inside."

Was he really going to pull that shit with her? "Ms. Soloman is under the protection of Wilde." She'd already given the guy her ID earlier. "We have reason to believe that a stalker gained access to her room..." *Definitely* to the hotel, if not her room.

The manager was blocking the room. "No one is inside." He stepped forward, waving his hand toward her. "So, until I can personally talk to Ms. Soloman, you will need to get back on the elevator and go downstairs—"

"The lock is broken." Her voice was flat and hard. When he'd stepped forward, she'd finally gotten a good look at the door—and the lock that had been smashed.

The manager—Brock Gordon—blinked. His head whipped back. When he saw the broken lock, he blanched and wiped his sweaty brow. "Oh, dear heaven."

Yes, *hello, scandal.* "The perp could still be in there. I'd advise you to step back, Mr. Gordon."

The door was open, so didn't that mean they could just walk in? As far as she was concerned, yes. That was exactly what it meant.

And Brock was dazedly following her command of stepping back, so she took that opportunity to lead her team inside. They entered with a hard and fast rush.

It didn't take long to realize that the perp wasn't there. A quick and thorough search was all that they needed. It also didn't take long to realize the bastard had left his mark.

A phone had been placed right in the middle of the massive, king-size bed. Gwen Soloman's bed. And the safe in her closet hung open—an empty safe. What had been inside?

They'd need to bag and tag that phone. "I want to see your security footage," she snapped as she whirled for Mr. Gordon. "Every single bit of footage you have."

He was sweating even more now. "Can we keep this quiet?" His voice sounded like a croaking frog as perspiration lined his upper lip. "Just between us?"

Julia locked her back teeth. People and scandals. They were always willing to do just about anything to keep up their fake appearances.

***

"Hell, yes, get it checked for prints," Simon said as he raked a hand through his thick hair. "Doubt the techs will find anything. And you say he broke the lock?"

Gwen tip-toed forward. The towel was wrapped around her body, and her wet hair slid over her shoulders.

"Yeah, I know what was in the safe. And I wanted it. Shit. Of course, get as many agents as you need to help with the security footage. Maybe the dumbass screwed up and we can see his face. I'll want to Gwen to take a look at the footage, too. We'll find out if anyone pops for her." A pause. Then he turned.

And his eyes fell on Gwen.

She saw his stare widen. And then that gorgeous green gaze of his slid down her body. He swallowed.

She'd come out to tell him that she wanted to borrow a t-shirt. But she'd found him on the phone and since he was talking about her, eavesdropping had seemed like a good plan.

He gave a little growl. A sexy, rough sound. That was Simon. So Simon. He'd always been on the primitive side. Some things hadn't changed.

"I've got her," he said as his gaze rose back to pin Gwen's. "You can bet she's safe for the night. I'll keep my eyes on her. No one will get past me."

His eyes were very much on her right then. And the towel felt way too small on her.

He ended the call. Blew out a breath. "He was there...left a phone on your bed."

She inched forward. Her toes—painted a hot pink—curled into the wooden floor.

"Your hotel safe was empty."

"He took the photos." She shook her head. "Why would he do that?" He'd *given* the photos to her.

"Because he didn't want me to see them. Maybe he doctored them. Or maybe there's something in them that would have given away his identity."

She didn't think the photos had been fake. But maybe...could there have been something in them that gave away her stalker? She'd been so shocked when she'd received them.

"Agents are talking to the hotel staff members. They're going to review the security footage. He got away tonight, but we *will* catch him, Gwen. Count on it." His fingers curled around the phone as he advanced toward her.

She couldn't help but tense. The shower hadn't exactly helped with the adrenaline rush. She was still too tense, too shaky, and her heartbeat kicked up even more as he approached her.

When he drew in close, she thought that he'd touch her. He didn't. And she could admit—to herself—that she was disappointed. Jeez. She was so messed up when it came to Simon.

"You're safe here," he swore.

Safe. Right. But hadn't she always thought safety was an illusion? Who was ever really safe? Monsters were always hiding just beyond the door.

"It's good that you came here with me instead of going back to your hotel room. That bastard could have been waiting for you."

A thought that she'd already had. "How are we going to catch him?"

We. Because she didn't plan on just sitting on the sidelines.

His head cocked as he gazed down at her. "First step in situations like this...I learn your secrets."

She didn't let herself tense.

"Every single one, baby. That's the way it has to be. This guy is preying on your past, on the things you want to keep hidden—so you have to tell me all of those things. I get your past, and then I start pushing into the rest of your life."

That didn't sound good. Way too ominous.

"I learn the secrets that your friends have. The secrets your lovers have. I investigate those closest to you in order to make certain your stalker isn't right beside you."

Simon was the only one beside her. Close enough to touch. Only he wasn't touching. And if he wasn't touching her now—

When he finds out my dark secrets, he'll never want me again.

"We have to fully bring the cops in on this. I'm sorry, but that shit has to be done. I know you want as much kept from the press as you can—"

She gave a mocking laugh. "I think the press learned about my stalker when my car ignited."

Simon didn't argue. "I'm not worried about the press."

He should be. They could be bloodthirsty and vicious.

"It's the cops we have to focus on. They don't know that this piece of crap is blackmailing you about Xavier."

Her body gave a small jerk. She couldn't help that. "Will they reopen the investigation on him?" *No, no, please say—*

"It's possible. But the stalker is just jerking you around. Obviously, you didn't kill Xavier."

Obviously. "I'm going to bed." She needed to think. A lot. "Good night." Forget borrowing a shirt—she'd just sleep in the nude. Screw it. She stepped around him—

But he moved into her path. "What are you hiding from me?"

Secrets that you don't want to know.

"Gwen, you used to tell me everything."

Yes, she had. She forced herself to stare into his eyes. "That was before you left me." Before he'd decided she wasn't enough. He had to go out and save the world.

And she'd saved herself. Could she tell him the truth? Did she dare?

His jaw hardened. "I had nothing to give you."

Ah, that was where he was wrong. To her, he *had* been everything. But she wasn't going down that path again. Oh, no. A woman had her pride. Better for him to just realize everything that he'd lost. Better for the guy to suffer and *wish* that things had been different.

She was a wee bit vindictive. A broken heart would do that. She wanted him to hurt, just a little. After all, she'd hurt plenty.

She'd had a few fantasies about Simon over the years. Most of them involved him begging her to take him back. She'd imagined him showing up on her doorstep, roses in hand, with his eyes so desperate and hopeful...

Right before she slammed the door in his face. *Bam, baby, bam.*

Revenge fantasy 101. "This didn't work out like I thought."

A furrow appeared between his brows. "Gwen?"

They were having this whole weird conversation while she was in a *towel*. "You were supposed to come begging at my door. Holding my favorite flowers. Telling me that life without me just wasn't worth living." Okay, sure that was a tad bit dramatic, but...

She'd made a life out of drama.

"Gwen..."

"But I was the one who showed up at *your* door. And instead of flowers, I brought all kinds of danger with me. A crazy stalker, a bomb, and who knows what else?" She bit her lower lip. "Why didn't you just tell me to screw off when you saw me in Wilde?"

He shook his head. "I'd never say that to you."

Liar, liar. Wasn't that exactly what he'd done years ago?

"My job is to help people who need me," he continued, seeming both earnest and grim. "You need me. I can make problems like yours *vanish.*"

Check. He was just doing his job. Not helping because he was still desperately hung up on her or anything. So what if he'd been her first lover? She'd had other lovers since him. Not like she was mooning over the one who got away. She had moved on. Her last lover had been voted as the sexiest man on the planet, for goodness sake. *Moved. On.* Time to get back to the matter at hand. "I thought Wilde was discreet. If you go to the cops and tell them *everything—*"

"I'm not telling them everything. We are discreet. It will be strictly need to know."

Okay, that was better. Some of the tension slid from her body.

"This is hard," he growled.

Now her brows rose.

"You're in a towel, and you look like every wet dream I've ever had."

Her lips parted.

"You know I still want you. You're a fucking hard act for anyone to follow, Gwen."

But he wasn't touching her. Simon was keeping that careful distance between them. She found herself wanting to push him. Wanting to push herself.

And if I'm so hard to follow...why did you leave?

Only she knew the answer. They'd been kids. He'd just been fooling around. She was the one who'd mistakenly thought it was more. "I'm in a towel because I don't have anything else to wear." She gave him a tired smile. "It's not so I can tempt you."

He growled.

She thought about letting the towel drop. Seriously, just letting that baby fall. Her life was out of control, insane, and the adrenaline and fear were making her *crazy*. For one wild moment, her hand rose and clutched the top of the towel. She wanted to drop it. *See what you've been missing, Simon. See what you let slip away.*

But his eyes became angry—and maybe lustful—green slits as if he'd read her mind. "Don't. Do *not* do it."

He should have remembered one thing about her. Even after all of this time, he should have remembered one very important thing.

"I'll get a t-shirt for you," he offered quickly. "Just do not—"

She hated being told what to do. Gwen let the towel fall. Her life was out of control? Yes, absolutely. So maybe everything should just go beyond control.

The towel slithered to the floor.

"Sweet fuck." His gaze immediately dropped to her body. She had to work out four to five freaking times a week, so he'd better be enjoying the view.

And he was...because her gaze dropped down *his* body, and Gwen saw the unmistakable arousal shoving at the front of his pants.

"Forget the shirt," Gwen announced as she straightened her spine. "I'll sleep in the nude."

Then she turned and walked away. She didn't run—though she kind of wanted to run. She just took her time, walking like she was on a runway. He'd been the one to walk away before, now it was her turn.

And he got to see exactly what he'd been missing.

***

Holy fuck.

Simon stood, absolutely rooted to the spot as the most perfect, heart-shaped ass he'd ever seen disappeared into his bedroom.

Do not rush after her. Do not fucking beg. But he was already drooling.

His dick was rock hard and shoving at the front of his pants, and he couldn't believe that Gwen had just stripped in front of him.

His heart felt like a jackhammer in his chest. The soft click of the bedroom door closing seemed to echo around him.

Gwen. *His* Gwen. Naked.

He sucked in a breath and then marched for the bathroom. He yanked on the shower. Only the cold water. He was going to need one extremely cold shower in order to get through the night. His hands were jerky as he began to yank off his clothes.

And with every move that he made, Simon still saw *her*.

Always, her.

CHAPTER SIX

The couch was hard as hell, and so, unfortunately, was he. Simon glowered at the big, round clock on his wall. One a.m. He'd been on the couch for over an hour, and he hadn't been able to sleep a wink. Every time that he closed his eyes, he saw Gwen.

Gwen's breasts.

Gwen's curving body.

Her shaved sex.

Sonofabitch!

He lunged up on the couch. He was wearing an old, faded pair of jeans and a paper-thin t-shirt because he hadn't wanted to be naked if she came out of the bedroom. He'd found the jeans and ancient shirt stuffed in a storage closet. Going into the bedroom and getting other clothes hadn't been an option for him. If he'd gone in there, seen her naked in his bed...that would have been both hell and heaven.

He still wanted Gwen. Not a big surprise. He'd pretty much always wanted her. The first time he'd had sex, it had been with Gwen. He'd been nervous as fuck, but he'd wanted her more than breath. And the more he'd been with her, the more he'd wanted.

Until he'd realized…

He had absolutely jack shit to offer her. His way out had been with the strength he'd always had—join the Navy. Become a SEAL. Change the world.

Be good enough for Gwen.

So he'd enlisted, and she'd been devastated.

"*Don't go.*" Her plea, but it had already been too late. You didn't get to back out on Uncle Sam, and he'd had these stupid plans. Plans to come home to her. To show her how mature and tough he was. To provide for her. Gwen had gotten a scholarship to Florida State University, and he'd *wanted* her to take that scholarship. A theater scholarship because the woman had always been incredible on a stage. So, yeah, he'd planned to go in the Navy, his eye on becoming a SEAL, and he'd thought he could come back and get a second chance. Live the dream.

Instead, I screwed everything to hell. Because a nineteen-year-old kid didn't understand just how lucky he was to be with a girl like Gwen in the first place. And there was no way she was just going to wait around on his dumbass to come back.

When he'd come back, she'd been gone. Not to FSU. But to Hollywood. And if he'd thought she was too good for him before…

When her face was on billboards, when she was in every movie theater around town, the woman was even more out of his reach. A million miles away.

The bedroom door creaked open.

Instantly, his body went on high alert.

Faint light spilled out from the bedroom. He kept sitting on the couch, but every muscle in his body was rock hard with tension.

Gwen tip-toed out of the bedroom.

He'd always had good night vision, and since he'd been awake on the couch, his eyes had long since adjusted to the darkness. With the extra light from the bedroom, he could see her perfectly.

Not naked this time, but wearing one of his shirts. A white button-up that fell to mid-thigh. She'd rolled it up at the sleeves. She advanced a bit, then stilled.

Was she going to the bathroom?

She crept forward, past the bathroom.

He knew she hadn't been able to get a look at him. He was cloaked in darkness. She was still in the light.

Huh. Story of their freaking lives.

Perhaps she was going to the kitchen...

No, she turned her body—toward him.

She inched closer. The floor gave a groan beneath her feet. And then... "Simon?"

"Yes?" His voice came out low and rough and fully awake.

Gwen gave a quick jump. "I, um, can't sleep."

Join the club, baby.

"I don't strip for random men."

Very good to know. "I'm not random."

"No, you're not." A pause. "I wanted you to know that's not a habit for me. I don't think I'm quite myself tonight." She pushed her hair behind her shoulder. "You really helped me today—or yesterday, I have no idea what time it is—and I just...I wanted to say I'm grateful."

Now he stood up. Slowly unwound his body from the couch as he rose and stared at Gwen. His bare feet pressed into the slightly cold floor. She was still the most beautiful thing he'd ever seen. She always *would* be the most beautiful to him. "I don't want your gratitude."

She came a touch closer. Brought her sweet vanilla scent with her. Had his cock aching even more. "Then what do you want?"

The same thing he'd always wanted. *Her.* The same thing he'd never been able to keep. *Her.* He cleared his throat. "You should go back to bed."

"Why? I'll just stay in there and stare up at the ceiling." Her breath sighed out. "I think I'm still riding that adrenaline high." Her voice was low. Husky. Sexy. "Every time I close my eyes, I see my car burning."

Tension tightened his muscles even more. He hated her fear. If he had his way, Gwen would never fear anyone or anything. "We're going to find him."

"I believe you. Wilde is supposed to be the best in the business."

"That why you came to the office? Because you had friends who told you we were good?"

"I do know people who've used the company before, but, no I came to Wilde just because of you."

Baby, be careful saying things like that.

She was almost right in front of him. Their bodies were bare inches apart.

"Can I tell you a secret?" Her voice had dropped.

"You can tell me anything."

"Once I could. Once, I felt like I could tell you every secret, every sin, and you'd never judge me."

I still won't.

"You always made me feel safe." Gwen's words came out in a rush. "I know we were both kids back then, but, God, if anyone so much as looked at me sideways, you were there. I often felt like you were standing between me and the whole world. Until...you weren't. You weren't there at all."

He reached for her hand. She gave a little start when his fingers curled around hers, but she didn't pull away. "Consider it my new job to stand between you and any threat. Until this guy is caught, I'm going to be with you. I'll keep you safe."

"You're the VP of Wilde. Eric was trying to explain to me that you don't take field work—"

"I take anything that involves you." Flat. True. "You think I'd trust you with someone else?" Did he want some other Wilde agent spending his nights with Gwen? Hell, poor Dennis had been fawning all over her. "They're too star struck by you. They won't see the threats coming." His fingers slid up her wrist. Traced lightly over her racing pulse point. "They'll only see you."

Her breath whispered out. "What do you see?"

"I see the star power, too. Hard to miss Gwen Soloman, celebrity."

"Oh."

Did she seem disappointed? "But I also see the girl I remember. Not the woman who wears those sexy-as-hell high heels, though I like her, too. I see the girl who used to run barefoot on a beach. The same girl who tempted me into skinny dipping even though I knew it was a bad idea. I'm pretty sure that when I came out of the water, I mooned a whole dolphin cruise full of people."

A small laugh came from her. "You're the one who tempted *me*."

He found himself pulling her against him. "You sure about that? I think I remember things differently."

She stared up at him. Her scent surrounded him. "I used to think..." Her voice had dropped more. "That you'd come looking for me. You know, one day. I had this crazy idea. You'd rush to my door. Tell me what a horrible, terrible mistake you'd made. That you never should have left me."

Baby, I never should have left you. You think I don't know that shit?

Now she pulled her hand away from him and stepped back.

Instantly, he missed her. Wasn't that the way it was for him, though? He fucking *missed* her. He had every single one of her movies in his place. He'd watch them sometimes, just to torture himself with what he'd lost. Yeah, he knew he had a problem.

"You didn't come to my door," Gwen whispered.

Oh, that's where you're wrong. But by the time he'd gotten there, she'd moved on.

Gwen turned away. "It's for the best, I'm sure. We're different people now. Way different. I'm certain all of those feelings are dead and buried for us both. It's just, you know, I guess your first is always supposed to be special or something." Her hand raked through her hair.

His head tilted as he studied her. "Things didn't feel dead and buried when you kissed me." Not even close.

She stilled. Glanced back at him. Stared a moment in silence. Gwen cleared her throat. "To be clear, *you* kissed me."

"Did I?"

"Simon..."

His overeager cock jerked. "God, I always loved it when you said my name."

She tensed.

And he'd said the wrong thing. Dammit. It was late, his control was shot, and his personal fantasy was right in front of him. "Your voice would go all breathy and sexy, and you'd turn me on...just by saying my name." Never happened with another woman.

"I should go to bed." But she didn't move toward the bedroom.

"You just said you couldn't sleep." He rolled back his shoulders. "I still want you."

She crept a little closer to him. Him, not the bedroom.

"Let's just get all of that out in the open, okay?" Why hold back? "Like I said, I still want you. Half the planet probably does, so I expect this is nothing new to you. But I want you. When we kissed, the desire was just as strong as it's always been. You want that part to be dead and buried, though? Fine, it can be. I assure you, I can keep this professional. Your safety will come first to me." She needed to hear this. He wanted her to trust him. He'd keep his dick zipped up and his hands off her. "I will do the job. I'll take down the bastard out there, and I won't touch you. Okay?"

She shook her head. "No, it's not okay. Very much *not*."

Simon had meant to reassure her, not to screw things up more. "Gwen—"

She rushed toward him. A fast tumble of steps. Her hands flew up and curled around his shoulders. "I lied."

"Gwen?"

"I still want you, too. The kiss mattered. It shouldn't, you know? It's been too long. We're different, but when I kissed you, I wanted you. I wanted you then, and I still want you right now."

Fucking *hell*. No, heaven. "What are we going to do about that?" No, that wasn't the right question. "What do *you* want to do about that?" He knew exactly what he wanted to do—her.

So much darkness clung around them. He wished that he could see her eyes better.

"I want to kiss you again."

Like she had to say that line twice. His head lowered, and, being careful because this was Gwen and if he was getting a second chance, he sure didn't want to ruin it, Simon brushed his lips against hers. Soft. Light.

Her lips parted beneath his. Her sexy little tongue slipped out.

A groan built in his throat.

His hands slid around her waist. He pulled her closer. The kiss went deeper. Became harder. He'd wanted her before she'd even stepped out of the bedroom. Having her pressed against his body, his hands on her, his mouth taking hers...

Desire deepened, gutted. The kiss changed. Stopped being so easy and light as the ravenous need that he'd fought to hold in check slipped through the cracks of his control. This was Gwen. His Gwen. Back in his arms. Wanting him. Kissing him.

In that moment, he could have devoured her. Simon wanted to taste every single inch of her. He felt like a starving man.

But her hands pushed between them.

His head lifted. He stared down at her even as his heart raced.

"It's still there," Gwen whispered.

Yes, it was. The need. For them, he thought it would always be there.

"You said...dirty, rough sex got rid of adrenaline."

He said a lot of real stupid sh—

"Just how dirty are you thinking?"

For a moment, he absolutely couldn't move. Maybe he was afraid to move because if he moved, this whole illusion before him might shatter. Gwen might vanish. She might pull away. She might—

She licked her lower lip. "Because I want you, Simon." Now she rose onto her toes. Her hands lifted and curled around his neck. "I want you very badly, and I'm done pretending. The need is there, for both of us. I'm not involved with anyone." A startled pause. "Are...are you?"

If he was involved with someone, he wouldn't have his hands on Gwen. That wasn't how he worked. "Only you."

She didn't get how true those words were for him.

He felt the tension slide from Gwen as her body softened. Her mouth slid over his collarbone in a light, sensual caress.

And that was just it. She wanted him? She was offering her delectable body to him? Did he look stupid? Hell, no.

Simon lifted her up, raising her easily into the air.

She gave a light, startled laugh. Her hands fell onto his shoulders. He'd lifted her straight up, and she stared down at him.

He hated the darkness around them. He wanted to see every single inch of her. He wanted to *taste* every single inch of her.

And he would.

He carried her toward the bedroom. Lowered her and kissed her and got her inside that room. The covers were pulled back on the bed. He put her down, just long enough to undo the buttons on her shirt, but his hands were too rough, the need too strong, and he sent those buttons flying.

Whatever.

Gwen laughed. The lamp was on near the bed and he could see her features and she *laughed*. She was smiling at him, staring at him with her deep, gorgeous eyes.

He kissed her and tumbled her back onto the bed. His mouth feasted on hers even as he pulled open her shirt. Then his mouth blazed a path down her neck. Gwen had always liked it when he licked her there, when he nipped right *there.*

She gave a gasp and arched up against him.

He kept licking and kissing. He made his way to her breasts. Her breasts were even fuller now. Curving and lush with tight, dusky nipples. He had to suck. Had to kiss. Had to lick. And she moaned when his mouth took her. Her hips arched up against him. His legs were between hers, and when she arched up, her sex pressed over the thick bulge of his arousal. He wanted his jeans gone. Wanted to be skin to skin with her. Wanted *in* her.

No, do this shit right. Slow down. A second chance only comes around once...

If it came around at all.

His fingers slid along her body. Over the silken curve of her stomach, down to her sex. Soft, bare. His fingers pushed between her legs. She was wet for him. Already. Hell, yes. He stroked two fingers inside of her, and she rocked against his hand. Her body was tight with tension, and he knew she was approaching her first orgasm.

He had to make this good for Gwen. So good...

Because he didn't want a one-and-done deal with her. Oh, no, he had much bigger plans.

He moved down the bed. Pushed her legs farther apart. For a moment, he just stared at her sex. So pretty.

"Simon?"

His head lowered. He had to taste. His tongue licked over her.

"*Simon!*" Her hands flew down. Her nails bit into his shoulders.

He licked again. Kissed. Stroked. Even as his mouth worked her, his fingers were sliding inside. She was moaning and arching against him, and he didn't let up. He wanted to taste her when she came. Wanted the pleasure to sweep over her and make Gwen forget *everything* else. He needed to give her that. Had to give—

"*Oh, God, Simon!*" She came against his mouth. He kept licking her, wanting the pleasure to last and last as she rode out her release.

She shivered against him. Moaned.

He licked her again. Her taste was incredible. Addictive. He lifted his head and stared at her. Her hair was spread out over his pillow, her lips parted, her breath coming in quick pants.

His dick was hard as steel in his pants. So hard the zipper had probably left an impression on him. He wanted nothing more than to drive into her, to have her legs wrapped around him as he pounded into Gwen and found his own release...

No, that wasn't true. There was one thing he wanted more.

Jaw locking, muscles tight, he eased away from Gwen. His hands grabbed the sheets nearby and fisted around them.

"Simon?"

He'd squeezed his eyes shut. Mostly because staring at her was a temptation in itself.

"Don't you...want me?"

His eyes flew open. "More than I've ever wanted anyone." An absolute truth.

"Then why..." Her words trailed away. She took a breath. "Why are you still wearing your jeans? They really get in the way."

God, even now, the woman made him want to smile. "If the jeans come off, I'm a fucking goner. I'll be in you two seconds later, buried as far as I can go."

"That doesn't sound like a bad plan to me."

If he weren't playing for the end game, yeah, it would be a *great* plan. But... "You're scared. You had the shock of your life tonight. And the adrenaline rush is about to crash on you any moment." Crash hard. He made himself let go of the sheets. Made himself get out of the bed. He needed to put some distance between them before he pounced on her again. "I don't want you waking up in the morning and regretting what happened between us."

She sat up, but didn't pull the covers with her. Her shirt—*his* shirt—slid over to mostly cover her breasts but still revealed just enough to make his cock twitch. "You think I'd regret sleeping with you?"

"I think we haven't been together in a while. I think you're scared. I think—"

"I know what I want, Simon. Life is too short for regrets. Trust me, it's a lesson I know well. You can regret the things you did. You can also sure as hell regret the things you didn't do."

Like hold tight to the girl you loved when you were nineteen?

"You can spend too many hours and too many days regretting everything. Regret wastes energy and saps your hope. I don't have time for it." Her shoulders straightened. "Fuck it."

"Gwen..."

"You want me? Then ditch the jeans. I want you, understand that. I know what I want in this world, and I will not be waking up in the morning regretting what happened. This isn't some marriage proposal. It's sex. Dirty, rough, and wild, isn't that what was promised?"

His hands dropped to the waist of his jeans. He was trying here, but he was no saint. Every movement of her body sent the shirt sliding a little bit, revealing Gwen's gorgeous breasts. Making him ache.

"I want you. We're adults, why can't we take what we want? I mean, unless there is some rule at Wilde about you *not* mixing business and pleasure..."

Actually, there probably was but...

She gave a little shrug. The shirt dipped open more. "I suspect that we already broke that rule when I was screaming your name."

He'd loved it when she'd screamed his name.

"There are lots of guys who want to fuck me." Said flatly. "They want the rush of saying they've scored with a star. Want to tell all their friends about what sex with me was like—"

He growled and clenched his hands into fists. "Want me to teach them some fucking manners?" Where he came from, a man never kissed and told. He didn't brag about screwing. He didn't—

She climbed from the bed. Stood in front of him. "That's the thing about you. Always wanting to be the hero. The protector. No one in my life wanted to protect me, not until you. And you're still doing it, aren't you? The first time I have trouble, I came running to you."

Don't touch. Don't touch. If he touched her, he was done for. He'd dive dick deep in her and never look back. He was *trying* to do this the right way.

Her hand lifted. Caressed his chest. Pressed right over his racing heart and seemed to scorch him through the shirt. "I had to be careful with my lovers."

He didn't want to talk about her lovers. He wanted to drive his fist into the lucky bastards who'd had her. Maybe break their perfect faces. Or their hands—for touching her.

That shit isn't normal. It's not sane. That's the kind of shit that will scare her away. He'd always been far too primitive when it came to Gwen. When it came to her, he felt too much. Needed too much.

"When I choose a new lover, I have to pick a man I can count on. I have to weed the guy out from the ones who just want the woman they see in the movies. From the ones who don't really want *me*." Her hand stroked across his chest. "But I know what I'm getting with you. You wanted me when I had nothing."

"I will always want you." Statement of simple fact. He'd be ninety, pushing a walker, and still wanting her.

Her head tilted back. "Then why turn away when I am offering myself to you right now?"

He'd tried. *Tried* to do this the right way. His control was shredding beneath her touch.

Her hand slid down and she caught the edge of his t-shirt. Gwen pushed it up. He helped her, yanking it over his head and dropping it to the floor. Her hands slid over him. Soft fingertips stroked over his chest. His chest was covered with scars from battles he'd like to forget. She didn't question him about the marks. Just softly kissed some of the wounds. And her fingers trailed down, down...she caught the snap of his jeans.

"Gwen..."

Her answer was another kiss on his shoulder.

She unhooked the jeans and slid down the zipper. His cock sprang forward, thrusting into her hands. When she touched his cock, he was gone. He kissed his control good-bye because there was no hope for him.

Wild and rough? Yes. Hell, yes.

He kissed her. Took her mouth and thrust his tongue inside. He caught her hands and pulled them away, the better for him to strip and kick his jeans across the room. He tumbled her onto the bed. She laughed. *Laughed.* He pulled away just long enough to grab a condom from the bedside drawer. He ripped open the packet and rolled the condom on his cock in record time. He dragged Gwen to the edge of the bed. Her legs hung over the side of the mattress—those long, gorgeous legs. He lifted up her hips and exposed her sex completely.

And he drove into her as deeply as he could go.

Her neck arched back, and her eyes closed. "Simon!" Her legs wrapped around his hips.

He leaned over the bed, slamming his hands down beside her and grabbing the sheets. He withdrew, then plunged deep, and nearly went out of his mind. Tight, wet, hot. He was lost in her, his control utterly gone. The bed jerked as he pounded into her, and her name fell from his lips.

He'd been addicted to her since he was nineteen years old. He'd tried to tell himself that he was wrong. That it hadn't been that good. That she hadn't been that good...

Gwen was better than good. Fucking fantastic.

She came again, bucking beneath him. He grabbed her legs and looped them over his shoulders, wanting to sink even deeper into her. Then his fingers went to her clit.

"Simon, it's too much—no, dammit, do *not* stop! Too much in a good way, good, good, *good!*"

He worked her clit until she came a third time. Hell, yes. Their bodies were slick with sweat. He kissed her. He licked her neck. He bit lightly and he erupted into her, coming on a wave of release that left his knees shaking.

He should have been sated. The pleasure had just filled every single cell in his body. He wasn't sated. Not even close.

He withdrew from her. Slowly. Put her legs down. "Don't move."

She blinked up at him.

He rolled off the condom even as he stormed for the bathroom. He threw the condom in the trash and grabbed a cloth. He wiped it over his cock—his dick was already hard again. *Because it is Gwen.*

His breath sawed in and out of his lungs as he stared at his reflection. He looked insane. Eyes blazing, jaw locked, stubble thick on his jaw even as his hair was a wreck. The woman should have run screaming from him.

She hadn't. She'd given herself to him again. She'd screamed *for* him as she came.

He spun away from the mirror.

Gwen was still on the bed. *His* bed. Waiting for him.

The nightstand drawer was open. He reached inside and yanked out another condom. The rip of the packet seemed loud in the silence of the room.

"Again?" Gwen asked, voice husky and sensual.

Again? With her, always. He had years to make up. Too many fantasies and not enough reality.

He rolled on the condom.

Gwen scrambled back.

Simon froze. Lust pounded through his veins and he tried to think through the thick fog. This was Gwen. *Gwen.* He couldn't scare her. Couldn't fuck up with her.

She went to her knees, crouching in the middle of the bed. "You look like you could eat me alive." There was the faintest quiver in her words.

Maybe she was realizing just how badly he wanted her.

He didn't take another step toward her. "Did I hurt you?" He'd been too desperate for her.

Gwen shook her head. Her body turned a little and she pressed her palms to the headboard. Then she smiled at him. "This way...this time." Her hips lifted toward him.

Sexy as hell.

He climbed onto the bed behind her.

Her palms rose until she was gripping the top of the wooden headboard. He curled his body along hers. He positioned his cock, got it right at the entrance to her body. His mouth moved toward her ear. He licked the lobe, then whispered, "Tell me if I hurt you."

"You won't."

He drove into her. And even as his cock filled her, his hand reached around her body. He found her clit. Stroked her. Wanted her to feel the same wild pleasure that he did. He wanted to hook Gwen on him. Get her as addicted as he was on her.

The rhythm was fierce. The headboard banged into the wall, and it was good thing that he didn't have neighbors. She was loud and he loved it when she called his name. Her hips drove back against him, and he felt her coming, felt the hard contractions all along his cock as he thrust into her. And as she came, he climaxed, too. Surged into her and never, ever wanted to let her go.

Because how did you let go of the dream that you'd always had?

Your one, perfect fucking dream.

***

Her scream woke Simon hours later. He was wrapped around her, her body snug to his side, but her scream tore him from sleep.

"Gwen?"

She struggled against him and bolted upright. "*Stop, stop!*" Gwen's voice was frantic.

"Baby, it's just a bad dream." He sat up and carefully wrapped his arms around her.

Her body shuddered, and he knew she was back with him. He'd turned off the lamp long ago, but right then, he wished he had enough light to see her face.

"Sorry." Her voice was wooden.

"Was it the fire? Did you have a nightmare about the car exploding?"

"Yes." A quick response. "It was the fire."

Why did he feel like she was lying to him? "Gwen?"

She slid back down in the bed. "Sorry I woke you. It won't happen again."

"I don't fucking care if you wake me up a million times. I just don't want you scared." He eased back down, too. He kept his arm around her. Kept her close. "Do you want to talk about it?"

She was stiff beside him. "No. Why give it any power? It was just a bad dream."

But he remembered what she'd said...*Stop*. Stop the flames? Stop the explosion? "You can trust me," he told her softly.

She didn't say anything. Her body was soft and warm against him, but Simon had the sudden feeling that Gwen was a million miles away.

***

When she thought he was asleep, Gwen slid from the bed. She tip-toed across the room and made it to the bathroom without so much as a creak of sound. She shut the door behind her. Locked it. Didn't look at herself in the mirror.

With shaking fingers, she yanked on the shower. The water poured out, hot and strong, with steam soon filling the bathroom. She hurried under the spray. Let it hit her...

And let her tears slide right away with the water.

She'd told Simon that she'd just had a bad dream. She'd lied to him. It hadn't been a dream. It had been a memory. The same one that had haunted her for years.

It was time to tell him the truth. Maybe he'd walk away. Maybe he'd turn her over to the cops.

Perhaps she should have told him the truth before they'd crossed the line and had sex again. But she'd needed to be with him, before she told Simon her dark secrets. Before she changed the way he looked at her. The way he felt about her.

Before she changed everything.

CHAPTER SEVEN

She was cooking when Simon strolled his sexy self out of the shower. Gwen had poked around in his cabinets, found a frying pan, and gotten some eggs ready to go. She made enough for Simon because, well, it was his stuff, after all. A thank you breakfast seemed like the least she could do.

And she also had an old habit...when she was nervous, she cooked. There was something about the whole process that soothed her. Always had.

Maybe it was left over from growing up with her grandmother. Her grandmother had always loved to cook in their small kitchen. She'd cook and she'd hum, and she'd make Gwen feel like the world was a safe place. Gwen had never known her dad. Her mother had cut out when she'd been a kid, and Gwen had found herself raised by her grandmother.

"Something smells amazing."

She stiffened at his deep, rumbling voice.

"But, baby, you sure as hell didn't need to cook."

She scooped the eggs onto a plate. Some for her, some for him. She'd sprinkled vegetables and cheese into the eggs. Not super fancy, but good enough. "I had to eat, so I figured I could cook, too." Gwen turned toward him, her grip a little too tight as she held the plates. "Though I know I should have asked before I went plundering in your fridge and cabinets. Sorry—"

Simon shook his head. "You don't have to ask me for anything."

She eased out a breath and put the plates down on the nearby table. He pulled back the chair for her, holding it out all gentleman-like. After casting a quick glance at him, Gwen sat down. He was dressed in jeans and a t-shirt—one that his wide shoulders and powerful arms stretched. His hair was still wet from the shower, and he'd shaved the stubble off his hard jaw. Dammit. She'd rather liked that rough stubble.

She was wearing one of his shirts. She'd showered, too, earlier, and done her best to tame her hair. It was thick and heavy, and it was supposed to be part of her "look" so her agent would have a heart attack if Gwen cut it off...something she had been tempted to do on more than one occasion.

They ate in silence, and even though she'd been starving when she woke up, Gwen could barely make herself chew and swallow. The fear was too heavy. Fear that came because she knew what was going to happen next. Her big confession.

"God, this is fucking delicious." He ate like a starving man. "You always could make anything taste like a dream. When I cook, the damn eggs just burn."

She smiled, remembering that about him. The guy truly had horrible cooking skills. She'd seen him absolutely blacken toast once—and make the toaster explode.

"Take-out keeps me alive," he told her, flashing a grin that showed his even, white teeth. "But your stuff is one hell of a lot better."

"It's easy," she said as she pushed around the eggs that she now couldn't eat. "You just follow the directions."

He laughed. "Trust me, I've tried. You have a gift."

Her hands slid off the table and into her lap. She liked his laugh. It was warm and rough. And it made her want to laugh back with him.

He'd already cleared his plate. "An agent will be bringing your clothes by first thing this morning. Then we will head to Wilde. I'll need you to talk to my team. I know it's personal, but I have to know about the people in your life. Friends, associates, ex-lovers."

She shook her head. "They aren't doing this to me."

"You never know. In stalker situations, it's often people close to you who—"

"No," she interrupted flatly. "It's not them. They didn't know about Xavier." *No one knows what I've done.* Only... Xavier.

The dead man.

"Your agent and your assistant will be called in, too. We have to question everyone close to you."

Because he thought they were all suspects.

GUARDING GWEN   111

Simon drummed his fingers on the table and watched her with narrowed eyes. "Are we going to talk about it?"

Her heart gave a fast, hard thud. "It?"

"Last night. The sex that was fucking mind-blowing."

It had been pretty mind-blowing. But talking about it? Not on her agenda. "There's something you need to know."

His expression tightened. "If you're about to tell me that you're involved with someone, that you have a lover who—"

"I killed a man." There. She'd just shared the darkest secret of her life. The one that haunted her. The one that made her wake up screaming. And, holy hell, but she'd never said those words out loud. Never allowed herself to tell anyone that painful secret.

But she'd blurted it over breakfast with Simon. Way to not have tact.

Barely breathing, Gwen waited for Simon's response.

He shook his head.

"What?" She jumped to her feet. Of all the things she'd expected, a negative head shake wasn't it. "You don't believe me?"

"You're hardly the cold-blooded killer type, Gwen. I mean, you used to relocate spiders. I don't think you'd kill—"

"Someone who was trying to attack me?" Gwen cut in, her voice brittle. "You don't think I'd fight back? That I wouldn't do any damn thing necessary to save myself?" Her chin notched up. "Think again. I would. I did."

His face changed. She saw the shock first, then...rage. A dark, burning rage that filled his eyes, turning them so very dark as his pupils expanded. Then she saw the fury in the flaring of his nostrils, in the hardening of his jaw and the flattening of his mouth. He rose, pushing his hands flat against the table. "Who?"

Who did he think? Who was this mess all about? "Xavier Gray."

A snarl came from him. "I told that sonofabitch to stay the hell away from you—"

"Right, yes, you did." Her voice was brittle. She was brittle. But Gwen was working hard at holding her shit together. *Story of my life these days.* "You beat the crap out of him when he got too handsy with me. Played the protector just great. But then you know what you did?" And anger was there, an anger she'd had buried inside for a long time. "You *left.*"

He backed up. The chair went crashing to the floor, and the sharp sound made her flinch.

"You left," Gwen continued coldly. "And I was still there. He was there. And one night, I was walking home from work by myself. I'd been waiting tables all day, trying to get extra tips for when I left for college in the fall. I was exhausted and alone, and he was there." *You weren't.* She didn't say those words, but the hurt was there. The absolute fury and pain that had burned inside of her for so long. "He came out of the shadows. He slammed into me, rammed me hard with his whole body, and my head hit the wall of a nearby building. Everything went black."

Simon lunged toward her.

"Stop! No!" Her voice fired out with the force of her fury as she lifted her hand toward him.

Simon froze.

"It's hard enough saying this, okay? Don't touch me. Don't come close to me, or I won't be able to get these words out. I haven't told *anyone* this stuff. I buried this secret down deep, and I tried to pretend like hell that it hadn't happened." She sucked in a deep breath. Her hand fisted and fell back to her side. "When I opened my eyes again, I was on his boat. We were in the middle of the freaking Gulf, and he was laughing, telling me that no one was close. That no one was going to come rushing to my rescue. That he'd watched me and wanted me for years, and he was going to have what he wanted. That his father had told him he could *always* have everything he wanted. In this world, he simply had to take it."

A muscle jerked along Simon's jaw. If possible, his eyes went even darker.

"He seemed surprised the first time I hit him. I mean, what did he think? That I was just going to sit there and let him do anything he wanted?" She shook her head at the memory. "He took a step back, like the shock was that huge, and I ran. I ran past him, and he *laughed* again. Xavier told me there was nowhere I could go, not unless I thought I could swim all the way back to the shore." Another deep breath. "I remember wondering if he'd done this before. Because...he was so confident. So certain that I couldn't get away. That he could do what he wanted for as long as he wanted..." She blinked. "He didn't have that right." Her voice sounded lost to her own ears.

"Baby..."

Gwen flinched again. She cleared her throat. "It was a yacht, one of those thirty-footers that some of those rich assholes always kept at the main marina. It had a cabin and I ran inside, thinking I could lock the door and figure some shit out about escaping. I had this half-hearted plan of using the radio to call for help. I'd barricade myself in there, radio for help, and the cops would come for him." Goosebumps were on her arms. "But he grabbed me before I could shut the door. He was yanking at my top, saying he'd waited for me to wake up because he wanted me to know everything he was doing. My hands flew out, and I-I grabbed a fire extinguisher."

Silence.

But in her head...she could hear the sound of waves and—

Thud. A rough, almost hollow sound.

"I slammed the extinguisher into the side of his head." Blood had poured from the wound. He'd blinked owlishly at her. "Xavier stumbled back, and I followed him. I held that fire extinguisher as tightly as I could. And then he reached for me again." Her lower lip trembled. Dammit, she hated that tremble. "When he reached for me again, I hit him once more. As hard as I could. He fell back, and Xavier fell right over the side of the boat."

She'd done it. She'd told Simon.

Now she turned away from him as Gwen rubbed her arms. "At first, I kept my grip on that fire extinguisher, thinking he'd come back up. I knew I should get on the radio and call for help. I knew it but then..." Her words trailed away.

She heard Simon take a step toward her.

Gwen whirled. Faced Simon once more. "He didn't come up." There. "Each second seemed to last forever. I was counting and holding my own breath, but he didn't come up. After ten minutes, I realized he *wasn't* coming up. I realized I'd killed him."

"Self-defense," he growled.

"It was." She nodded. "Yes, yes, it was. But..." Now one shoulder moved in a careless roll. "Who was going to believe that? Xavier's family had more money than God. I had a bedroom drawer full of tips that I'd saved up from my waitressing jobs. I was on his boat. Would the cops believe that he'd knocked me out and brought me out there? Or would they think I'd come willingly? That I had some plan to hurt him?" And this was the part that had been so big and scary in her mind. "You'd attacked him the week before when he made a move on me. Everyone at the beach saw the fight that day. They saw me between the two of you. They *saw*. They'd heard him yelling that I wanted him. And now he was dead. I'd killed him. I was eighteen and scared out of my mind, and you..."

No.

"I was gone," Simon rasped.

Her spine straightened. "I dropped the fire extinguisher overboard. I wasn't trying to destroy evidence, I swear, I wasn't. I remember it just felt so heavy as I stood there. The boat was rocking hard beneath me. The waves were crashing into the side over and over again. I could taste salt water on my lips, and the extinguisher just seemed so *heavy,*" Gwen said again. "It fell, and I didn't even realize it until I heard the crash of it hitting the water."

"Gwen..." His voice was thick. Rough. "Baby, you're crying."

What? Her hand lifted and swiped across her left cheek. "When it crashed into the water, something seemed to break inside of me. I stared at the waves and knew I couldn't be found on his boat. I had to get out of there. His family was going to destroy me. My grandmother was dead." She'd buried her grandmother a week before graduation. A *week.* "You were gone. I had *nothing.* No one but myself. So, I had to keep surviving. I had to get out." Her heart slammed into her chest. "I jumped into the water."

Simon swore. "You could have *died.*"

"I was always a good swimmer," she whispered. "But my head was hurting. I didn't even realize that I had this giant knot on my temple, not until later. It came from when he'd slammed me into that building. Maybe a good lawyer could have argued that I wasn't thinking clearly because of that blow, that I had a concussion but...well, it wasn't like I could afford a good lawyer back then."

His body seemed carved from stone.

"The waves pulled at me, and I remember being so cold. So freaking cold. I swam and I swam, and then sometimes..." A rough laugh. "I just floated on my back. When I could barely breathe and I just needed a minute, I floated on my back and I stared up at the stars, and I tried to figure out what the hell I was going to do. I stared at those stars, and I wished that I could be someone else. That I could get out of there—that city, that town that seemed to suck me dry. I just wanted *out*." The night had seemed to last forever.

"What happened next?" There was no emotion in his voice. Or on his face. Not any longer. But his eyes still blazed. He'd done a fairly good job at hiding his feelings. Her acting coach would've said he had potential.

"When my feet finally touched sand, I was so shocked that I think I screamed. I stumbled onto the beach and fell, and the sand was in my mouth. It was on my face, my hands, on every inch of me. I sat on that beach. I stared out at the waves, and I realized…I'd made it." That was when the hope had grown inside of her. "If I'd made it to shore, then maybe Xavier had, too. Maybe he'd swam to shore. Maybe he'd been afraid to come back on the yacht because he thought I would attack him again. Maybe he was okay. Maybe…" Her words were too fast. "Maybe he was afraid of me. So I thought that if I just went home, I might wake up the next day, and everything would be normal again. He'd stay away from me. I'd stay away from him. I'd go to college like I'd planned. Everything would be *fine*."

She backed away from Simon. Part of Gwen couldn't believe that she'd just told Simon her secret. He could go to the cops. He could destroy her. But…there was no choice here. "For two days after that, things were normal. And then the first report came about Xavier's boat being found abandoned by the Coast Guard." She'd been working at the restaurant when the news aired. She'd heard the reporter's words and dropped the tray she'd been carrying. Way to not look suspicious. The plates and glasses had shattered when they'd hit the floor.

Even as she had that thought, that memory, her gaze darted to the table where she and Simon had just eaten breakfast. To the plates still on the table. She grabbed them and took them toward the sink. Her hands were shaking. *Don't drop these plates like you did that day. Don't—*

His fingers wrapped around hers. "Leave them."

The plates clattered into the sink as she yanked away from him.

"Gwen?"

She glanced up at the ceiling as she avoided his stare. She was *not* crying again. But she was going to finish this story. "The cops were asking for information. Asking if anyone knew any details about that night. God, I was so scared. I was sure the cops were going to come for me any moment. I left work, and I went to the beach. To the same spot I'd been in the other night when I'd finally reached shore." For a moment, she could almost feel the wind on her skin. "I stood there, staring out at the waves, and I knew I had to turn myself in. I didn't want to be hunted. I watched all those cop shows while I was growing up. There was probably DNA on the boat. Stuff that could incriminate me. Xavier's family would destroy me, but I didn't have a choice. The knot and bruising had already faded from my temple. I wasn't going to have any physical proof that I had been assaulted, and I knew I was going to jail, I knew—"

"*You never called me.*"

Her gaze darted to his face. "Why drag you down with me?"

Simon grabbed her shoulders. His grip was tight but not painful. Never painful. "I would have helped you."

She could only shake her head. "You were off being all you could be. I had to help myself. I had to stand on my own. And...I did." His touch seemed to singe her. "Stop touching me. It's hard enough without you touching me."

Immediately, he freed her and backed away. "I'm sorry." There was so much pain in his voice.

Was he apologizing for touching her? Or something more?

"I was on that beach, trying to figure out my next move...and then everything changed." She released a long, slow breath. "Life does that, you know? You think one thing is going to happen...and then it flips in an instant." That was the way it had been for her. The world changed. "A movie was filming. I'd just accidentally walked into their shot, and...the director came running toward me. He said I was..." Now she laughed. "'Projecting sorrow.' That was the term he used, and yeah, I was. Serious understatement. Whatever. He liked what he saw. He asked me if I'd ever done any acting." A bitter laugh escaped her. "I mean, that was a million-to-one chance. I'd even auditioned for a bit part in that movie the week before. I hadn't gotten it, but right then, this guy was saying he wanted me. He got me to read a few lines. They filmed me. It wasn't going to be anything huge, but for a few hours that day, I was able to forget the nightmare around me."

She'd been able to pretend that everything was okay. That she was someone else. She liked pretending to be someone else. She'd always liked that. When your own life sucked, escaping into another one was the best way to survive.

"Eveline was on set. She was repping one of the stars, and she came up to me when I finished filming. Eveline offered me representation on the spot. Said she could make me famous." A smile twisted her lips. "Even more importantly, she told me the magic words, 'I can get you out of this town.' I signed with her and didn't look back." Her shoulders slumped. She'd done it. Told her biggest, darkest secret.

Now it was time for her to wait.

Her arms curled around her stomach. It would sure be a whole lot better if she had on actual clothes and not just his shirt. Gwen felt vulnerable enough as it was. With the shirt, and her legs on display, she felt like too much was—

"What do you think I'm going to do now?" Simon's voice was a low rumble.

"I'm not sure." She rocked back onto her heels. "I confessed to murder, so I guess the normal thing to do in this situation would be to call the cops."

"Normal?" Simon seemed to strangle on that one word. "Sweetheart, there is nothing *normal* about this." He took a hard step toward her.

She backed up, an instinctive response.

He stilled. That muscle flexed along his jaw again. "Do you think I would *ever* do anything to hurt you?"

"Yes."

Shock flashed on his face. "Baby—"

"It gutted me when you left me before. That *hurt*. Physical hurt? No, I don't think you would, but there are lots of ways to be hurt in this world. And I knew that when I confessed to you, there was a chance you'd turn me over to the cops. I *murdered* a man."

"No." A snarl. "You acted in self-defense. You didn't murder anyone. So don't say that again, okay? Don't think it. *You acted in self-defense.* And a good lawyer will tell you, if there's no body, there's no crime."

What? She blinked in confusion.

"I know a good lawyer. If we need him, I'll bring Kendrick in, but I am *not* turning you over to the cops." Simon shook his head in what appeared to be real confusion. "Is that what you thought? That I am such a fucking bastard I'd have sex with you one night and then drag you to the police station the next morning?"

"No." Yes? Well, not that he was a fucking bastard but—

A furrow appeared between his brows. "Or did you think..." Now his voice was even lower. "Did you think if you slept with me again...I *wouldn't* turn you in?"

He was twisting things. "Simon—"

"Because, baby, you didn't need to sleep with me in order for that to happen. You don't need to try and manipulate me. I would *never* throw you to the wolves. Let's just be clear on that." His eyes held hers. "You think I don't know that I made the worst mistake of my life when I walked away from you years ago?"

I made the worst mistake of my life when I walked away from you years ago. She shook her head. He couldn't have said those words. The words straight out of one of her fantasies.

Only, she wasn't slamming anything. She wasn't sure she could even move in that moment. Gwen felt rooted to the spot.

"And now to hear what happened to you while I was gone...to know the nightmare you went through without me...how could you ever believe I would do anything but help you?"

How could she believe it? "Because people change. And we're not talking about some simple crime here. It's not like I stole a loaf of bread or spray painted some graffiti some place. I was—"

"You were a victim, and it is my fucking fault." Simon yanked a hand through his hair. "I stirred Xavier's anger. I'm the one who pissed him off and humiliated him in front of the town. And, shit, I even got calls from the cops after he vanished."

He'd what? Simon hadn't mentioned—

"They came to me, questioned me with my superior officers present, but I had an iron-clad alibi, so I didn't even think a damn thing about Xavier being gone. I figured he'd drank too much and fallen off his yacht. Told the cops the same thing. That's what everyone figured." His hand dropped, and Simon appeared sick. "If I had known for an instant what happened to you, what you were going through..."

Her spine stiffened. "You know now."

He winced.

"And I need you now. I need your help. After hearing my story, you understand why someone blackmailing me about Xavier's death scared the hell out of me—even before the car bomb. No one should know what I did. No one should know about that night. Unless..." She was almost too scared to say the rest.

His eyes narrowed.

"Maybe Xavier isn't dead," she whispered. "Do you think it's even possible?"

His lips parted, but then an alarm began to sound. A slow, low beep. She gave a little jerk.

"Easy." Simon pulled out his phone. Swiped his finger over the screen and stared down at it. "That's just Dennis. I talked to him a little while ago. He's bringing some clothes by for you." He typed in a code on his phone, and the alarm stopped.

Then Simon glanced back up at her. "I don't know what's possible." Determination hardened his voice. "I'll find out, though, you can count on it."

Her shoulders seemed to feel lighter.

He took a slow step toward her. Held up his hands, palms out. "I'm not going to touch you."

A shiver slid over her whole body.

"I'm so sorry. So fucking sorry you went through that all alone. You won't be alone again, understand? I'm here. I'm in this thing with you until the end. We're going to find out who is doing this to you. We're going to stop him. Whether it's Xavier Gray or some other asshole—I will stop him."

It took her a moment to realize what she was feeling. Relief. There was anger in his eyes, fury, but it wasn't directed at her. He wasn't looking at her like she was some kind of monster.

And that was what she'd feared. That he'd stare at her with hate or rage or look at her in disgust. But he wasn't.

You were the victim.

Simon's head cocked. "You seriously thought I'd turn you over to the cops?" His lips twisted. "Baby, don't you get it? That's not who I am to you."

"Who are you?"

"I'm the guy that you come to when you need shit taken care of. You want a body hidden? I'll bury it. You want me to take down the bastard hurting you? I'll destroy him. Ride or fucking die, that's what I am to you. I will never choose anyone over you. And I *won't* make the same mistakes again this time. You can count on it." A determined nod. "I learned to fight hard and to fight dirty when I was a SEAL. There is nothing I won't do to protect you. No line I won't cross. If you believe nothing else, I say, believe this...*you will come first for me.*"

"Because I'm your client?"

"No, because you're everything. And one day, you'll realize you always were."

No, not possible. He didn't know her anymore. She wasn't the same girl. He wasn't the same boy. There was so much they didn't know about each other. More secrets. More lies.

And a woman sure as hell wasn't everything to a man when he walked away and never looked back.

Don't believe him. Don't give him too much of yourself again. Use him...because it's what you have to do.

"I want to hold you. Kiss you." His hands flexed into fists and then released. "We aren't done, you understand that?"

Done? No, they weren't done. "You're my bodyguard. You stay with me until it's over." Now that he wasn't, you know, phoning the cops on her ass. She wanted him to stay close. She liked having him near because he could make her feel so safe. She had to blink away tears of absolute relief.

"I'm one hell of a lot more than that, sweetheart. When you were in my arms last night, screaming my name, I wasn't just your bodyguard."

Her cheeks burned. "You were yelling out my name, too."

"Hell, yes, I was. Because it's always you, baby. *Always.*"

What?

His phone vibrated. "I have to let Dennis inside. Shit timing." He turned away from her.

She lunged forward and grabbed his arm. "You're not telling him?" No, wait, that sounded like a question. Wrong, *wrong.* "You're not telling him." Better. That statement had sounded firm and confident. Maybe.

He looked down at her hand as it gripped his arm.

"You *can't* tell him." A desperate edge entered her voice. "You might not want to turn me in, but how do I know Dennis won't sell me out? This is a major story, and the tabloids would pay hundreds of thousands of dollars for it." And she was not exaggerating. One of her co-stars had just had a secret baby exposed. And the person who'd shared all the dirty details had gotten four hundred grand for the story.

"I'm not telling Dennis," Simon assured her.

Her breath expelled in relief.

"But I *will* have to tell Eric."

No. She could feel all of the color draining from her face.

"Baby, *let* me touch you. I'm afraid you're about to fall at my feet."

No, she wasn't. She didn't fall at anyone's feet. The world was supposed to be at her feet now. She'd dragged herself up. Worked twenty-hour days, seven days a week. Never complained on set. Worked until her feet bled in her high heels. Proven herself time and time again to the roughest directors in the businesses. "I won't fall." She pulled away. "But if you tell Eric, then it's over for me."

"Client confidentiality."

A mocking laugh escaped her. "Confidentiality to cover murder? I didn't realize just how all-purpose Wilde really was!" And she'd specifically *asked* about confidentiality when she'd been in Eric's office. The guy had responded that confidentiality depended on the crime.

They were talking about murder. Call her crazy, but she didn't see Eric Wilde viewing murder as a not-so-serious crime.

Simon's green gaze glinted. "No body, no crime. You're our client. And I told you, *if* I see that you need a lawyer, I know a good one. Self-defense isn't murder."

The scandal alone could destroy everything she'd built, even if she never set foot in a jail cell. She'd known the risk she took telling him, but...she'd *had* to give him the truth. Especially after last night's car bombing.

The stalker out there wasn't playing some game. He was dead serious.

Simon's phone vibrated again. "I have to let Dennis inside. You stay here. I'll bring the clothes up."

She swiped her hand over her cheek once more. No more tears had leaked out. That was good.

"Gwen."

Her head snapped up.

"*Trust me.*"

She wanted to, but the truth of the matter was that she hadn't completely trusted anyone, not since she was eighteen years old.

***

Simon stalked onto the elevator. The doors slid closed. His breath sawed in and out.

Gwen had been attacked. That prick Xavier had gone after her again. She'd been alone. At his mercy. She could have *died*.

And Simon had been gone. Off to protect the rest of the world, while *his* world was left by herself. Unguarded.

His right hand fisted. Rage burned inside of him, nearly choking Simon. She'd stood before him, her body so stiff, her chin up, and her voice trembling faintly. He'd wanted to haul her into his arms. Wanted to hold her as tightly as he could.

But she hadn't wanted him to touch her.

Because I failed her. I wasn't there when she needed me the most. I pissed off the bastard, and he took out his rage on her.

Simon wished he could do things differently. He wished he could go back. Change everything. And if he could...

He would kill Xavier Gray himself.

Rage burst from him, and Simon slammed his fist into the elevator wall. Once, twice...

The doors opened.

His fist hit the wall a third time.

"OhmyGod." Dennis gaped at him. The guy's eyes were huge behind the lenses of his glasses. "What did the wall do to you?"

Simon snarled at him.

Dennis gulped and backed up. He lifted the bags he carried. "All new stuff—everything in her size. Her agent put in the order at a local boutique for the things Gwen would want. Eveline said she knew Gwen's style."

And I don't know her at all anymore.

He snatched the bags from Dennis.

"Uh, I could have taken them to her." Dennis was dressed in what looked like a new suit. And his hair had been carefully styled back from his forehead.

Was that...was the guy even growing a little stubble on his jaw? Since when did Dennis sport facial hair?

Since he wanted to hit on Gwen.

Simon sucked in a breath and counted to ten. "I've got it."

Dennis gave him a doubting stare. "You don't even look like you've got your shit together, man."

Simon growled. Seriously? Dennis wanted to push him?

Dennis sprang back. "Hey, sorry! I just wanted to help Ms. Soloman!" He twisted his hands together. "God, I loved her in *The Wrong Alibi.* She was such a convincing killer, you know? Like, I felt absolutely sorry for her during the whole movie. I was convinced she was this poor victim who'd been wronged and then..." He smiled. Sighed. "Wham. Last five minutes of the movie, I realized she'd been the guilty party all along. She'd played the cops, played her lover, and had everyone believing she was broken when she was a stone-cold killer." He gave a hum of appreciation. "That woman can act."

Simon's hold tightened on the bags. "Yes." His voice was wooden. "She can."

Dennis squinted at him. "You okay? 'Cause, seriously, you were pounding a wall like twenty seconds ago."

Simon turned away. "The wall pissed me off."

"Uh, that makes *no* sense—"

"Security will engage again in five minutes. Be gone by then." He slanted a last glance over his shoulder at Dennis. "I'll be bringing Gwen into the office once she's had a chance to freshen up."

Dennis smiled. "I'll see her there—"

The elevator doors closed.

That woman can act. Those words played through Simon's head again, and for some reason, his heart ached.

CHAPTER EIGHT

"Here are your clothes."

Gwen reached to take the bags from Simon, but then she tensed. He saw her nibble on her delectable lower lip before she asked, "What happened?"

Simon forced a shrug. "Dennis made a delivery." He'd noted the high-end name on the bags. "Your agent called in your sizes to the boutique and—"

She took the bags. Dropped them. Then reached for his right hand. "I mean...what happened to your knuckles? They're red and scratched." She gaped up at him. "Did you *punch* that kid Dennis?"

"First, he's not a kid." Her fingers were soft as silk against him. "And no, I didn't punch him. In the elevator, I...slipped and my hand hit the wall."

Her hold tightened on him. "How many times did you hit that wall?" She was so close. If he moved two inches, he could put his mouth on hers.

He didn't move.

That woman can act.

"I don't know." It didn't matter. "Like I said, I slipped."

"You don't ever slip. You're the least clumsy person I've ever met." She was still holding his hand.

And he was still liking it far too much. "Anyone's control can slip."

She lifted his hand to her lips. Pressed a kiss to his knuckles.

Fuck. "Gwen." Her name was savage.

She let him go. Stepped back. "Sorry."

"Why the hell did you do that?"

She reached for the bags. "Why the hell did you—apparently—punch a wall multiple times?"

"Because I was mad as hell that I wasn't there when you needed me the most. Because I let you down. Because you were hurt, and *I wasn't there.*"

"Oh." Her chin lifted. "You still shouldn't punch walls. That shit isn't healthy." She turned away.

"Why did you kiss my damn hand?"

She didn't look back at him. "Because you were hurt and I wanted you to feel better." Gwen headed for the bathroom.

His gaze drifted over her body. Those long legs, a beautiful gold. Her grandmother had been Italian, and Gwen's Italian roots were obvious in her thick, dark hair. In her golden skin.

Beautiful Gwen. She had curves for days. A body made for temptation and sin. That was his Gwen.

Is she still mine? When he'd had her in his bed, Gwen had certainly felt like she was his. "Why did you sleep with me last night?"

Her shoulders stiffened. "After everything I told you this morning…" Now she glanced over her shoulder. "That's what you want to know?"

It mattered.

"Fine. Whatever. I slept with you because I wanted you. Simple as that."

Nothing was ever simple in his world. She opened the bathroom door, but then stopped. Without looking at him, Gwen asked, "Why did you sleep with me?"

"Oh, baby, that one is easy…"

But he didn't finish that sentence, not until her gaze found his.

"I want you more than breath. So, when you offer me a taste of paradise, I'm always going to accept."

***

"She confessed to what?" Eric pinched the bridge of his nose. "Jesus. *Jesus*."

"Self-defense," Simon snapped. "Obviously."

"Uh, nothing is obvious." Eric dropped his hand and gaped at Simon. "Your *ex* walks in yesterday, demands to work only with you, and then, bam she confesses to killing a man. That doesn't seem, I don't know—*odd*?"

"She trusts me. That's why she confessed. The bastard stalking her blew up her car last night. Gwen is scared, and she wants the help of someone she can count on."

Eric began to pace. "I don't like this."

"Yeah, well, I sure as shit don't, either. Gwen could have been killed last night—"

Eric stopped pacing and pointed at Simon. "You're too involved. You see only her, and that's dangerous. You aren't impartial, and I worry you won't be able to get the job done."

What. The. Hell. Simon gripped the edges of his chair. He and Eric had been friends—best friends—ever since Simon had stopped being a SEAL. Hell, Eric was part of the reason he'd stopped. Two members of Simon's team had betrayed their unit. The world had been going to hell in a blood-filled basket, and then back-up help had arrived to drag Simon out of that nightmare. The back-up hadn't come from Uncle Sam, though. Oh, no. A private company had come to his rescue. A company manned by the tech guru of the hour. A guy who had liked to get his hands dirty. Bloody. Eric Wilde.

There had been plenty of blood the day Eric had dragged Simon out of that war zone. Simon had paid the guy back, though. He'd saved Eric's ass more times than he could count. After all, you weren't supposed to keep a tab between friends.

"If you're not impartial, you can put her at greater risk." Eric's face was inscrutable.

Simon had to laugh. "Are you bullshitting me right now?" The guy must be. "Because you *married* the woman you were supposed to be protecting a while back. We both know you were never *impartial* when it came to Piper. You were obsessed!"

"Yeah, fine. Guilty. So, I'm telling you based of my own experience...*you need to step back*." Eric's eyes raked over him. "Because if you don't, you'll lose your mind. You won't see the threats coming because you'll just see her."

Eric was wrong. "No. No, I can keep her safe."

"Simon—"

"Gwen isn't going to trust any of the other agents the way she trusts me!" Wait, did she trust him? Gwen must, right? She'd told him her dark secret. A secret that enraged him every single time he thought about it and about the way he'd utterly failed her. "I can't let her down again."

Eric's brow furrowed. "What are you talking about?"

He was talking about how he'd been an arrogant, young ass. A kid who'd gone out to save the world, not realizing he'd left the biggest threat at home. "I should have been there when she needed me. I *will* be there this time."

"Oh, man, take it from someone who knows..." Eric exhaled on a long sigh. "You are so far gone."

Did the guy think he didn't realize that?

"How do you know she's telling you the truth?" Eric pushed. "The woman is an actress. How can you believe the story she told you?"

He wanted to say that he just did because it was Gwen. Because Gwen wouldn't lie to him. But...

He'd changed one hell of a lot over the years. Had she changed, too? "Wilde will be investigating. I want to see what we can uncover."

Eric scratched his chin. "And if we uncover evidence that says the gorgeous Gwen is a cold-blooded killer? What then? You just going to hand her over to the cops?"

Simon's back teeth clenched.

Eric nodded knowingly. "Yes, that's pretty much what I thought. See how we just circled back to you not being impartial? See how I did that? And do you understand where I might be coming from here, buddy?"

"I understand plenty." He pointed at his friend—and his boss. "If this was Piper, would you turn her over to the cops?"

Eric's gaze went cold and lethal in an instant. "I'd never let Piper spend so much as a day in jail. I'd do everything in my power to keep her safe."

Now Simon nodded. "Right. That's pretty much what *I—*"

"Because there is nothing in this world I love more than Piper. You feel the same way about Gwen? Is that what you're trying to tell me? You fell the same way about a woman who only walked in this office *yesterday* to request your services? Bull. I don't buy it."

Before Simon could respond—a very angry, shove-it-up-your-ass response—there was a quick knock on the door. A moment later, the door swung opened, and a tall, well-dressed blond guy strolled in like he owned the place.

But, despite the blond's attitude, Ben Wilde *didn't* own the company. His brother did. But Ben always liked to make himself at home there.

Ben shut the door behind him and glowered. "I'm so mad at you assholes." His blue stare darted between Simon and Eric. "You've been holding out on me. Friends don't do that to friends. That shit isn't cool."

Simon yanked a hand over his face. "What are you talking about?" He liked Ben, counted the guy among his closest friends, but right then, Simon was clueless about what Ben—

Ben held up his phone. Or, more specifically, a feed on his phone. "You see these photos?" He scrolled with his index finger. "Photos of *Gwenevere Soloman?*"

Hell.

Ben marched forward and shoved the phone into Simon's hand. "Take a good look. A long, hard look. Then tell me if you recognize the guy who has his arm around Gwen and is holding her extra tight."

Simon barely spared a glance at the screen. "It's me."

"Damn straight, it is. Because, apparently, Wilde is guarding my all-time favorite actress, and *no one bothered to tell me!*"

His all-time what? Simon glared. "Since when?"

"Uh, since that excellent bit of acting she did in *The Wrong Alibi.*" Ben's eyes took on a faraway look. "Did you not see her in that tiny, miniscule little red bikini when she—"

Simon surged toward his *ex*-friend.

"*Don't.*" Eric's snapping voice. "Look, Simon, if you think I don't understand the urge to attack Ben, then you know nothing about me. My brother sometimes speaks before he fully understands a situation."

Ben frowned down at his screen. Then he scrolled through some pics. "What's to understand? The woman is hot. And I want an introduction. Sure, the gossip sites are saying Simon is some 'Mystery Man' in her life who saved her last night." He looked up, smirking at Simon. "But I know the truth. No way you're dating Gwen Soloman. You're just pulling bodyguard duty."

"I'm *not* dating her?" Simon's brows shot up.

"Uh, you want to tell me that you *weren't* on bodyguard duty last night?" Ben threw right back.

"Yeah, I was, but—"

Ben slapped a hand on Simon's shoulder. "The woman is a million miles out of your league. I mean, you mostly just *growl* when you talk to the opposite sex. I've seen you in action, and the sight can be painful to watch."

"Move the hand."

He moved the hand. "A woman like her—she needs charm. She needs to be wined and dined. She needs seduction." Ben winked.

You need an ass kicking. Oh, but the temptation was strong.

"You can introduce me. Come on." Ben shoved his phone into his pocket. "I'm single, I'm handsome, I'm a—"

"Dick," Simon supplied helpfully.

Ben winced. Then he straightened his tie. "It's because I said she was out of your league. Sorry. That was harsh, I'll admit it. But, man, I just really like Gwen Soloman. She's like, one very hot fantasy of mine—"

"Oh, Jesus," Eric muttered. "Your funeral."

Simon surged toward Ben. "The fantasy is over. Consider it dead and buried. You're not dating Gwen. You're not charming her. You're not seducing her. You're doing *nothing* with her, got it?"

At his words, Ben squinted. For a moment, Ben stared at Simon as if he'd grown two heads. And then... "Oh, hell, you, too, huh?"

Remember he helped you move into your building. Remember he gave you a lift to work all week when your car was in the shop. Remember he is not always an asshole and don't attack. Remember when you first woke up in an Atlanta hospital, he was there. You didn't even know his name. He was just there to help.

The door opened again. Dennis bobbed his head inside. And behind him...Gwen appeared.

"I should have remembered." Now Ben looked a little uncomfortable as he grimaced at Simon. "All those movies at your place. You're like a Gwen super fan, huh?"

Eric seemed to be choking.

Ben hadn't even glanced back to see who'd entered the office. He'd just kept right on, running his mouth. Simon had to stop him before he said more. *"Ben."* A warning edge.

But Ben didn't heed the warning. "Hell, we even went together to see *The Wrong Alibi*. And you were like, dead quiet the whole time. Creepy quiet. I should have realized you were a—"

"Super fan?" Gwen's amused voice interrupted.

Simon was going to make Ben pay for this. So slowly. So painfully. Pay.

Ben's eyes doubled. He mouthed, *Oh, shit.* Then he spun around. "*I* am a super fan."

She gave a quick laugh. One that sounded like music to Simon's ears. Why'd she have to be so perfect? It just made him need to kick the asses of more guys.

She was wearing jeans that hugged her delectable legs like a second skin. Sexy heels—red because that had always been her favorite color. Her blouse was red, too. The top dipped low to reveal a hint of her truly sexy-as-hell breasts. With her thick mane of dark hair tumbling over her shoulders and her slick, red lips, she looked like a dream to Simon. And probably to the other jerks in the room, too.

Gwen gave a quick wink to Ben. "A super fan? That is wonderful to hear. I love super fans. I love fans. I love the folks who watch my movies so that I can keep doing my dream job."

Dennis just stared at her as if she was some kind of magical angel.

She wasn't. She was a flesh and blood woman. With some very dangerous problems that needed to be discussed privately.

"Dennis, give us a moment?" Simon asked quietly.

Gwen tossed a smile back at Dennis. "Thanks for the tour of the place. You are very knowledgeable."

His whole face turned beet red before Dennis stumbled out of the office and shut the door.

"And you..." Simon grabbed Ben's shoulder. Hell, he could give the guy an intro. *Only* that. "Gwen, this is Eric Wilde's brother, Ben."

Ben offered his hand to her.

Gwen took it, shaking briefly. "You're in security, too?"

"No, I'm an attorney, I'm—"

Surprise flashed on her face. Then she immediately glanced at Simon. "I thought you said pulling in a defense attorney might not be necessary yet, that I—"

"*Gwen,*" Simon spoke her name softly but with a distinct edge. "Ben is a divorce attorney."

"Oh." She pulled her hand back. Smiled brightly. "Nice to meet you, Ben."

Ben cocked his head. Like a shark, he'd smelled the blood in the water. "Why would you need a defense attorney, Ms. Soloman?"

"Please, just call me Gwen, and you know..." A shrug of her delicate shoulders. "Who doesn't need a defense attorney these days?"

"Someone who isn't charged with a crime," Ben responded instantly.

"Right, that kind of person." Her smile dimmed a little. "I suppose."

Ben looked even more fascinated by her. "You are so...interesting."

Seriously? *Stop flirting, buddy. Now.*

But Ben didn't stop. He poured on the charm as he added, "You're also even more beautiful in person than you are on the screen. That shouldn't be possible, but I swear, it is."

Red filled her cheeks. "Thank you."

She was blushing? Gwen didn't blush. Blushing for Ben?

Oh, hell, no. Simon positioned his body right next to hers. His shoulder brushed against Gwen's.

Ben's gaze finally slipped off Gwen, and it darted over to Simon. He gave a knowing little nod.

"Don't you agree, Simon?"

It took Simon a minute to realize that Ben was actually talking to him.

Simon frowned at the guy. Agree with what? That Ben was being a dick?

Ben cleared his throat. "Don't you agree that Gwen is even more beautiful in person?"

He gave a grim nod.

Ben winced. Then he looked at Gwen. "Charm isn't his strong suit."

Hold up. Was the guy *apologizing* for him?

Leaning forward a bit conspiratorially, Ben confessed, "You should see him when we go to clubs. A good wingman, he is not. The guy is so growly and tense. Hell, I can't even remember the last time that he had a girlfriend—"

"Okay, that's good," Eric finally intervened. Just in the nick of time because Simon had been about to attack the man's younger brother. Eric slapped his hand on the back of Ben's shoulder. "Great visit, brother, as always. But time for you to go. We have a case to discuss, and since it doesn't involve a divorce, we don't want to bore you with all the pesky, little details."

"I'm not bored." Ben shrugged Eric's hand away. Then glowered a bit at his older brother. "Actually, come to think of it, things have been a bit...slow in my life lately. You know, since you stole my best friend and all."

Eric stiffened. "I didn't steal her. I married her, and you seemed *fine* with—"

Simon cleared his throat. "Family drama later, okay? We need to talk about Gwen."

Eric and Ben swung their heads toward Gwen.

She waved at them.

"I want to help," Ben blurted.

Simon shook his head. "Oh, I think you've helped enough." *And I'll be sure and repay that help, later.*

After giving a long suffering sigh, Ben announced, "Fine, but if you change your mind..."

Simon didn't plan on changing his mind.

Ben offered his card to Gwen. "If you change your mind, I'm happy to help you anytime."

She took the card. Her fingers brushed Ben's. He smiled. His dimples flashed. Stupid dimples. Women always liked them too much.

Simon plucked the card from her hand. "We know how to get in touch with you."

Another sigh, and then Ben headed out of the office. The door closed behind him with a soft click. Simon tossed Ben's card into the nearest trash can. Gwen didn't need it.

She has me.

"Excuse my brother. He can be a bit...enthusiastic about things." Eric folded his arms over his chest. "He *will* not be working on your case, I assure you."

Her body still seemed tense.

"Before Ben arrived," Eric continued carefully, "Simon briefed me on your...situation."

Her stare cut to Simon. He saw the fear that flashed in her eyes, but the emotion vanished when she blinked. A mask seemed to slide over her face.

"We have agents who have already started interviewing the people who work with you. Your assistant, your agent, co-stars." Eric nodded decisively. "And we're sending investigators down to Pensacola."

"No!" The word tore from Gwen. "If people start poking around down there, they'll just raise suspicion—"

But Eric appeared even more determined. "I need to know what we're dealing with here. My team is very low profile, I assure you, but I have to understand more about Xavier Gray. I want to know what the authorities thought about his disappearance. I want to know who might have been able to tie that disappearance to you—"

"No." Now she stepped away from Simon and strode toward the window, her body filled with a tight tension. "You send someone down there, they ask the cops questions, and it will just stir the past up. Don't you see, it will—"

"Gwen."

She whirled toward Simon when he called her name.

"Baby, the past is stirred up. Somebody *knows* what happened, and that person is trying to hurt you. Keeping secrets won't help you right now."

"Well, the truth sure won't set me free! It's more likely to send me into a jail cell!" She shook her head. "This is a mistake. A huge, terrible mistake."

"Someone tried to kill you." Simon kept his voice flat. "Someone who knows about your past. Someone who knows you well enough that the bastard used Xavier as a way to threaten you."

She swallowed.

"Who did you tell?" Simon pushed. "We need names, Gwen. That's one of the reasons our team needs to go to Pensacola. We need to find out old friends who would know—"

"I didn't tell anyone there," she interrupted quickly. "I got out of that town as fast as I could. Do you really think I was gonna confess to someone there? You were the only one I trusted back then."

He could feel Eric's gaze swing toward him. His friend seemed to consider things a moment before Eric asked, "Who did you tell since then?"

"No one."

Simon eased out a low breath. Clients often tried to hold their secrets back. Pointless, because Wilde always found the truth. "Come on, Gwen. A lover, a friend, a—"

"No one. I didn't tell anyone until you. *You* are the one I trust." Her golden gaze held his.

Eric edged closer to her. "Someone has to know. The bastard tormenting you found out. Maybe...maybe he saw you with Xavier Gray that night."

"And he held onto the information all this time?" Gwen burst out. "Why? Why not use it sooner? And if the guy *did* see me with Xavier, then he saw Xavier knock me out and carry my body onto the boat."

"Fuck," Simon snarled.

Gwen flinched.

"Accomplice." Simon glanced at Eric to see if his friend was having the same thought.

Eric inclined his head. "Makes sense."

Gwen gave them both a quelling frown. "What? What accomplice? I didn't have an accomplice! I was walking home from my job, and Xavier attacked me. I didn't—"

"Maybe he wasn't alone."

At Eric's low words, all of the color seemed to leave Gwen's face.

"You just said he got you from the alley to the boat. Maybe someone helped him transport you. Maybe that person put two and two together when Xavier never came back. And now that the world knows you're one of the highest paid actresses in Hollywood, the guy wants to cash in on your fame."

"But he didn't just want money," she whispered.

A furrow appeared between Eric's brows. "Then what else did he want?"

Gwen licked her lower lip. "Me."

CHAPTER NINE

Simon wanted to grab Gwen and pull her into his arms. She looked fragile and scared, and her pain was pissing him off. Gwen shouldn't be frightened.

I won't let her down again.

"Our agents are professionals. They can do recon work down in Pensacola, and they won't arouse suspicion, I assure you, Gwen." Eric's expression was earnest. "And a lot of the work, I will handle personally. I can access details from the Pensacola Police Department's online database. I can get case notes and materials without anyone ever knowing."

She slid forward onto the balls of her feet. "That doesn't exactly sound legal."

Eric shrugged.

Yeah, that shit wasn't exactly legal.

Gwen shook her head. "I don't want anyone breaking the law for me. I just—I want this guy stopped. My assistant was hurt last night. I spoke to him this morning. He was lucky—just had a few stitches, but it could have been so much worse. If anyone else got hurt or killed because of me—"

"No." Simon couldn't stay away from her any longer. He closed the distance between them in an instant. "This isn't because of you. It's because of the jackass out there. You didn't set the bomb. You didn't make the car explode. This isn't on you. It's on him, and we will find the SOB."

"But we have to investigate." Eric was adamant. "We have to turn over the rocks and see what crawls out."

A wince from Gwen. "I never liked snakes."

"We need to know everything, baby," Simon told her.

Eric let out a low whistle. The glance he fired at Simon said he noticed the endearments that Simon kept dropping. Screw it. Screw him. Simon focused on Gwen. "If there are more secrets, you have to tell us. If there is *anyone* you might have confided in, even a little about this—"

"*There isn't.*"

"Lovers get close. You share secrets."

Her gaze held his. "I haven't shared this secret with any lover but you. And I was scared as hell to tell you." She tucked a lock of hair behind her ear. "Why is this happening now? Why after all of this time?"

There had to be a reason. "Maybe there was a trigger. Something happened that set the guy off." The more they learned about Gwen and her past, the more they'd understand. "The person we're after is tied to you and to Xavier. We have to explore both of your pasts to find the truth."

She gave a slow nod as sadness washed over her face. "The press will find out. Everyone will, won't they? I was crazy to think I could keep this all quiet."

They controlled the story, not the media. "The press knows someone blew up your car. They don't know anything else."

"When did you first get contact from the guy?" Eric wanted to know.

"About six months ago. That's when he first sent me the roses." Her brow crinkled. "But I guess he could have contacted me before then...maybe I didn't even know it." A long exhale. "My assistant usually handles all of my mail. And if things are, um, weird, he makes sure to keep those letters or emails separate because he knows I don't like to see them."

"You get a lot of threatening mail?" Simon didn't like that idea, not one bit. She'd mentioned to him before that Van kept the more—what had she called it?—"creepier" notes from her.

"I get more than I'd like. A lot more." Her gaze fell to the floor. "People don't like what I wear. They don't like how I act. Men think they can tell me all the things they want to do to me, and then strangers tell me that I ruined their lives. You name it, and I've probably gotten a letter about it."

"Damn." Eric frowned. "That doesn't bother you?"

"Of course, it does. It scared the ever-loving hell out of me the first time I got a hate letter, but my agent said it was part of the business. To ignore them. It was her idea for Van to start keeping the bad material separate from the stuff I saw. She said there was no point in letting that get into my head."

Oh, Simon would definitely be having a long chat with the agent. And with Gwen's assistant. "We'll need to see those letters, emails, everything."

Her shoulders slumped. "I guess there's no part of my life that will be kept secret from you, is there?"

He waited for her eyes to lift. Waited for her golden gaze to meet his. "No, sweetheart," Simon told her softly. "There's not."

She swallowed. "The team that you send to Pensacola—will they know what I did?"

He shook his head.

Eric spoke up. "That intel won't leave this room. We are purely doing recon, trying to find out as much as we can about Xavier Gray and your time in that area."

"The ghosts from the past." A faint smile curved her lips. A smile that held no humor. "They are the deadliest ones."

Yes, they were. "I'll need to stay close to you." As if Simon would have it any other way. "Until we figure out what's happening, you can't trust others in your life."

A furrow appeared between her dark brows. "I can trust Van. I can trust Eveline—"

"No. Your agent, your assistant, your exes—they'll have to be cleared by our team. For all we know, the person trying to hurt you could already be in your life. Killing close."

She shook her head. "No, no. I *know* Van and Eveline. They wouldn't do this to me."

Her pain was breaking his heart.

She looked down at the floor again. No, he needed Gwen to see him. His fingers curved gently around her chin, and he forced her to look toward him.

"I get it." And he did. He'd seen it before. "You don't want to think someone in your inner circle— a friend or a lover—would hurt you. But, baby, those are often the people who will hurt you the most. We've seen it time and time again. Until we can work down our list of suspects, until I can guarantee your safety, I am going to stand between you and everyone else. You came to me for protection, and protection is exactly what you are going to get. Twenty-four, seven, sweetheart. I'll be at your side all the time, and you will *not* be hurt, not on my watch."

***

"Just how personal is this?" Eric's voice was low.

Gwen stood just a few feet away, talking with Dennis.

Simon didn't glance his way. He kept his gaze on Gwen. The view was far better.

"I told you, man," intensity deepened Eric's voice, "you have to be careful when you're intimately involved. And the way you're looking at her right now...shit, I think you're already too lost in her."

He'd been lost in Gwen for years. "No one will hurt her."

***

Simon shut the door to the conference room and stared at his prey.

Van Hart lounged in one of the chairs, a mug of coffee to the right of him. He was dressed in jeans and a sweatshirt, and his hair was styled in that fake messy mop again. This time, though, he was sporting a bandage on his forehead.

The stitches. Right. The guy had strolled into the building a few moments ago, and he hadn't seen Gwen, not yet. Simon had wanted to talk to him first.

But Van frowned at him. "I thought I was coming in to see you *and* Gwen..."

Gwen was busy with Eric, signing paperwork, answering questions. Blah. Blah. Blah. Simon pulled out a chair, spun it around, straddled it, and stared hard at Van.

Van gulped. "Everything...okay?"

"Gwen's car blew up last night. I definitely don't consider that *okay*."

Excitement lit Van's eyes. "Can you believe that shit went down?" His voice rose a little. Not with fear—definitely more like excitement. "A bomb! Man, it made all the celebrity gossip sites. Gwen lit them up!"

She hadn't lit them up. She'd nearly died. And so had Van—only the guy sounded more pumped than scared.

Simon pinned Van with a hard stare. "Gwen told me that you handle her fan interactions."

"I do." Pride shone as Van straightened his shoulders. "I oversee all her social media accounts and her physical mail and her guest appearances and—"

"She said you take out the threats. The darker notes."

"I...do?" Now Van's voice was more hesitant.

"I want all the threats. I want to know the name of any person who's called or stalked or threatened Gwen either online or in person. You're going to hand over every bit of that data to me and my associates here at Wilde."

"What?"

"Every bit. Someone out there wants to hurt Gwen, and I'm going to stop him."

A nervous laugh escaped Van. "That's just...fans, people saying things. No one would actually hurt—"

"Someone blew up her car. Yeah, someone actually wants to hurt her."

"This...this shit is real?"

What kind of question was that? "As real as the stitches in your forehead."

Van's hand lifted to touch the bandage. He didn't seem quite as excited any longer.

**

"Where is Gwen?"

Interrogation number two. Simon strolled inside the next room to find Eveline Jacobson waiting for him. Her long, perfectly manicured nails tapped against the top of the table in front of her.

"Gwen isn't coming in for this chat," he told her as he settled into a nearby chair. "I wanted to speak with you privately."

Her gaze raked him. A spark of...interest lit her eyes. "Speak away."

"You've been Gwen's agent ever since she left Pensacola."

"Hmm. I know talent when I see it." Again, her gaze darted over him. "You have a whole dark and dangerous vibe going on. I like it."

He stared at her. Just stared until her gaze came back to his face.

"What?" She shrugged.

"Gwen's life is in danger. My job is to protect her. Not to fucking flirt with you."

Eveline laughed. "Not interested, huh? Already taken?"

"Something like that."

"Pity." Her attention shifted to the closed door. "How long will this take?"

As long as it fucking takes. "You told Gwen's assistant to keep track of any threatening materials that were sent to her."

"Yes. Gwen can get...emotional. She worries too much so it just seemed easier to take that worry away for her." A shrug. "That's my job, you know. To make things easier for my clients."

"Someone tried to kill Gwen last night."

Her head tilted as she focused on him again. "You're her bodyguard. One she hired *without* consulting me. Shouldn't you have done a better job of keeping her safe? As far as I'm concerned, the car bombing should never have happened. If Gwen had just come to me in the first place—"

"What would you have done?"

"Made the problem vanish. It's what I do."

Her fingernails were tapping against the table. "What other problems have you made vanish for Gwen?" Suspicion slid through him.

She flashed a shark's smile. "Gwen was nothing when I found her."

He stiffened.

"I made her into what she is. I gave her fame. I got her the roles that turned Gwen into a household name. I got her fortune. I got the world at her feet." Eveline laughed dismissively. "You think I couldn't make a stalker vanish? Please."

"You're wrong."

Her eyes turned to slits.

"Gwen has never been nothing. So don't fucking act like you *made* her." Anger boiled in his gut. "If anything, she made you. What big clients did you have *before* Gwen?"

Silence. The air seemed to become ice cold. "I'm here as a courtesy to my *friend* Gwen. I don't think she'd like the way you're talking to me."

"What makes you think I give a damn what Gwen likes?" He held her stare. "My job is to keep her safe. Not to make her happy."

"It feels like you're investigating me. Questioning *me—*"

"I am. Because you're close to Gwen. Close enough to hurt her."

Her fingers flattened on the table. "Well, that would just be dumb on my part. Gwen is the reason I have my mansion in Beverly Hills, why I have three BMWs, and a house in France." That shark smile came again. "I would never hurt my money train, so maybe go try investigating someone else."

No, he'd keep investigating the agent. Wilde was already looking into her finances. "Who would hurt her?"

"I don't know." Her hand waved vaguely. "She likes dangerous men. Those guys who seem to get off on adrenaline kicks." A smirk. "Probably guys like you. No wonder the press took one look at you and pegged you as the boyfriend and not just a guard. You're totally her type."

He didn't let his expression alter. "There a particular ex-lover who stands out to you?"

"Sure. That rock star asshole she dated last year. Guy went ballistic when Gwen dumped him. Destroyed four guitars and got kicked out of the best club in Hollywood." She looked expectantly at him. "You know the guy I'm talking about, right?"

Yeah, he did.

"Bran Copper," she said, almost with relish. "But he's on tour now, somewhere in Europe, I think, so I doubt he's taking secret trips to the US in order to put car bombs in Gwen's ride."

The rock star would be checked out. "Why did you pick him?"

"Other than the fact that Bran likes to break things?" Her brows rose. "Because when they split up, Bran said that he'd see Gwen in hell before he ever let her go to another man."

CHAPTER TEN

"We'll need you in five minutes, Ms. Soloman." The woman gave a quick nod as she pulled Gwen's dressing room door shut.

"This is bullshit."

Simon's anger practically blasted at her.

"Your car *exploded* here on set yesterday. And now you're back tonight?"

Back and pretty exhausted. She'd spent the day at Wilde, answering question after question and trying to act as if she was completely in control and not seriously freaking out because her life was being ripped apart. She'd even gone down to the police station so the cops could have their turn questioning her about the car bombing.

She knew that Simon had grilled her agent. And her assistant. She was pretty sure Wilde had even interrogated most of the crew members on set. Simon and Eric viewed everyone as suspects, and Gwen was starting to stare around herself with the same suspicion. *Who can I trust?*

She wanted to run and hide, but that wasn't exactly an option. Not when there was work to do. Not when the cast and crew were counting on her. It was time to get to work, and no one would stop her from doing her job. "I'm primary in this scene. If I didn't show up, then I'd delay production for everyone. All of those people are out there to do a job, and I won't be the reason this project is delayed."

"*A car bomb.*"

She stared at her reflection. Her makeup had been carefully applied by a team of two women and a man—the same team that had made her hair fall in loose curls over her shoulders. Perfect curls that she could never, not in a million years, recreate without them. "Wilde is checking all the vehicles, right? And the studio said they doubled the security. No one will be on set without express permission from the folks in charge here."

He growled. A sound that shouldn't have been sexy, but it was. Everything about the guy was sexy to her.

"I don't like this, Gwen."

Now she turned to stare at him. He was glaring. Looking all fierce and kick-ass and sexy. Lickably sexy. She'd always had a weakness for tall, dark, and handsome guys—a weakness she fully blamed on him. "I don't like it, either," Gwen told him bluntly. "But I can't run away from this." That was one of the reasons she'd gone to Wilde in the first place. To fight, not to give in to the blackmailer. "People count on me. If I back out, that's work that doesn't get done. Salaries that might not get paid. I'll do what I'm scheduled to do, then we'll leave." She rose, the robe she wore sliding over her thighs. "Besides, I have you."

His eyes narrowed on her. "Yes, you have me."

Gwen faltered. *No, I don't. I haven't had you, not really, in years.* But a woman could pretend. She was very good at pretending. "You'll keep me safe." She believed that. "You'll see the threats coming."

"I didn't see the threat last night. I'm not Superman, though when it comes to you, I wish that I was."

She tried a smile to lighten the mood. "But he's not perfect. He has his kryptonite weakness."

"That's exactly what you are."

She backed up, not expecting that hit. Her hip bumped into the chair. And his words pierced straight to her heart. The weak heart that he'd always been able to touch.

His brow furrowed. "Gwen?"

She rallied fast. Never let it be said that she couldn't rally. "Is that what I am? Some kind of weakness to you?"

"Yes."

Jeez. The guy wasn't pulling punches with her. So, she wouldn't pull punches with him. "That why you had sex with me last night? Because I'm an old weakness?" As soon as the words fired out, she regretted them. Why was she still talking? What was wrong with her? Since when had she turned into some kind of glutton for punishment? She didn't want to hear—

"It would take a real dumbass to turn away from a woman like you."

Gwen shoved her hands into the pockets of her robe. Head held high, she brushed past him and marched for the door. "I'm needed on set."

His hand flew out and curled around her shoulder. He spun her back to face him. "You're running from me." The furrow between his brows had gotten deeper.

"I'm going to do my job. Getting my ass on set and not being late."

His gaze searched hers. "You're... mad?"

"Give the man a freaking cookie," she snapped. Mad, hurt—lots of things. *Kryptonite, my ass.*

He blinked.

"Every woman *loves* being told she's kryptonite. Because that's sexy and romantic." She jerked away from him. Lifted her chin. "Just so you know, it cuts both ways. You think I *want* to still need you this way? You think I like it that you can touch me and my body goes all crazy? I *don't.* I thought I could come to you and get you to help me with this stalker. I thought we'd keep our hands off each other. I thought that part of us was dead and buried." She was breathing too hard. Talking too quickly. Her heart was pounding too fast. Dammit, dammit, dammit!

Simon just shook his head and looked even sexier. "Not dead. Not even close." He gazed into her eyes. "I want you more now than I think I ever have."

She felt the same way. It shouldn't have happened. They should have worked each other out of their systems long ago. And last night—it should have been, like—hell, she didn't know. For old times' sake or something. Not life-altering. Not change-everything-amazing.

Her life was already burning down around her. She hadn't counted on the way she felt about Simon. But...

When she was in his arms, it was almost the only time she did feel normal. Safe.

And he thought she was kryptonite.

His head lowered toward her. As if he was about to kiss her—

Kryptonite.

Her hand flew up and shoved against his chest. "The team just spent thirty minutes doing my makeup. You aren't messing it up now just because kryptonite is in your path."

He stilled. "That pissed you off."

You think?

"I meant it as a compliment."

Like she was going to believe—

"I've never wanted another woman as much as I want you. Never have and I know I never will again. There is something special about you. You make me need. You make me want. You make me go absolutely insane so that nothing else matters but you. That kind of desire can't be contained or controlled. It will make a man desperate. Make him weak."

What was she supposed to say to that? And why the hell was she rising onto her toes like she was about to kiss *him?*

A rap sounded at the door.

She jumped.

"Call time, Ms. Soloman!"

Yes, right, thank goodness. Saved by the knock before she made another mistake.

"I'll be watching you, Gwen," Simon rasped. "If anything happens, if anything on set makes you nervous, you just motion to me. I'll be there."

She slid out of the robe. She'd almost forgotten that she was wearing it. Once the robe was gone, she glanced down. The curve-hugging, black dress fit like a second skin. And the thing barely reached the tops of her thighs. She looked back up at Simon.

His gaze was on the dress. "Jesus. It's going to be a *long* night."

"Simon—"

"You're fucking beautiful. And I know you have a job to do. Just like I do." His gaze returned to hold hers. "Nothing will hurt you. Not while I'm close, okay?"

She nodded. *But you hurt me, Simon. I forgot about the pain you presented to me.*

That pain wouldn't kill her. The stalker out there, though, he just might.

***

She did the same scene thirty times, and each time, she acted as if it was the first. The set had been designed to resemble a club, a seedy club on the wrong side of town. She and her co-star were there for intel, and Gwen did a perfect job of seducing the intel straight from the men there.

"She's incredible," Van said. "A total professional. I could watch her all night."

So could I. Simon didn't take his gaze off Gwen. For the moment, they were doing the regular scene shooting, but her stunt double had just been brought in. The woman wore the same dress Gwen wore, and her dark hair looked *exactly* like Gwen's. When the double approached Gwen, hell, it almost looked as if she had a twin. The woman even seemed to have Gwen's mannerisms down pat.

"I mean...like, not in a weird way," Van added quickly, stuttering a bit. "I'm not her stalker, and, uh, shit, you got all that material I sent to Wilde, didn't you?"

The emails. The creepy notes. The threats. Too much. Enough to turn Simon's stomach again and again. Enough for him to want to grab Gwen and carry her far away from the danger that seemed to be everywhere. "I got the stuff." And it was being reviewed—very, very carefully—by the techs at Wilde.

He kept his gaze on Gwen and on the stunt double.

"That's Raven. She always works with Gwen." Van still sounded shaken. "I mean, you probably already know that. You're getting reports on everyone, aren't you? Checking us all out."

Gwen looked toward Simon right then.

He gave a slow nod. No threats. She was good.

He saw tension slide from her shoulders.

Van inched closer. "You're...gonna keep her safe?" A quick, nervous question as his fingers fluttered toward his bandage. "Nothing can happen to Gwen."

"Nothing is going to happen to her." *I won't let it.*

Gwen backed away from the scene as her stunt double took over.

Her co-star sidled closer. Austin Quest leaned down to whisper something in Gwen's ear. She laughed and Austin's hand brushed over her arm.

Simon tilted his head and when Austin finally glanced his way....*Hello, asshole. We'll be having a nice, private chat soon.*

Austin jerked his hand from Gwen and hurriedly backed away.

***

He waited until Gwen was pulled into a talk with the director, then Simon took his time closing in on Austin. The guy saw him coming at the last moment and stiffened.

Simon kept heading for his target.

"Man, I am *not* hitting on Gwen." Austin put his hands up. "It's acting. You know what that is, don't you?"

Simon didn't roll his eyes. He also didn't deck the jerk. Double win.

"I see the way you watch her. You two are like—a thing, right? But you need to calm down. Man, Gwen is so not my type."

Simon just waited. So far, he hadn't even needed to say a word. Austin seemed to enjoy talking too much to interrupt.

"I don't share the spotlight, so I *don't* date other celebrities. I have a big rule about that."

Simon crossed his arms over his chest.

"Not that Gwen isn't hot. She is!" Austin rushed to say. "But we're not a thing. We're—"

"You're not going to be a thing," Simon finally interrupted to say. "Because Gwen is with me." He was sticking to her like glue, and the folks there could see him the same way the press did—as Gwen's lover. Lover, protector, investigator—he'd be whatever she needed.

Austin swallowed. "Is that a gun? Are you wearing a gun right now? Like, a real one?"

Austin was going to get on his last nerve.

"Are you an ex-cop?" Now Austin eyed him with more interest. "Or like...a special agent? Because, you know, I played a spy in—"

"I know."

Austin swallowed. His voice dropped, "Military, huh? It's all in the way you move. I did some prep work with a dude who was an ex-Ranger. He taught me some crazy shit."

Interesting.

"You a Ranger?"

Simon didn't respond.

"Something else? Got to be special ops. Were you a sniper? Demolitions? Oh, wait, were you a SEAL? 'Cause that would be really bad-ass. A—"

Simon stepped closer to the guy. "What I was doesn't matter. What I am *now*...That matters. I'm the guy who is going to be guarding Gwen. I'm the guy keeping her close and safe. And you? You're gonna be the guy who doesn't get in my way."

"Not in your way. *Not*." A quick shake of his head.

"Have you seen anyone around set who didn't belong? Before I got here...before the bombing last night? Did you see anything that looked suspicious to you?"

"I...no?"

"Is that a question or an answer?"

"No. N-no, I didn't see anything."

Austin looked nervous as hell. "There something you're hiding? Because if so, just know that I *will* find the truth."

"I was busy fucking someone last night, okay?" He heaved out a breath. "Didn't notice a damn thing except her. She left me a few minutes before I heard the explosion."

The director called for Austin.

Simon didn't move out of the fellow's way, not yet. "I'll need a name."

"Raven, okay? I was fucking Raven. I told you...I don't do celebrities, but sexy stunt women? They're sure as shit fair game." Austin hurried around him.

Such a dick. The fellow was so much better in the movies than he was in real life.

***

Raven Charles was riding one major high. She'd nailed her stunts that night, and Gwen had even told her that there was already talk of a follow-up movie. A movie the folks in charge wanted Raven to work on.

Hell, yes. She'd been waiting for her big break. After years of grinding away, it was *her* time.

So, she slung her bag over her shoulder, she yanked off the long, dark wig that she'd worn for the shoots, and she got herself ready to have some fun.

The best clubs were just opening. Starting at midnight was part of the plan. She'd party it up and celebrate until dawn. This was *her* night.

Her night to shine.

She waved to the security guards as she hurried past them. Security was extra tight because of that crazy shit that had gone down with Gwen. The guards had even offered to take Raven home—no way. She didn't need a babysitter. Not for that night.

Raven rounded the corner and—

Mr. Tall, Dark, and Dangerous stepped into her path. She stopped, frowning. He was the guy she'd seen watching Gwen all night. The one with that hot, intense vibe.

She raised a brow at him. "Bodyguard?" Her gaze dipped over him. "Or lover?" He was built and bad-ass and normally, so her type. But this guy, he'd only had eyes for Gwen.

And I won't be a stand-in. Because, unfortunately, she'd done that shit before. And she didn't just mean on set. She'd even had a jackass request that she wear the wig in the bedroom.

"I'm the man with Gwen."

Oh, damn, his voice even sounded like sex to her. Well, if you counted rough and gravelly as sex, and she did.

But then Raven realized Gwen was behind him. *Not playtime.*

Gwen slid to the guy's side. Gwen—the chick was way too soft for Hollywood. Raven doubted that Gwen could so much as hurt a fly. If Gwen didn't harden up, the others would eat her alive. It was only a matter of time.

"I want you to be extra careful," Gwen said. Her voice was always so good. Soft and seductive, even when she didn't intend for it to be. That was one of Raven's problems. She was working on speech and acting classes, but her voice still came out too sharp and with a Chicago edge that she couldn't quite shake.

Gwen continued, "The jerk who came after me...I wanted to warn you to just be on guard. I don't know what he's capable of doing. And I don't want anyone else getting caught in the crossfire."

Raven had to laugh. The day she needed protection, well, that day hadn't come. She was a *stunt woman*. She worked out like a beast, and she practiced martial arts just for extra fun because she loved to kick ass. "I'm good, thanks."

"Raven, this is serious. Someone could get hurt—"

"You mean like Van?" She'd seen him and his stupid Band-Aid. "Dumbass deserved to get singed. He is such a prick."

Gwen didn't argue. Neither did Tall, Dark, and Dangerous.

"You were here last night," he said.

She could listen to his voice forever. Totally reminded her of Vin Diesel. Yum.

"Did you see anyone who didn't belong?"

Raven smiled at him. "The only new face I saw..." Her hand lifted because she just had to touch the dark shadow on his jaw. "Was yours." Her hand fell. "But I'm guessing you're not the one who tried to blow up Gwen?"

"No."

"Good. I kind of need her. Without Gwen, I don't exactly have a job. I mean, if Gwen is gone, why need a double? So, be a love and keep her alive, would you?" She gave a little hum. "I like her." And she did. Raven winked at Gwen. "Don't go exploding on me."

Gwen's expression tightened, and for the first time, Raven realized that Gwen...she looked afraid.

Raven lost her smile. "Gwen?"

It was the guy who said, "If you remember anything about last night, you let me know, okay?" He passed her a card. "Right away."

She tucked the card into her bra. Safest spot. "Sure thing." Some of her earlier excitement had started to wane. Not cool. Maybe clubbing wasn't the best idea. Maybe she should try for something else.

"Do you need a ride?" Gwen asked.

Why did everyone want to give her a ride? "I got this." Besides, Gwen was the one with the exploding car. Who'd want to ride with her? "The night is waiting. See you both later." Rolling her hips as she walked—just in case Tall, Dark, and Dangerous was watching—she strode out. The night was still young, and so was she.

Sometimes, it sure seemed like the party would never end.

God, she hoped it didn't.

***

"Without the hair, she doesn't look much like you."

Gwen glanced up at Simon. His eyes were on her.

"You ready?"

It was so late that most of the reporters were gone—though the production crew had done a good job of keeping them off the set, anyway. She knew Simon's ride was waiting in the back. Waiting under guard.

She'd worn three-inch heels for the last six hours, and she'd stood on her feet for pretty much the whole time. She was dead tired, scared as hell, and, yes, way, way past ready to leave.

She followed him to the SUV without a word and slid gratefully into the passenger seat. Distantly, Gwen heard him talking to the guard who'd been watching the ride. When Simon climbed into the vehicle, Gwen turned toward him. "Is the guard with Wilde or—"

"He's with me." Simon cranked the SUV.

Right. Heat blasted out at her.

"I had your personal belongings from the hotel suite brought to my place while you were filming. And, Gwen, my home *is* the safest place for you tonight."

Did he think she was going to argue? Nope, too dead tired. They had the next two days off from filming, and she was hoping that by the time she returned to the set...

Will this nightmare be over?

Maybe it would be. Maybe she'd go back to her life. Simon would go back to his. It would all be over. Everything would just be done.

He drove them out of there as she slumped in the seat. She was oddly nervous to be alone with him again. God, last night, the things they'd done together...so much for thinking she'd exaggerated the way he'd made her feel, that she'd been building the past up too much in her mind.

The guy *was* as good as she remembered. Better. It sucked when your first lover turned out to be the best one you ever had. Or maybe...maybe it didn't suck. Maybe it just meant your timing was absolute shit.

"We have a problem." His voice was low. Rough.

She lifted her lashes and turned toward him.

"We're being followed."

Gwen jerked, her body jolting, and the seatbelt yanked into her shoulder. She whipped around, staring behind her. Sure, in the distance, there were headlights but... "Are you certain?"

He turned at the next corner.

The other car turned, too.

"Absolutely, fucking positive."

CHAPTER ELEVEN

"If we're being followed, *why* are you stopping?" Because that sounded like the worst plan ever to Gwen.

"Because I'm not taking that bastard back to my place. And if it's the prick after you, this shit ends right now." He'd whipped the SUV onto a side street. Then he did some kind of fast maneuver that made her dizzy, turning the vehicle so that it was now facing the driver who was headed toward them.

This was so bad.

"Cage him in from behind."

Her head whipped toward Simon. Was he talking to her? Uh, no, he was talking on his phone. When had he yanked that thing out?

"This bastard isn't getting away." Simon shoved down his phone and turned to her. "Duck. Get below the dash. And don't even think of getting out of this vehicle until I come back."

For the moment, she ignored the bossy and demanding tone. Obviously, this was his whole area of expertise. Wasn't that why she'd gone to him for help? However...*big* however...having

Simon just run up to the car that had followed them seemed crazy scary to her.

Headlights hit them. She heard the squeal of brakes.

The guy tailing them was there.

And Simon had just pulled out a gun. Where in the hell had that thing been? Yes, she'd noticed his holster earlier, but he'd removed it when he'd gotten in the SUV. Simon had sure grabbed the gun fast. He shoved his other hand on her back. "Get down, baby. Stay down."

"Simon—"

He pushed open the door and leapt out of the vehicle.

Oh, God. She was down, trying to turn her body into a pretzel and absolutely freaking out. The SUV's driver side door slammed.

Then she heard the rush of footsteps. A raised voice.

No gunshots. I don't want to hear any gunshots.

More squealing tires. Was that whoever Simon had been talking with on the phone? Part of his team? The person who was supposed to help cage in the other driver?

"Let me go! I have a right to be here!" A man's voice bellowed. *"It's public property, and I'm the press!"*

She shifted a bit.

"Get your hands off me!"

That wasn't Simon's yell. He'd told her to stay down but...

Gwen lifted her head, peeking just a little bit through the front windshield. When she peeked, she saw that Simon had some guy pinned across the hood of an old sedan. And there was another fellow with Simon. Big and burly—with a gun gripped in his hand.

Her nervous gaze darted around the scene. The sedan's headlights were on, blasting at full power, and...oh, no. Was that a camera on the ground? It was. One of those big, expensive cameras with the long lens that most people didn't use any longer because everyone filmed on their phones these days.

Everyone but...

Certain reporters. Tabloid reporters. A few specific ones came to mind. And that sedan. It was familiar to her. As familiar as...

As the jerk Simon was about to punch.

This scene was turning into a serious nightmare.

Gwen cracked open the door. She had to stop this before it got worse. "Simon!"

"Stay back, Gwen!" A fierce shout.

"You need to come here, now!" Gwen shouted right back.

His head swung toward her.

"I know him," she added, her voice carrying and breaking a bit in the night.

"Yeah! She knows me!" The paparazzi reporter was still trapped on the hood of his car. "So, call off your goon, Gwen, before I get the cops out here and sue him for assault!"

Crap. They didn't need this to become even more of a circus.

She left the SUV and hurried toward them. Simon held the reporter—a man she'd encountered too many times named Andy Flint—down with just one hand. She was relieved to see that Simon's other hand didn't grip his gun. He must have already tucked that away someplace.

"Simon, he's a piece of crap but he's...harmless." Technically, though, she supposed it depended on your definition of harmless.

"The new lover is batshit crazy, Gwen." Andy panted and gazed up at Simon. "Even more messed up than Bran, and everyone knows that guy was mental." He grunted. "I'll be running with the story about how you just can't help but fall for the crazy ones—and that this fucker is *over the top*."

She grabbed Simon's arm. The muscles were like steel beneath her touch. "Let him go."

He didn't.

"Please," Gwen added softly.

Simon shoved away from the reporter. "You were following us."

Andy got up, slowly, straightening his sweatshirt before scooping to pick up his camera. "Damn straight, I was. That shit's my job. I always follow Gwen. It pays the bills." He rubbed his camera against his sweatshirt and glared at Simon. "If you broke my baby, I am suing your ass."

No, she didn't want Simon dragged into this mess because of her. "Forget this night, Andy, and I'll give you exclusive access at the next premiere I do."

Andy's head whipped toward her. "I do like exclusives, but red carpets are boring. I'm gonna need more." He lifted the camera, as if he were about to snap a pic—

Simon ripped the camera right out of the guy's hand. "You been taking pics of her during the filming she's been doing in town?"

"Give me my camera back!"

"I want the photos. I want every single photo you've taken."

"Oh, yeah, tough guy?" Andy jutted out his chin. "Then go look on the website like every-fucking-one else."

A shiver shook Gwen's body. This was not going well.

"Another possessive-ass lover who thinks he can control a celeb." Andy grunted in disgust. "Did you seriously not learn anything from Bran? Like I haven't seen this shit before, like I haven't—"

"Someone tried to *kill* Gwen last night," Simon snarled. "So, yeah, I think I have reason to be *protective* of her."

"Publicity stunt!" Andy tried to grab his camera, but Simon just held it out of his reach. Andy huffed and put his hands on his hips as he whirled for Gwen. "You think I'm not smart enough to realize it was a PR play? You weren't hurt, and your assistant got a scratch. But now you're on every news channel and your movie will be on everyone's lips."

"It wasn't a stunt," Gwen denied flatly.

"Whatever. Your agent is a friggin' barracuda. The woman plans things like this in her sleep."

"No." Gwen was adamant. "You're wrong."

Andy glared at her, then he turned his attention to Simon—and the quiet guy who shadowed Simon. "What's the deal? You the bodyguard?" He addressed the man who hadn't spoken. The man who'd now holstered his gun. The big, muscled, scary dude in the shadows.

The guy still didn't speak.

"I *want* my camera." Andy's voice sounded strangled.

"And I don't *want* dumbass tabloid guys following Gwen," Simon fired right back. "Guess we're both getting disappointed tonight, huh?"

"I'll buy it," Gwen blurted before this could get any more out of hand. "Name your price, Andy, and I'll buy the camera."

"My price..." Andy said this with relish, "I want set pics. You know folks will salivate over those. Maybe you and your co-star getting all cozy." He slanted a glance at Simon. "Sorry, new boyfriend, but that shit sells. Pics of her and Austin are worth way more than pics of her and a nobody."

"He's not a nobody," Gwen immediately snapped back. *Never had been. Never would be.*

"What the fuck ever!" Andy grabbed for the camera.

Simon held it out of reach.

And Gwen blurted, "I'll see what I can do."

Andy glowered.

"You know my word is good." Gwen fought her desperation. "I stuck to our deal in the past, didn't I?"

He gave a grudging nod.

Simon just watched them.

"Then trust me now. I'll make good on this, Andy. Just...do what Simon says, okay? If he wants your photos, give him access. Someone is really trying to screw me over, and not in a good way. I'm...scared." She let the fear—the very real fear—slip into her voice because while Andy might be an asshole most days, he also had a soft heart. It was just a very, very small heart. Grinch-size. "If you got photos that might show who planted that bomb, that might show someone on set who didn't belong there, we can use them."

He smiled. "It'll cost you."

"It always does. Send them to me, okay? Along with the bill."

He laughed. "Told you already, they're up on the website. I don't sit on news. I go straight to posting."

She knew this story would be posted, too. Dammit. Whatever. At least she'd tried.

She reached for Simon's hand again. "Let's go. You can't... you can't steal his camera. If he's not giving it to you—"

Simon's head turned toward her. His left hand lifted and pushed back the hair that had slid over her cheek even as his right continued to hold the camera. "Oh, baby..." His voice was low and tender. "I can steal. I can lie." His mouth came toward her ear and he whispered—for her alone, "For you, I would do just about anything."

Another shiver slid over Gwen.

His lips brushed her cheek. "Go back to the car."

Okay, now she was extra worried. Her gaze darted to Andy.

"Uh, Gwen..." Andy began. "How about...*don't leave?*"

"Your buddy Andy and I need to talk, Gwen," Simon added. "Lars, take her back for me, will you?"

And the security agent who'd been dead silent took Gwen's arm.

"Gwen?" Andy croaked.

Simon wasn't going to hurt Andy. Andy might be an annoyance but...

"Trust me," Simon told her.

Right. She was supposed to be doing that, wasn't she? Trust. Gwen nodded quickly and let Lars lead her back to the SUV. He opened the passenger door for her and guided her into the seat. Not that she needed guiding. She knew how to get in a damn seat, but Lars gave her a quick, apologetic smile.

Then he shut the door. And took up a position right beside it. Probably to make certain she didn't go springing out again.

She peered through the windshield and saw Simon close in on Andy. She knew the men were talking, but their voices were low—no more wild shouts from Andy, so whatever they were saying, she couldn't hear them.

But, surely, everything was okay. It was *Simon*. A former SEAL. A hero. A protector. And if she couldn't trust anyone else, she could at least trust him.

***

"You put so much as a finger on me again, and I will make your life a nightmare," the reporter blustered.

Hell, Simon wasn't even sure the guy *was* a reporter. Simon's hand flew out and yep, he touched the guy. So the fuck what? Simon snatched the jerk's wallet and scanned the ID. "Andy Flint."

Andy grabbed his wallet...

Simon let Andy retrieve his wallet, but Simon still didn't give up the camera, not yet. "You scared Gwen tonight, Andy."

"I was doing my *job*."

"You were stalking her."

"Yeah, well..." Andy shoved his wallet into his pocket. "That's my job. I follow celebs. I take their pics. The world is hungry to hear about them, to see them, and I feed that need."

"You're a jackass."

Andy shrugged. "So the fuck are you."

"How many times have you stalked Gwen?"

Another shrug.

That means too many to count. "Someone wants to hurt her, Andy. If I find out that someone is you..." Simon leaned in close. "I will destroy you."

"Like I'm scared, like I'm—"

"You should be scared. If you were smart, you would be. But I'm not so sure you are the brightest freaking bulb. I think you're a dumbass parasite who gets off on taking pictures of people when they aren't aware you are there watching."

Andy fell silent.

Simon opened the camera and took out the memory card.

"Hey, asshole—" Andy blustered.

"You'll be compensated," Simon said flatly. He tossed the camera at Andy. The guy grabbed it, then nearly dropped it in the next instant. Such a dumbass.

Andy let loose a furious snarl. "You'll be sorry you messed with me—"

"I'm not sorry about many things in this world." *Only Gwen. Only her.* Only for walking away when he should've held tight to the one thing that mattered most. "So, screw that shit. You'll be the one who is sorry if you cross my path again. Stop stalking Gwen. Leave her alone."

"No way, man. She's big business. Sorry if you can't handle the fact that most of the guys in the US jerk off to her but—"

Simon shoved an arm under the guy's neck, freezing his speech. Freezing Andy. "You don't know me." His voice was low and lethal and ice cold. "Don't assume I play by the same rules that everyone else does. Gwen is mine. You don't talk shit about her. No one talks shit about her when I'm near, not unless that fool wants an ass kicking, do you understand me?"

Andy gave a half-nod.

"This is the last warning you're gonna get from me. Stay the hell away from Gwen." He glared at Andy, waiting for the message and his deadly intent to sink in. "I won't be so friendly if our paths cross again."

Simon let him go and Andy scrambled to get inside his car.

Simon turned his back on the jackass and stalked to the waiting SUV.

"That handled?" Lars drawled, not sounding overly concerned.

For the time being. Yeah. It was handled. "I'm taking her home."

"I'll tail you until you have her secure."

Good. He didn't want any other unwelcome guests entering the game. He climbed into the vehicle, slammed the door, and Gwen's scent hit him immediately. Sweet vanilla. Woman. Sin.

Jesus.

He grabbed the steering wheel.

"Simon?"

Breathe. Don't snarl. Breathe. But... "You didn't stay in the car."

"Uh, no, I didn't."

Breathe. "He could've had a fucking gun."

"I *know* Andy. He's a dick most days, but he's not violent. He's not some threat. He's—"

Screw breathing. "When we get home, we're talking about rules." He cranked the SUV. Got them the hell out of there with a squeal of the tires. Andy was busy hauling ass, too.

"I've never been very big on rules," Gwen admitted softly.

"Too damn bad, baby. Because these rules might just save that sweet ass of yours." And help him keep his sanity.

***

Andy went back to the movie set, hoping he could at least score some shots of the other actors leaving. Maybe a money shot of Austin and the chick he'd been screwing the other night. Oh, yeah, Andy had seen them together, but he hadn't been able to get close enough for a pic.

So far, this night was shit. *Shit.* And that big bruiser of a new boyfriend that Gwen had?

That fucker was scary. Scary and crazy. Andy *would* be finding out the guy's secrets. Oh, hell, yes. No one messed with Andy Flint. No one treated him like garbage. Not these days.

He put a new memory card in his camera and focused his lens. He scanned the area, looking for some action. Looking for—

Pay dirt. Hells, yes. That was the co-star, Austin Quest, up against the side of the alley, with his tongue down some chick's throat. Austin had a routine—he liked to have sex outside, rough and fast, so Andy had known that he didn't even need to try and get past security on the set. He just needed to find the right dark spot and wait. He could use his lens to zoom in for great shots.

Andy hit the button on his camera, snap, snap, snapping, and knowing that he'd be scoring some serious cash for this one.

Screw Gwen. Screw her boyfriend. This was his business and he'd come out on top.

He always did.

***

Don't flip the fuck out. Don't flip the fuck out.
Simon paced the length of the den. Again and again. His gaze jerked toward the bathroom.

Gwen had gone straight in there, not saying a word.

He had plenty to say to her. This wasn't some game. He wasn't giving orders for shits and giggles. This was about her safety. He had to know that she'd do exactly what he said, when he said it. Her life was on the line. One wrong move...

I won't lose her the way I lost my team.

He stopped, his body tensing even as he slammed the mental door shut on that memory. No, dammit, *no.* This was not the time to take a fun stroll through the memory of his personal hell.

The bathroom door opened. Steam drifted out. Gwen stood there, her body wrapped in a towel, and her wet hair tumbling all over her shoulders.

"Hell, no." He shook his head, hard.

Gwen blinked. "What are you talking about?"

"You're not coming out, looking like my favorite fantasy, so that you can get past my anger. That shit isn't happening."

Her lips parted. Her eyes widened.

He whirled and marched for the bedroom. Her clothes were in there, but, hell, they were probably skimpy clothes. Sexy clothes. Clothes that would just make her look even more beautiful.

The floor creaked. She'd followed him.

"Simon, I think you're being a wee bit...crazy."

Yeah, he was. "That's because you're close to me. Whenever you're close, I lose my goddamn sanity. Always a side-effect of Gwen Soloman."

He heard her quick inhale. "That's an asshole thing to say."

He yanked out a sweatshirt from his drawer. Forget her clothes. He'd cover her in his. Simon strode toward her. "It's a hard truth I learned long ago." He handed her the sweatshirt. "Put this on."

She looked at the shirt. Then looked at him.

"Please," he gritted out. She didn't get it. His dick was shoving against the front of his jeans. A drop of water was sliding down her collarbone, and he wanted to lick it away.

"Let me get this straight," Gwen muttered. "*I* have to get dressed in your old clothes because you can't control yourself around me?"

Well, Jesus, when she put it that way—

She shoved the shirt at him. "Maybe deal with your issues better, Simon. Maybe just back the hell out of this room and leave me alone."

Leave her alone? "When the hell have I ever been able to do that?" He spun away from her and tried to freaking deal with his issues better. His fingers fisted around the sweatshirt. "Wanna know my number one issue?" He didn't look back at her. "It's that I've always wanted you more than I've ever wanted any other woman." A bitter laugh escaped him. "Truth be told, I think you ruined me for others. I tried...I tried to get past you. You want to hear how many women I've been with since we were together?"

"No." Her voice was brittle. "I don't want to hear that crap. Just like I don't want to tell you how many lovers I've had. This isn't some contest."

No, it wasn't because he would be the loser. *I lost when I let her go.* "Baby, no one compared to you." So he hadn't wasted a lot of time on comparison. What did she think? That he had some giant list of lovers? Uh, no. Ben had been right when he said that Simon didn't exactly ooze charm. Sure, he went with Ben to clubs, but Simon didn't make a habit of hooking up with anyone. He didn't flirt. He didn't charm. Because—

Those women aren't Gwen.

He heard a rustle behind him. *Oh, shit, is she dropping the towel?* Like she'd done last night?

He whirled. She still wore the towel. He was relieved.

Nah, he was soul-deep disappointed.

"Want to know my number one issue?" Gwen asked him.

The woman was about to make him insane.

"It's that I still want you just as much now as I ever did. Even though you walked away. Even though you were out of my life for years. Even though you probably think I'm some horrible person, some terrible killer—"

What?

"I still want you, and I'm not putting on that damn shirt. Because if you want me, too, then come here. Come to me, come to me because—"

Like he had to be told more than once? He was on her in an instant. He threw down the sweatshirt and grabbed Gwen. He pulled Gwen close as his mouth feasted on hers. He was angry and scared, and he *needed* her. Last night, he'd savored every single inch of her.

This wasn't the time for savoring. His control was absolutely gone. All it had taken had been those sweet words—okay, angry words—spilling from her lips.

If you want me, too, then come here—

He feasted on her mouth even as he yanked away the towel. It hit the floor, and he didn't give it another thought. Her hands were on his shoulders, digging in tight. Her body—naked and perfect—pushed against his.

Take. Take. Take.

He lifted her into his arms and carried her to the bed. Simon stopped kissing her only long enough to grab for a condom from his night stand. It was a good thing he had those things there, just in case. Her breath panted out and her silken fingers took the condom from him.

"Not yet," Gwen whispered.

"Gwen—"

Her fingers went to the snap of his jeans. She unhooked the snap and pulled down his zipper with a hiss of sound. His cock sprang toward her. When her fingers closed around him—

His eyes squeezed closed. He stood at the edge of the bed, his knees locked, and every muscle in his body tight with tension. She stroked him, fisting her fingers around him and pumping from root to tip.

"I missed you," Gwen said. Her voice was husky and sexy and just straight up tempting.

Then she put her mouth on him.

Holy fuck. Her mouth was tight and wet and hot.

Gwen Soloman was going down on him. *His* Gwen. His fantasy from the time he was a teen.

And he was about to explode in her mouth.

No. Simon wanted to be buried balls deep in her sex. Wanted her coming around him. Wanted her as lost to the pleasure as he was. "*Gwen,*" he growled her name and with hands that shook, Simon pushed her back.

She licked her lips. Her golden gaze gleamed with desire.

Did she realize that she owned him? "I'm going to fuck you so hard, baby."

Gwen gave him a wide, slow smile. "Promises, promises..."

He'd kept his promise. To her. Always to her.

He yanked the condom on. She tumbled back on the bed and spread her legs for him. He lodged his cock at the entrance to her body. She was open and ready and quivering beneath him. Her hands reached eagerly for Simon—

He caught her wrists. Pinned them over her head with one of his hands. Kissed her hard and deep and he drove into her, sinking into the hot heaven of her body and *never* wanting to let her go.

He withdrew, keeping just the tip of his cock in her, and he lifted his mouth, gazing at her. Beautiful, perfect Gwen.

Her eyes opened. She squirmed beneath him. Arched her hips. Tempted him. "Simon!"

All he wanted was to sink into her. To go wild with her. All he wanted...

Her. Alive. Safe. "The next time..." His voice was a guttural snarl. That was pretty much all he could manage when his dick was dipping in paradise. "I give an order...you follow it..."

Her lips parted. Her eyes widened. "You are..." *Pant.* "Not talking about this *now!*"

He drove into her. Had to do it. She was hot and perfect and pushing him to the edge of sanity. "*Your safety...*" God, he could barely talk. He wanted her too much. "Comes...first..."

Her legs locked around him as she tried to pull him back inside. "*Simon!*"

"*You*...come first."

Then he let go. He pounded into her, giving her everything that he had, and making absolutely sure that, yes, indeed, Gwen came first. She screamed when the pleasure ripped into her, her whole body bucked, and he felt the contractions of her sex around his cock. He rode out her orgasm, thrusting harder and deeper because he knew it would make the pleasure even stronger for her. When she sighed out his name, he surrendered to his own climax. Simon came on a swell of pleasure that shook his body. His heart thundered, pounding harder than any drum, and the whole world seemed to fall away.

When the pleasure ended, he should have been spent.

Instead, his eager dick was already getting hard again.

He withdrew from her. Realized that he still held her wrists together. Her breath came slower, and her long, thick lashes lifted so that she was staring straight at him.

Simon hadn't intended to fuck her. He'd planned for them to talk. To go over the rules of this case and his role as her—her what? Security agent? Bodyguard? Lover? All of the above?

Shit. *Shit*. He'd crossed every line, and the hard truth was that Simon wasn't a bit sorry for it. He'd take Gwen any day. Take her any way that he could get her.

He went to the bathroom. Trashed the condom and came back with a warm cloth for her.

Only...

Gwen's lashes were closed. She'd turned onto her side, curling away.

Hell.

He put down the cloth and slid into bed beside her. When he did, she immediately rolled toward him, moving in her sleep. Putting her body against his with total trust, as if she knew he'd keep her safe.

And I will. "But you have to listen to me. You can't put yourself at risk." Because if something happened to Gwen, what the hell would he do then?

***

"You know where Gwen Soloman is hiding."

Andy jerked at the low, rough words that came from right the hell behind him. He whirled around, his grip on his camera tight, as he tried to peer through the shadows and see just who had sprang up behind him.

But he couldn't get a look at the person's face. And he didn't know that voice. Did he? It was pitched so low, barely above a whisper.

"I'll pay you, make it very worth your while, if you tell me where she is."

Andy laughed. "What? You think you can give me a hundred bucks and I'm supposed to be impressed?" Had to be some fan, hanging around the set. Fool was probably Gwen-obsessed.

"I'll pay a whole lot more than a hundred."

Andy rolled his eyes. This night was such a shit show.

"You followed her tonight. I bet you followed her last night, too."

Actually, he had.

"Tell me where she is."

Andy thought of the big bruiser who'd come at him earlier that night. He couldn't see this jerk in the shadows but when it came to threats...

I'm more afraid of the guy with Gwen. Because he didn't think that fellow had been making a threat. It had been a promise. "Trust me on this. You don't want to get anywhere near Gwen or that crazy-ass lover she has. He'll rip you apart."

He'd gotten plenty of shots. Austin and his lover and their tryst against the side of the alley would be all over the internet soon. Huh. Maybe he actually *owed* Gwen's lover for this bounty. If the psycho hadn't sent him back to the set, he would have missed out on the shots of a lifetime.

Andy turned away, glancing down at his camera. He needed to get back to his place with these. Hell, yes. He'd upload them right away.

He needed—

Something sharp and hard drove into Andy's back. It took a moment for the pain to hit, and when it did, at first, it was like an icy cold spreading through his body. Then...then the blood started pumping out. "Wh-what...the—"

The knife—*a freaking knife!*—twisted in his back. "You're not going anywhere." The voice was different now. Stronger. Clearer. "You're telling me where Gwen is so I can make that bitch pay. She knew what I wanted. She was supposed to give it to me!"

Holy...The car bombing. The attack on Gwen. It had been real? All of it? It had been—

The blade pulled out.

Andy's body slumped forward, but he didn't hit the ground. The attacker held him in a tight grip.

"I'll *make* you tell me."

Andy wanted to scream but...who was around? The set was closed now. Austin had left long ago, right after he'd finished up his screw. Andy had lingered, in case something else happened on set. But no one else was there and Andy...

He dropped his camera. It crashed onto the ground, shattering.

CHAPTER TWELVE

"Don't! Stop!"

Gwen's voice woke Simon. He turned toward her, pulling her close against him once more.

But she shoved against him. *"Don't! Let me go!"* Her voice was fitful, a bit smothered, as if talking was hard for her.

He knew she was having another nightmare. Just like the one she'd had the previous night. Only...

Is it a dream or a memory?

"Gwen? Baby?" Simon spoke softly and gently ran his fingers over her cheek. "Wake up."

She gave a gasp, and he felt a shudder run the length of her body.

"You back with me?"

"I'm sorry." Her words were too high now. "Was I talking again?"

"You don't have to be sorry for a damn thing. I just need to know you're okay."

She shook her head.

"Baby?"

"I didn't mean to wake you." Now her voice was small. Almost...ashamed.

Hell, no.

He sat up in bed. Turned on the nearby lamp.

She blinked and immediately yanked the covers up over her breasts. She clutched the covers to her chest, her grip too tight.

"How often do you have the same dream?"

Her knuckles turned white as she gripped the sheet.

"Only it's not a dream, is it?" Simon pushed her.

Gwen shook her head.

He was trying to tread so carefully with her. "Do you want to tell me about it?"

Her breath sighed out. "I already did. I told you everything that happened on the boat." Her eyes were so deep and sad. "And, no, I don't have the dream all the time. If I did, I'd probably go insane. I hadn't...it's just because of the stress. Because I'm scared. I'm sure that's why it's come back."

The nightmares had come back because the jerk out there was threatening her with the past. "We're going to find him," Simon promised. "We're going to—"

An alarm beeped, the signal coming first from his phone and then from the security area just down the hall. Simon tensed.

"What is it?" Gwen asked.

Trouble. Simon leapt from the bed. Yanked on his jeans and then grabbed for his phone. His fingers flew over the screen.

One of the motion sensors outside of his building had just been triggered.

His fingers tapped against the screen. He wanted to see who was out there, and he pulled up a camera feed—

The old sedan was familiar. A sight that pissed him off. Andy hadn't gotten the message.

Simon had been afraid this would happen. If the guy had followed him *this* time, odds were good the jackass might have followed them the night before, too.

"What is it?" Gwen perched on the edge of the bed. "*Who* is it?"

"The photographer asshole." Someone who had been warned. Simon stared hard at Gwen. "You can watch the feed in the security area, but under no circumstances are you to come outside."

"Simon—"

"My orders, Gwen."

"But I'm the one paying Wilde!"

"And I am the one who will do anything to keep you safe." As far as paying Wilde, screw that shit. He'd make sure her bills were covered with Eric. "You don't leave the security of this place, got me?" He leaned toward her, letting her see his intent. "If you put yourself at risk, you don't even want to know how pissed I'd be."

Her chin notched up. "Maybe Andy is just going to snap some pics and leave."

"If he gets pics of the exterior, then this location is compromised. If he puts the pics up on his site, if he tags you on social media, everyone will know where you are." Simon had screwed up. He should have noticed a tail the night before.

Maybe Eric—damn him—had been right. Because Simon wasn't impartial on this case. Not even close. He saw Gwen. He was blinded by her.

And his obsession was putting her in danger.

"Stay here," he ordered, knowing the words sounded hard and grim.

She nodded.

He turned away—

But Gwen's hand flew out and curled around his wrist. "You'll be careful, though? You'll be safe?"

She was worried? That was progress.

"And you won't...hurt him?"

That wasn't a promise Simon would make. "The code to access the security feed is 1028. You can pull up all the exterior cameras and watch them on my monitors."

"10...28? That's my birthday."

Yeah.

Her hold tightened. "Simon."

"I have to go, Gwen. He's still fucking outside. For all I know, he's giving away your location right now." Simon leaned down and kissed her. Hard and fast. "*Stay safe.*"

He pulled on a shirt and shoes before rushing from the room, and he made sure to get his weapon, too, right before he slid into the elevator. Fury hardened his body. Andy had been warned. Now the guy was compromising Gwen's safety.

He'd pay.

***

Gwen slid from the bed. She grabbed Simon's sweatshirt—the one he'd tried to get her to wear before, and she pulled it over her head. The shirt was massive, falling to mid-thigh on her and surprisingly soft.

She hurried out of the bedroom and toward the security area, fear giving her extra speed. Simon had already vanished on the elevator, and she'd seen him grab his gun.

As she stood in front of the row of monitors, Gwen shifted nervously from foot to foot. She leaned forward and typed in the access code—*her* birthday—and watched as all the monitors lit up. Her gaze darted around them, seeing all the exterior views. Seeing...

The sedan. Its headlights were on and shining at Simon's building. She leaned forward and squinted her eyes. Was Andy in the car? She couldn't tell for certain.

As she watched, Simon appeared. He jogged from the building and headed straight for the sedan. Her breath caught as she waited.

He slowed when he was right beside the car. Was he saying something? She couldn't tell, not from that angle. And the sedan's doors were still closed.

What was happening down there? Where was Andy?

***

Simon glared at the figure slumped behind the steering wheel. "Come out, Andy," he snarled. "Right the hell now."

The man didn't move.

Simon's eyes narrowed. He could see the camera on the dashboard. *Sonofabitch.* "This isn't a joke." He grabbed for the handle of the driver's side door. "I *warned* you." Simon yanked open the door.

The vehicle's interior light immediately flooded the sedan with illumination, and Simon got a good look at Andy Flint.

Or rather, at Andy Flint's *dead* body.

The guy's chest was covered with blood. His face looked like it had been beat to hell and back.

Simon didn't need to check Andy's pulse to know he was dead. Simon backed away immediately, not wanting to contaminate the scene even as he drew his gun and searched for the threat that he knew *had* to be there.

Andy sure as hell hadn't driven himself to the scene. Someone else had done it, then shoved Andy behind the steering wheel.

Simon's gaze flew over the street. "Where the hell are you?"

***

Simon had taken out his gun. Gwen's heart squeezed in her chest when he rushed away from the vehicle, with his gun out. She didn't know what was happening or why he'd suddenly—

He was spinning around, searching the street.

But no one else was out there. Just him and Andy...right? Only Andy hadn't gotten out of the sedan. And Simon was scaring the crap out of her.

He glanced back at the sedan. Took a slow step toward the vehicle. God, this scene was terrifying her.

Simon stalked toward the sedan's open door once more. Was he going to reach inside? She leaned even closer, and her nose almost touched the monitor before her. Was he—

The sedan exploded, and Gwen screamed.

CHAPTER THIRTEEN

She'd run straight to the elevator. Her hands slammed into the control panel even as her whole body shook with fear and rage. The explosion had been huge. And right after she'd seen the ball of fire erupt, all of the feeds on the monitors had died.

Simon. He wasn't dead, though. He couldn't be dead. No way. No!

The elevator descended, and a few frantic moments later, the doors opened. She lunged forward.

Hard hands caught her and shoved her back. Gwen opened her mouth to scream even as she kicked out at her attacker—

"Gwen!"

Simon?

A bleeding, clothes-torn, furious Simon had a fierce grip on her. "I told you to stay the hell inside!"

He was alive. She was so happy she almost cried.

His hold tightened on her. "*You were supposed to stay inside!*"

She was still inside, technically. "And you were supposed to stay safe!"

He slammed one hand into the elevator's control panel. "He's dead."

"If he was in the car, yes, he is! Because I saw the flames and you were right there, and I was afraid you—" *Were dead.* Her lips pressed together.

"Andy Flint was dead long before the fire got to him."

His shirt was singed. Blood dripped down Simon's cheek. She wanted to throw her arms around him and hug him as tightly as she could.

"He'd been stabbed. Tortured from the look of things." Each word hit her with brutal force. "Andy was put out there as bait, Gwen." The elevator was moving.

Her knees almost buckled.

"The killer set the scene. He knew I'd see the sedan on the security feed. The car was there to draw me out of the building."

The doors opened.

He caught her hand and hauled her out of the elevator. She stumbled, her legs not seeming to work just right.

"Andy's camera was on the dashboard. I thought he might have snapped a pic of the bastard who'd attacked him. I started to grab for it, then realized it was too perfect. The camera being *right* there. To get it, I'd have to duck hard into the car. And all I could think was...*it's bait to pull me in.* He wants me inside so that he can blow me to hell."

OhmyGod.

"I was running even as the car blew. Didn't you *see* that?"

"No, I saw the explosion." They were in the den. "Then all the feeds went dark."

He stiffened. "Say that again?"

"All of the feeds stopped. I couldn't see *anything*. I needed to know that you were okay. I had to be sure—that's why I was going outside!" Her voice was rising to an alarming degree. She had to get that shit back under control. "I was scared. Nothing can happen to you. *Nothing*."

He dragged her close. Kissed her hard and deep and some of the terrifying cold finally left her body.

"He's trying to get to you," Simon growled against her mouth. "And that won't happen, I swear it. You're staying with me until we catch him. At my side. I'm not letting you out of my sight again."

Did he think she was going to let him go? He'd nearly died—while trying to protect her.

A phone was ringing.

His phone? But she didn't remember Simon taking his phone when he left—he'd grabbed his gun and—

The phone was ringing in the bedroom.

Simon's fingers twined with hers as they rushed to the bedroom. His phone was on the nightstand. She saw the number on the screen, but then Simon grabbed the phone.

Before he could answer it, she demanded, "I want to hear, too." This was her life. Her nightmare.

He nodded and put the call on speaker. "Who the fuck is this?"

Laughter. Then a distorted voice said, "A mutual friend gave me your number. He happened to have your card on him when we...talked."

Nausea rolled over Gwen.

"I told Gwen what I wanted. She should have paid the price. His death is on her."

"Fucking asshole!" Gwen shouted. "This is all because you wanted nude pics of me? You wanted a hundred grand? You're insane! You *killed* a man, you—"

"So did you, Gwen. So the hell did you." A low, rough snarl. "I know, you understand? *I know.* You should pay the price. You should do every single thing that I want. Or I *will* make this house of cards come tumbling down on you. Down, down, it falls. Until there is nothing left." More grating laughter. "And it's not a hundred grand any longer. It's a million."

She looked up at Simon. His face was rock hard. His fingers slid over the screen, and she realized he was texting someone while they were talking to that freak killer.

And...in the distance, she could hear the scream of sirens.

Because a car exploded outside. Because there's a dead man. Because everything is wrecked! Everything!

"A million dollars and...you, dear Gwen. I want you. Not just pictures. Not just video. *You.* You'll come to me..."

"You're not touching Gwen," Simon's voice was cold and flat. Totally emotionless. "*I'm* coming for you. My team is coming for you. You're going to pay for what you did."

Laughter. "If I pay, so does Gwen. It all goes back to Gwen. You gonna let her get thrown in jail? I don't think so." The voice was disguised, but the rage was clear. "Big, bad hero, back in Gwen's life. You still want her just as badly, don't you? You don't get her this time. This time...I win. I control everything, I—"

The sirens were louder. And she could...wait, could she hear the sirens coming from the phone? Gwen's eyes widened. She *could*. The sirens were echoing from the phone because that bastard was close by! He was still out there, waiting, watching—

"I know you're close," Simon said. "You had to be, so that you could detonate the bomb. Just waited for me to go in the car. Did you realize, you sonofabitch, that I got the camera? The memory card is still inside it. You're such a dumbass. The camera was broken, yes, but the card is intact."

She knew he was bluffing. He hadn't gotten the camera. But maybe he could scare the stalker into thinking that they had it.

"You're gonna be on the card. Andy always got the shot. That was his deal, wasn't it? I'll see your face. The world will see. You'll be the one on all the TVs now. And I'll come for you. I will *end* you."

The line went dead.

Gwen's breathing seemed too loud. Too ragged. "He's outside," she whispered. Somewhere, hiding close in the dark. The man who hated her. The man who knew all of her secrets.

He'd found her. He'd killed. And...

"He won't get in, Gwen." Simon still gripped his phone. "My team is almost here. The cops are coming. The firefighters. The area is going to be searched. We're going to get him."

She nodded. And she wanted to believe him. *They will get the killer.*

Her hands twisted in front of her and rubbed against his sweatshirt. "I have to tell." She understood that. Maybe she'd always understood. "I have to tell everything." To the cops. To the world. She had to take away this bastard's power.

"Gwen..."

Her head tilted back.

"Gwen, he knows me. He knows you." Simon's voice was low and intense. "He knew us both *back then*. The guy is someone who has been in our lives. Both of our lives."

Yes, he and Eric had thought that before, it was why they'd sent a team to Florida but...

Who could hate her so much?

So much...that the stalker had murdered a man.

***

"I need to confess." Gwen sat at the interrogation table. And, really, it was just like a movie set. Just like a scene from *The Wrong Alibi*. The slightly scarred table top. The one-way mirror on the wall. The chair with the legs that were uneven. Every time she leaned forward, the chair

rocked. The temperature in the room was icy—
that hadn't been the case on the set of *The Wrong
Alibi*. But...but they'd had a cup of coffee for her
on set. And there was a cup of coffee on the table,
too. Really dark, really cold coffee.

If she just focused, she could pretend this was
another role. That she was acting. She could do
this. She could get through this night.

"Confess?" The pretty detective lifted both
her eyebrows as she cast a questioning glance at
Simon. "Seriously? What in the hell is going on? I
thought you told me she was a victim."

"She *is*." Simon was adamant. His arm slid
around the back of Gwen's chair, brushing against
her. "She's just had one hell of a night."

"Hmm." The detective—Layla Lopez—cocked
her head. Her dark eyes swept over Gwen. "I bet I
can think of one person who had a rougher night."
She tapped her chin with one long, light blue
fingernail. "That would be *my* vic. The poor
bastard who was torched right outside of *your*..."
Now her gaze drifted to Simon. "Place."

"I told you—Andy Flint was dead before the
fire got to him. He'd been stabbed—hell, I think
about eight times. Someone put him in that car.
Someone left him for me to find."

"The man who is stalking me," Gwen added
fiercely. "*He* did this!"

Layla nodded. "I'm a homicide detective. The
poor dead bastard? He's my vic. And I am going
to do everything in my power to find his killer."
She waited a beat. "So, how about you give me
your full confession, Ms. Soloman, and we'll go
from—"

The interrogation room door opened.

Ben Wilde poked his head inside.

Layla rolled her eyes. "Jesus Christ. Not you again."

Gwen frowned at Simon. Why was Ben there?

"Tell me you aren't this woman's attorney," Detective Lopez instructed.

Uh, no, he wasn't. Ben had told Gwen that he was a divorce—

"*I'm* her attorney," a very clear, very sharp male voice announced. A voice that had come from behind Ben.

Ben stepped out of the way.

Gwen caught sight of the tall, well-dressed man behind him. A guy in a truly impeccable suit, his long, lean fingers gripping a leather briefcase. He flashed a broad smile, showing his perfectly white and even teeth. His skin was a warm, pure dark cream. And that smile—it was almost wicked. "Hello, Detective Lopez."

The detective sighed. "Of course, I should have known that you'd be close, Mr. Shaw. Let me guess, you smelled blood in the water and you had to follow that delicious scent?"

Gwen was totally lost. What was happening?

Ben cleared his throat. "Actually, I called Kendrick. Asked him to come down and rep Gwen because my brother told me she might need a hand tonight."

A hand—a whole body. She needed as much help as she could get.

The man in the great suit strode toward Gwen. She stood as he offered his hand.

"Ms. Soloman?" That smile of his was pure perfection. "I'm Kendrick Shaw, and I'm the best criminal defense attorney you've ever seen."

Should she tell him that he was the only one she'd seen? In real life, anyway. No, probably not. She shook his hand. "Thank...you?" Yes, the words sounded like a question because she felt so utterly lost.

He winked and the little wink oddly soothed her. Then Kendrick squeezed her hand. Let her go. "There will be no confessions. Not about anything."

"But—" Gwen began.

"Not until I've talked with my client and I've been fully brought up to speed on this case." He put his briefcase on the table. "Detective Lopez, I need a moment to confer with my client."

Gwen's head was splitting. And spinning.

"Fine," the detective snapped. "I'll give you five minutes, and then I want to know exactly what in the hell is going on." She strode from the interrogation room.

The door slammed shut behind her.

Gwen swallowed. Then she pointed to the one-way mirror. "Can't she just be in there, watching?" *Listening?*

Kendrick's perfect smile was gone. "Only if she wants a lawsuit from me."

Gwen released a low breath.

"The dead man—" Kendrick began, his brows pulling low.

"I didn't kill him!" Gwen exclaimed. "Neither did Simon!"

"Jesus," Ben muttered. "This case went bad, fast." He was pacing near the door.

"Good to know," Kendrick told Gwen, "though, for the future, I will never ask you—specifically—if you have committed a crime. It's better for me not to do that, okay?"

Simon's hand slapped down on the table. "That reporter followed us. I told him to get his ass lost, and the next thing I knew—"

The door flew open.

Detective Lopez filled the doorway. Hadn't she *just* left?

"Yes, I know that I'm charming and amazing." Kendrick made a show of looking at his watch. "But you didn't need to rush back. You *did* promise me five minutes and I don't think it's even been one—"

The detective held up her phone. "Guess what just appeared on Andy Flint's website? Or rather, that wannabe news site that he worked for?"

Gwen was afraid to find out.

The detective put her phone on the table. Hit play and...

Gwen saw the sedan. She saw Andy—she saw...*Simon?* Yes, yes, it was the whole scene from earlier, when Andy had first followed them. She even came into the video as she grabbed Simon's arm and tried to pull him away from Andy.

"This was earlier in the night," Gwen whispered. "Simon didn't hurt Andy then. He just—"

"I told him to stay the hell away from Gwen," Simon fired out bluntly. "Or I'd make him pay."

"Oh, shit." Ben huddled close so he could view the footage, too. "You don't admit crap like that, not with the cops present."

"No," Kendrick agreed quietly. "You don't."

The video changed. Suddenly, a new location. The sedan, but this time...

Gwen's breath left her in a fast rush. *This time, the sedan was outside of Simon's place.* Simon was reaching into the car. He seemed to grab something before he surged back.

The sedan exploded.

"You threaten the victim, then he gets blown to hell." The detective's voice held a world of suspicion. "Maybe Ms. Soloman isn't the one who needs the lawyer. Maybe it's you, Simon. Maybe it's *you.*"

Simon shook his head.

"I know about you, Simon." Layla put her hands on her hips. "*You're* the one with demolitions training, aren't you? I think you told me that, one night when I was out with you and Eric Wilde. You did demo work as a SEAL."

Gwen didn't even understand what was happening. Why was the detective accusing Simon? And why had she been out with Simon and Eric? "He hasn't done anything wrong!"

"Eric was so excited to get you on his team," Layla continued, "because of your—what did he tell me? Ah, yes. 'Your multiple-levels of expertise.' You're an expert at hand-to-hand combat, you can build a bomb in moments, and, oh, I bet you know all about torture techniques, don't you?"

"Stop," Gwen snapped.

Kendrick put his hand on her shoulder. "She's trying to trick you."

The detective was pissing her off. "He was a SEAL!" Gwen's temples throbbed harder. "He didn't torture people. Simon helped people. He—"

Layla turned her head toward Gwen. "When did you hire him?"

The question caught her off guard. "Two days ago." Was that right? She was a little fuzzy on time. They'd been in that interrogation room for hours. Was it still night? Or day? She tried to get a glimpse of the clock but—

"How can you possibly know anything about him in such a short period of time?"

"Because—" *Because I loved him when I was eighteen. I knew him completely and totally, and a man doesn't change that much.*

"I know him." Layla gave a grim nod. "This isn't the first time our paths have crossed, is it, Simon?"

"You know I didn't kill that poor bastard." Simon's expression showed his fury.

"I know there is a whole lot more to you than meets the eye." Layla pointed to her phone. "You were pissed at that guy. Mad because he was following Ms. Soloman. I'm curious...when you are leaning in close to him, what are you saying? Just what are you threatening to do to him?"

Enough. "Stop!" Gwen's voice had gone cold and hard.

Everyone looked at her.

"Simon didn't kill Andy Flint. The freak stalking me did that. He *called* while Simon was right in front of me. The guy confessed. Said that he was going to destroy me. That he was going to take everything away from me." She wouldn't look down at the video again. "If he put the video up on Andy's site, then he must have gotten Andy's password and credentials *before* he killed the guy. Then he kept right on filming. Recording every moment. He put the scenes up on that website—I don't know why. To rip apart my life more. To hurt Simon. To get attention. He's a sadistic bastard, and I'm here because I thought the cops would help us to stop him." She was nearly shaking with rage. "Simon said you were a great detective, that we could count on you."

The detective raised her brows. "Is that what he said?"

"Simon didn't kill Andy. The bastard who bombed my car—he's the one who killed Andy. And he's the one who called right after the crime and said that he wasn't going to stop. He thinks I owe him—that I'm *his* somehow, and I'm absolutely terrified of what he's going to do next."

There. She'd put it all out in the open. Well, almost all of it.

Silence ticked past in that small room.

"I have the full video footage," Simon revealed. "You know, just in case you want to see what actually went down."

Gwen's head turned. Why had he held back that particular bit of information?

Simon stared at the detective. "The SOB tried to cut the security feed to my place right after Andy's car blew up. The cameras stopped recording then, but all of the data that had been collected up *until* that point is still saved."

Gwen's attention darted back to the detective.

Layla frowned at him. "Why didn't you say this shit before?"

Totally my question.

"Because you can't identify a damn thing about the guy in the video." Now Simon brought out his own phone. Tapped on the screen. Gwen leaned in close, holding her breath as she watched. The sedan slowly drove down the street. Braked. A guy hopped out of the driver's side—right before he reached back in and yanked Andy's dead body—presumably, moving it behind the steering wheel. Then the jerk in the hoodie and ski mask bent to shove something under the car.

"The bomb?" Layla asked.

"That's what I figure. We're gonna need to get a ballistics expert to examine the remains. Bomb-makers have signatures that can give them away."

"That's true," Gwen said, feeling cold and wooden. "My agent and I consulted with a bomb expert when I was working on *The Wrong Alibi*. He said some bombs were so personal they might as well have fingerprints on them."

Simon's head whipped toward her. "There was no bomb scene in *The Wrong Alibi*."

"Super fan," Ben noted. "You would remember every scene."

Simon ignored him.

"The scene wasn't in the movie," Gwen agreed. "It got cut. For the end, I was supposed to put a bomb under my husband's car. I was going to blow him and the Benz to hell. As the fire raged,

I would drive off into the sunset for the final shot." *Oh, shit.* She cleared a suddenly thick throat. "Test audiences didn't like that, so we had to reshoot. My character was captured by the cops and the bombing never made it to the final movie."

"Who was the bomb expert that you talked with?" Simon and Layla both asked at the same time.

"I...his name was Dale. Dale Sanders."

"Have you had any contact with Dale since the filming?" Lopez asked.

"No, but...maybe my agent has. She's the one who first contacted him. She can tell you how to find him."

A few moments later, the detective had left the interrogation room. Simon was on his phone, barking orders at whoever was on the other end of the line, and Gwen found herself trapped between two lawyers.

"I don't want you talking to the cops unless I'm present," Kendrick advised her. His voice was low and warm, and his stare was direct. "Better safe than sorry."

"I'm...I'm not charged with any crime. I mean, are you *sure* I need your services?" She just wanted to get out of there.

Kendrick nodded. "We're going to talk when we're alone. My instincts say, hell, yes, you need me...and the fact that Ben and Eric Wilde called me in..."

Gwen's hands twisted together. "We'll talk soon." And, yes, she'd be taking his services.

Because she very well might be facing a murder charge one day.

He grabbed his briefcase. "I want to go see what Lopez is discovering about this case. I'm assuming that Simon will be taking you out of here?" His attention slid to Simon.

Simon moved the phone away from his mouth. "Damn straight."

"But not back to your place," Gwen blurted.

Simon's jaw hardened. "No, not there. Don't worry, baby, I'm working on a safe house for you right now."

Kendrick squeezed her hand. "Simon will take care of you. He's one of the good guys."

They knew each other well? She felt so out of the loop.

Kendrick hurried out of the room, taking his leather briefcase with him.

Ben frowned at her. "You look pale. When is the last time you had something to eat?"

She had no clue. "What time is it?"

"Nearly nine a.m."

Oh, damn.

"And, in case you're curious, yes, it does look like a circus outside of this station. Reporters are camped out for blocks. I recommend heading out the back door."

"We tried that already," she mumbled. "And the guy who followed us wound up dead."

"*I got him.*"

Gwen glanced up at Simon's fierce growl.

"Found Dale. The guy is *in* the area."

What? Since when? When they'd worked together before, he'd been in LA.

"He has a place just outside of Atlanta." Simon shoved his phone into his pocket. "And I'm betting Layla is discovering the same intel right about now."

Gwen stood up. "You think Dale is involved in this?"

"A bomb expert with a connection to you? A guy who just *happens* to be in the area? After *two* bombs have been set off? Yeah, sweetheart, this is something I won't ignore. I can't buy coincidence on this."

"But it doesn't make sense." Her hands fisted at her sides. "Dale isn't connected to my past! The first time I met him, I was working on *The Wrong Alibi*. He has no clue about anything I've done—" She stopped, glancing at Ben.

Ben blinked. "Are you about to make a confession?"

Um, no.

He tilted his head and asked, "Am I supposed to promise you confidentiality right now?"

"No, I don't want you to promise me anything. I just want this to stop. A man is dead, and I don't want anyone else hurt because of *my* secrets." She wanted this mess over with. *Finished.*

Simon edged closer to her. "Wilde has a safe house ready for you. It's on the edge of town. I'll take you there now and get you settled."

"So, I'm supposed to hide?" Gwen shook her head. "You heard the guy on the phone, Simon. He wants a million dollars—"

Ben let out a low whistle.

"And the man wants *me*."

Simon's face appeared to have been cut from stone. "He's not getting you."

"I can't have him hurting someone else! And if I run and hide, that could be exactly what he does. But maybe if I go public with the story about Xavier, I can take away his power." It was her hope.

Ben had fallen silent.

Simon exhaled. "This guy isn't going to stop if you turn to the press. Don't you see that, baby? He's killed now. For all we know, he could have killed before this, too. He's after *you*. And he's not going to stop because you destroy your life by spilling the past. He's not going to stop until we make him stop."

A shiver slid over her.

"The cops will go have a chat with Dale Sanders. Layla will grill the guy and get the truth from him. Maybe he's the SOB who's been after you. If he is, then this can all end by nightfall."

Her nervous gaze darted to Ben. She found him watching her so very carefully. She knew he had questions, but Ben wasn't asking them. And she couldn't help but feel incredibly grateful.

Simon laced his fingers with hers. "Let's get you to a safe place. Once you're secured, we'll figure out the next step."

She didn't like hiding. And she sure as hell didn't like people dying.

CHAPTER FOURTEEN

"So..." Ben drawled as he lounged on the couch. "Just what did Gwen do? What deep, dark sin is she hiding?"

Simon slanted a fast glance toward the hallway. Gwen was showering in the bathroom. He could hear the thunder of the water. He'd gotten her to the safe house, but Ben had tagged along. And, honestly, he was glad to have someone with him that he could trust.

But as far as Gwen's sins..."You don't need to know, man."

"You keep the best secrets from me." Ben's lips pulled down. "Like the fact that you and a movie star were lovers. Here I thought you'd never have a chance in hell with her, but you'd already claimed her long ago."

Simon dropped into a nearby chair. He felt absolutely bone weary. "Eric has a big mouth."

"Nah, man. He didn't tell me jack shit." A smile flashed Ben's dimples. "I figured that out on my own. It was the way you looked at her in Eric's office."

Simon lifted his brows.

"Like you could eat her alive." A pause. "Like you *had* done that and couldn't wait to do it again."

"You are such an asshole."

Ben shrugged. "Yeah, but I'm an asshole who wants to help his friend. So tell me what I can do."

Simon glanced down at his phone. "When the bastard called me last time, he used Andy Flint's phone." He'd learned that while down at the police station.

"That call—was that when he said he wanted a million dollars? *And* your Gwen?"

Was she his? He wanted her to be. He sure felt like he was hers. "Yes, that's when he said that bull." He pinned his friend with a hard gaze. "I'm expecting another call from him. If he really wants the money, then he's going to want some sort of exchange. Some set up deal."

Ben nodded. "Unless..." His arm stretched out along the back of the couch. "Unless the bad guy is Dale Sanders. Then Layla can arrest his ass, and you can close this case."

When he closed the case, Gwen wouldn't need him any longer. She'd be safe. She'd go back to her world. He'd go back to his.

"What can I do?" Ben asked again. "I mean, sure, I get this isn't my area of expertise, but I'm here. Use me."

Simon opened his mouth to reply, but then he heard the rattle of the doorknob. Instantly, he was on high alert because no one should have just been able to march up to the front door without the security system going off. Not unless—

He bounded forward.

The door swung open to reveal Eric Wilde.

Of course, Eric would have been able to bypass the security system. He'd been the one to create the system.

Eric looked especially grim. Not a good sign.

"Where's Gwen?" Eric asked.

"Showering."

Eric's gaze darted toward the hallway. He nodded, as if satisfied, then he lifted the laptop bag he carried. "We need to talk. Now."

Simon's gut tightened.

"You're not going to like it, man. Not one bit. Your Gwen *isn't* who you think."

***

"Wait for my order." Layla pulled in a deep breath as she studied the small house before her. About fifteen minutes outside of Atlanta, the place had been hidden along a twisting dirt road and surrounded by tall pine trees. According to the info she'd obtained, Dale Sanders was renting the house. He'd been renting it ever since Gwen Soloman had come to town in order to film her new movie.

Every single instinct that Layla had was screaming at her. She'd brought her partner Mac and two uniforms with her. The uniforms were there as a precaution. She motioned to them now. "Go around the back of the house." The last thing she wanted was to deal with a runner. "Right now, we're just here to ask questions." No warrant, not yet. Mostly because they didn't have enough evidence to get one.

"Let's make this question and answer session fun," Mac muttered. As usual, his clothes were rumpled, like the guy had just crawled out of bed, but his eyes were sharp and focused. His fingers were already poised near his gun.

Fun. Not exactly.

She and Mac had been together for a while now, so when they moved forward, they did it in perfect sync. An old, beat-up truck was parked in the driveway. She put her hand on the hood. Cold. Their guy hadn't been driving recently. Her gaze darted down to the dirt road.

Tracks? Yes, she could see the grooves in the dirt. Seemed like Dale had recently entertained some company.

"Got a black sweatshirt inside," Mac announced quietly. "Looks like a ski mask, too." He was peering in the truck's passenger side window.

She risked a quick glance, too. *Looks just like the outfit the guy wore in Simon's security video.* Her fingers were poised close to her own gun.

They crept toward the front of the house. "Atlanta PD!" Mac called out. He lifted his hand and pounded on the door. "Dale Sanders, we want to talk with you!"

***

Simon shut the study door behind him. Ben had stayed in the den. He was supposed to keep Gwen occupied when she came out of the shower. *Please be wearing more than just a towel, sweetheart, or I'll have to kick his ass.*

Eric had already booted up the laptop. "The cops will find this information. It's only a matter of time." His fingers flew across the keys. "I got to it first because I am that good."

Simon sighed. "Just spit it out, man."

Eric glanced up. "I thought you'd want to see the proof for yourself."

Simon stalked forward. "I trust you. Tell me."

His lips thinned, but then Eric revealed, "I followed the money trail. Dale Sanders? He didn't just *happen* to be down here. He lived in LA. In order to come here, someone had to foot the bill."

Simon nodded. "Right. So, we find the person who paid—"

"She paid."

Simon didn't follow.

"Gwen. She paid. She transferred money from one of her private accounts to cover the cost of his rental house. She paid for him to come here. And she paid him extra—maybe for services rendered."

No, no, that didn't make sense.

"This is why I thought you'd want to see the evidence for yourself. That look on your face right now. The disbelief. I warned you before, man, that you were in too deep with her."

Yeah, he was in deep, and he also wasn't buying this story. "Gwen would have told me."

Eric lifted his eyebrows. "Because the woman has never kept a secret from you? That what you're saying? Because I thought Xavier Gray—"

Fuck that. Simon marched forward. He scanned the material on the screen. Saw the transfers. The money going from Gwen's account.

Heading right to Dale's. Sure, it wasn't her main account, looked like an old, smaller, private account that she'd set up years ago. One that hadn't seen any activity at all until the recent transfers.

"Celebrities like attention," Eric murmured.

Simon shook his head. "This *isn't* Gwen." He was one hundred percent certain. "Someone is setting her up."

Eric's expression didn't change. "You're really sure of that?"

"I'm sure of *her*."

"How? Why?" Eric shook his head. "The evidence is right here, and I—"

"I'm dead certain because I trust her. Gwen's fear is real. She didn't do this." He didn't care what the evidence said. His faith was in Gwen. "But someone wants to make it look like she's guilty as sin."

***

Gwen crept from the bathroom. She'd pulled on jeans and a loose blouse, and her bare toes curled against the floor. The safe house was huge, and the place felt strangely cold to her. Or maybe that cold was just coming *from* Gwen. Because ever since she'd left the police station, she'd felt as if ice covered her heart.

"Hey, there, Gwen."

Her head turned. Ben was on the couch. A faint, slightly nervous smile curved his lips and made his dimples wink.

"Simon is chatting with my brother for a bit." He motioned to the couch. "Why don't you sit down? We can get to know each other."

The guy was handsome. Sexy. Probably got women to do all sorts of things for him when he flashed those dimples of his. "They disarm the ladies, don't they?"

He blinked.

She took a slow step toward him. "The dimples. They make you look safe. Like you're the good guy."

His smile widened a little, making his dimples cut deeper. "I don't know what Simon has told you, but I promise, I *am* a good guy."

Was he? "Not sure I'm ready to buy that line." It was the eyes that told a different story. Those blue eyes of his were deep and gorgeous, but she'd noticed they could also turn cold. She'd seen it at the police station. There was a whole lot more to Ben Wilde than you tended to notice at first glance.

She didn't sit on the couch next to him. Instead, Gwen perched in a nearby chair. "Are you and Simon close?"

"We're good friends." He seemed to mull something over, then said, "When I first met him, he was wired to so many machines that I didn't know if he was ever going to open his eyes again."

What? Her whole body jolted as if she'd been hit with an electric shock.

"Happened on one of his missions," Ben continued, seeming to be all casual but she didn't think this was a casual conversation at all. "Two of his team members had betrayed Simon. Tried to take out the whole unit."

Her heart raced in her chest and that cold she'd felt? It got worse. A lot worse.

"My brother was doing some contract work back then. Shit he doesn't talk about much. Eric used to do all kinds of secret projects for Uncle Sam." He leaned forward, as if imparting deep, dark secrets. "Want to know the deadliest weapon in the world? I think it might be tech. Some of the things my brother used to make..." But Ben whistled and shook his head. "A story for another day. But, well, it was while Eric was working a covert op that he came across Simon. Dragged Simon out with the help of the contract agents Eric had working for him. When they made it back to the US, Eric made sure Simon had the best possible care until he got back on his feet."

Her breath heaved in and out. "I didn't know."

"Simon said he had no close family. His mom had died the previous year. And his dad—"

"His dad passed away when Simon was fifteen." He'd been a firefighter, and he'd died trying to save a family when their home ignited. He'd gotten out the two kids, but had died when he'd tried to rescue the mom.

And Simon had always wanted to be a hero. Just like his dad. Wasn't that why she'd thought he'd gone off to become a SEAL? Because he'd wanted to live up to his father's image. Wanted to help others.

And she couldn't hold him back.

Even though she'd wanted to grab tight and hold on with all of her strength.

"Are you all right, Gwen?" Ben's voice was soft. Concerned. "You're crying."

She swiped a hand over her cheek. She'd just realized that Simon could have died, and she wouldn't have known. "The world is better when he's in it." Her own voice was just as soft as Ben's had been. Even if Simon wasn't with her, she needed to know that he was out there. Somewhere. Gwen straightened her shoulders and stared straight at Ben. "If anything like that *ever* happens again...you call me, understand?"

"And if you're with someone else? You think your lover will be fine with you running off to check on Simon?" A wink of one dimple. "Not so sure about that, Gwen—"

"I'm sure." Her voice was flat. "Simon will always be important to me. I don't want him to *ever* be hurt. But if something should happen, I want to know. I want to be there with him. I want to hold his hand, and I want him to know that he's not alone. That he still has family." *He has me.*

Ben's smile turned just the faintest bit...satisfied. *Is the guy playing me?*

"So, you *do* care about him." Ben nodded.

"Never said I didn't."

"The big star...you aren't just playing around with your bodyguard?"

No. Not playing. Giving the man her heart a second time, when she knew there wasn't a future? *That* was what she was doing, yes. But it was her mistake to make. "It's not supposed to be possible."

"What isn't?"

"Finding the love of your life when you're only eighteen years old. People say it's just a crush. Just hormones. Just a million other things. It's not supposed to be forever." *But sometimes, it is.*

Before he could respond, a nearby door opened. Simon stalked out, and one look at his face told her he was absolutely enraged.

Gwen surged to her feet. "Simon? What's wrong?" Oh, God, had there been another attack?

His green eyes burned as they raked over her.

***

"I hear movement inside," Mac said as he glanced back at Layla.

She nodded. She'd heard the thuds, too.

Mac squared his shoulders. "Open the door!" he barked. "Or we will—"

A voice yelled, *"Come in!"*

Layla's hold tightened on her gun.

"Come in and help—"

Mac was already shoving open the door. A door that was unlocked. But the second he went inside—

Boom. An explosion blasted from deep within the house. Layla was staring at the back of Mac's head and body, and she saw him hurtle into the air. It was like the whole scene was happening in slow motion. Mac was big and burly, but his body flew up as if he weighed nothing. He flew back and hit her, and they both tumbled onto the ground even as heat blasted around them. She looked up, frantic, her whole body shaking, and Layla saw more flames bursting from the house.

She grabbed for Mac. "We have to get back!"

Boom. Boom.

Fire was everywhere. The uniformed cops were screaming behind her.

And her partner wasn't moving at all.

CHAPTER FIFTEEN

"I didn't do this." Gwen's voice was wooden. She looked up from the laptop and shook her head. "I swear, I didn't make any transfer to Dale."

Eric had just shown her the evidence. Simon had stood there and watched as rage pumped through his body.

Gwen's hair had dried after her shower. It tumbled over her shoulders, and her lips trembled a bit as she glanced back at him. "Please, Simon, tell me that you believe me."

Simon opened his mouth—

"That *is* your account, isn't it?" Eric pushed.

Gwen nodded. "Yes. That was one of the first accounts that my agent helped me to open when I started in the business. I swear, though, I'd almost forgotten about the thing. I don't use it."

"Someone used it." Ben paced closer to her. He'd been listening to the whole exchange, and his face had turned downright grim.

"That someone wasn't me." Her eyes were on Simon. "Do you believe me?"

Eric thought he was a fool. Fuck Eric. Simon closed the distance between him and Gwen. His hand lifted and sank into the thickness of her hair as he tipped back her head. "Yeah, baby, I do." His mouth lowered to hers. The kiss was hard and deep and claiming.

Her hands lifted and curled around his shoulders. Her body crowded closer and softened against him. All he wanted to do was lift her into his arms. Carry her to the nearest bedroom and make absolutely sure she understood—he was on her side.

Simple as that.

Did he trust her? Yes.

Would he risk everything he had for her? Hell, yes.

Why?

It was time that she knew. Time she understood. Time—

Ben cleared his throat. "Uh, want to tell me why?"

Simon lifted his mouth from Gwen's. No, he didn't want to tell Ben. He wanted to tell Gwen. Wanted to put everything on the table for her. He didn't want to do it in front of an audience. Not his style. Without looking away from Gwen, he said, "Someone is setting her up, obviously. Someone who has access to Gwen's account." And, for him, all the real evidence was pointing to one person.

The other person who'd had access to the account. A person intimately connected with Gwen's life. Someone who might want to get extra publicity for her.

He saw the same knowledge fill Gwen's eyes. "No," she said. "It's not *her*."

"Uh, yeah..." Ben drawled. "Want to clue me in about just who we think the bad guy is?"

"Her agent," Simon responded. "Eveline Jacobson. She's the one we need to talk with—right the hell now."

His phone rang, vibrating in his pocket. Frowning, Simon pulled it out and glanced at the screen. *Layla Lopez.* He put the phone to his ear. If she'd collared Dale Sanders and the guy was trying to point the finger at Gwen...*not on my watch.* "Listen, Layla, don't buy the shit that Dale Sanders is selling you—"

"He's dead." Her voice sounded distorted. Choked?

And had she just said the guy was dead?

"Blew himself to hell and back." Sirens echoed on the phone. "Tried to lure me and my partner inside so he could take us with him." Those sirens kept blasting. "My partner is on the way to the ER, and this house is still blazing." Static crackled. Voices shouted in the background. "Found pictures in the guy's truck. Looks like pics of Gwen."

The pictures that had been in Gwen's hotel room had been taken by her stalker. Were those the same pics that Layla had recovered?

"Pics of her on set. Pics of her walking in town. Pics of her shopping and...hell, even photos of the woman in her underwear."

Sonofabitch.

"They were in his truck. Along with Andy Flint's stolen cell phone."

Simon stared at Gwen. Her skin seemed too pale. She couldn't hear what Layla was saying, but he knew she feared the worst.

"Dale was the perp behind the bombs. The tool box on his truck was full of bomb making equipment. He must've known we were closing in...bastard tried to take us with him." Her voice was shaking. "My partner Mac...God, he's bad, Simon."

"Layla, I'm sorry." He swallowed. "What can I do?"

"Pray."

His eyes squeezed closed.

"I've got to go. Stay close to Gwen, just in case. I'll keep working this scene." Her sigh slid over the line. "Make sure nothing is missed..."

Layla didn't miss things. Soon enough, she'd realize there was a money trail connecting Gwen to Dale. "Layla, I think there is more to this. I don't think Dale was acting alone."

"What?" The crackle of static again. "Simon, what do you—"

"We think Gwen's agent is involved. There's a lot to go over, but...I suspect she paid Dale. I believe she brought him to town just so that he could terrorize Gwen." His eyes opened.

Gwen shook her head. She didn't want to believe her agent—her friend—had set up this mess. He got that. When the ones closest were the ones to hurt you, that shit would *gut* a person. But sometimes, that was what the truth did. It hurt. It destroyed.

It ripped your world apart.

***

"There's a mistake," Gwen said softly. "She wouldn't do this to me."

They were alone in the safe house. Ben and Eric had left. Eric had headed down to the police station because he wanted to check in with the cops and learn as much as possible about the explosion at Dale's rental house.

Layla had said that the uniforms would be picking up Eveline Jacobson. He knew Layla would grill her and find out the truth. Layla had ordered him to keep Gwen away from the station. And to make sure he kept his eyes on her at all times.

He didn't know if that was for Gwen's safety...or because Layla didn't completely trust her. Either way, he intended to make staying close to Gwen his number one priority.

"We'll get to the truth, Gwen." His voice was low but certain.

She turned toward him. Her arms were wrapped around her middle. They were in the den, and the safe house seemed so quiet around them. "The truth? That someone *paid* Dale to come down here? Paid him to set the bombs?" She shook her head. "It's not adding up. Eveline isn't tied to Xavier. She didn't know about that part of my life. And the stalker wanted me to send him a million dollars. You heard him. He wanted cash. He wanted me. He didn't want—"

"Attention."

She blinked.

"That could be what *she* wanted, Gwen. What she wanted for *you*, her star client. Think about it." He wanted to close the distance and pull her into his arms, but she seemed so brittle. Too breakable. "The first bomb—it was in *your* car. The stalker called you and said the trigger had been hit when you were far enough away from the car. The perp didn't intend for you to be hurt that time, just scared."

She licked her lower lip. "You're saying I wasn't in real danger."

He didn't think her agent would risk actually hurting her. The whole thing had been a setup. The stalker had never wanted money or Gwen. *Just attention.*

"What about Andy?" Gwen's voice rose. "*Why* kill him? Why—"

"Andy liked to stay in the shadows and take pictures. Maybe he took a picture of something he shouldn't have. Or of *someone* that he shouldn't have seen." Simon rolled one shoulder. "Maybe he snapped a pic of Eveline that would prove her guilt. So perhaps she had to stop him."

A little line appeared between Gwen's eyes.

Simon wasn't done. "All the calls and the threats—they were just that, baby. Threats. To make it all seem more real. She was using Dale and—"

"He's dead." Simon saw that her hands had fisted. "How is that part of the plan?"

Simon didn't know. "Maybe guilt got to him?" Simon was just tossing out ideas. He didn't know what in the hell had gone down with Dale. He'd find out, though. "The press reported that Andy

Flint died in a car explosion. The reporters got that detail *wrong*. He was dead before the car ignited, but maybe Dale didn't know that. Maybe he thought that his *partner* used one of his bombs to kill a man, and Dale couldn't handle the guilt. The cops were closing in, and he panicked." It was shit he'd seen criminals do before. Instead of spending the rest of his life in jail, Dale had chosen to go out in a blaze. And he'd tried to take good cops with him.

"Is the detective going to be okay?" Her voice was even softer.

He hoped to hell Mac would be. A Wilde agent was staying at the hospital and would be calling with updates. "He's getting the best care right now."

She rocked back on her heels. "All of this...and you think it's just because my agent wanted to get more attention for my movies? How the hell can a movie be worth more than these people's lives?"

There was so much pain on her face.

"And how can you trust me?" Her hands fell to her sides. "Didn't you suspect—at least a little—that maybe I did this myself?"

"Not even for a second." They were alone. Time to be crystal clear. No more standing back. He strode toward her.

Her shoulders tensed. "Simon?"

"I never suspected you. I trust what you've said to me. I trust you."

"I trust you, too."

He wanted to touch her so badly. But there were things she needed to know first. "I've lied to you."

Surprise flashed on her face. "What?"

"Since you've come back into my life, I've been holding back on you. You think I was helping you because of the past, don't you?"

"Y-yes..."

He shook his head.

"Then why have you been helping me?"

"Because the idea of anything happening to you tears me apart. Makes *me* want to tear someone else apart. Because I have to know that you're safe."

Something came and went—a flash of emotion—in her golden eyes. "I need to know you're safe, too." Her gaze fell to drift over his body. "I saw the scars on you. I touched them. I kissed them, but I didn't ask you about them."

No, she hadn't. "My body has been beaten to hell and back."

Her gaze rose once more. "You almost died."

Now he knew exactly what she and Ben had been talking about earlier. The guy should have kept that particular tidbit quiet. Gruesome details didn't need to be shared.

"You didn't call me, Simon. You never told me. If you'd died, I wouldn't have known."

"Baby—"

"It tears *me* apart," she was using his words now, and he felt the stab in his heart, "to know that you might not be safe."

His hand rose to press over his heart. The heart that ached. The heart that had always been hers.

But she wasn't done. "I didn't go to you because of the past. When my world started falling down, I didn't run to Wilde just because you were tied to me and Xavier." She shook her head. "I guess I lied, too, because that wasn't truly the reason."

He found himself sliding ever closer to her. "What was the real reason?" He hoped, oh, hell, yes, he hoped—

"I loved you when I was eighteen." Her smile held a sad, wistful edge. "But I should have stopped. I should have let you go." A pause. Then, "I didn't. I could never really let you go. A part of me has always needed you."

He shook his head because no way had she just said—

Gwen laughed. "I know you don't feel the same way. I mean, you never tried to find me. You never—"

"I went to your house in LA. I had just gotten out of the hospital, and I had cheated death. The *only* thing I wanted was to find you and beg you for a second chance."

Her lips parted. Gwen didn't speak.

"I left you at nineteen because I had nothing to offer you. I wanted to give you the world, and I could barely take you to the movies." That memory still stung. "When I came back on leave, I already knew I was a dumbass. *You* were in my head every single day, know that. You got me through training. And you got me through the hell that followed. On my first real leave, I wanted to see you. I needed you, but by then, you were already out of my reach."

"No—"

"I saw your face on one of the magazines in the airport." The memory was still there in his head. "Couldn't believe it. Snatched the thing up. And, yeah, it was you. Gorgeous Gwen."

"You didn't come to me. You *never* came to me."

"Not then, no. Because I'd realized you were even more out of my reach. I was still serving, and there wasn't anything I could give you."

The gold in her eyes deepened. "You have always been so wrong."

Tell her everything. Don't stop. "A mission went bad. My last one. I woke up in a hospital hooked to more tubes than I could count. Eric and Ben were there." He considered himself lucky to have their friendship even on the days he wanted to kick their asses. Friends—got to love them and fight them, right? "They didn't know me, but they were there to help. They pushed me to keep going. Pushed me to go after the things I wanted in this world."

Gwen waited.

"You were the one thing I wanted most. So as soon as I was cleared by the docs, I went out to LA. I was close, baby. So close...close enough to see that you had moved on."

Her eyes widened.

"Another actor. Wade Danton. I saw you two together at your place. Saw the way you touched him and the way he touched you. The media was saying you two were heavy in love, that an engagement was coming any day. And I thought— what the hell was I doing? Trying to jump into your life when I had no part in it anymore? That wasn't right. That wasn't fair. You didn't want some ghost from your past coming back."

Gwen shook her head.

"Yeah, you think I don't know that shit makes me seem like a stalker? That I got close enough to see you with him?" Gwen had always been his weakness. She'd been under his skin and in his very blood for so long. "But I wanted you happy. That's what I've always wanted. So I backed the hell away."

"You didn't give me the chance to slam the door on you."

"What?" His brows lowered even as his body tightened.

"I had this fantasy. For such a long time. You were going to come back. Tell me how sorry you were. Beg me to take you back." Her hair slid over her shoulder. "And I was going to slam the door in your face."

He took a step back. Her pain. Her anger. He deserved it all. "I'm sorry." He realized how blind and foolish he'd been. When he'd been spending all of this time with her, when he'd been making love with her at his place, he'd thought...

Shit, forget what he'd thought.

Gwen might be screwing him, but she wasn't looking for more. The fantasy of *more* was his. Gwen didn't want that. She didn't want more than a strong bodyguard and a sensual distraction. He turned away, trying to get his act together. Or, hell—it was too late for that. He'd started this shit, so he'd end it. But he couldn't look into her eyes when he did it. That would just take too much. "I'm sorry I hurt you. I left when I was nineteen because I wanted to become more—I wanted to be a guy you'd be proud to be with."

"Simon—"

"And I stayed away because I knew I could never compete with the world you live in now. I mean, you have everything. Why do you need some grumpy asshole ex-SEAL?" He released a long breath. "Even if that asshole loves you more than he'll ever love anything else in this whole world."

She grabbed his shoulder and spun him back around. "What?"

"I love you, baby." His smile was sad. "I loved you when I was a dumb kid, and I love you even more now. But you don't love me back, and I get that. I burned that bridge, and if I could take it back, if I could change the past, believe me, I would. *I would do anything for you.* Know that. Because nothing in this world is more important to me than you are. Nothing will *ever* be more important. You're it for me. Slam any door in my face that you want. I get it. I do. But know that I'll still love you—I always will."

Her gaze searched his. She didn't say that she loved him back. Of course, she didn't say that. He hadn't expected her to—

Gwen shot up onto her toes. Her hands yanked him toward her. Her mouth crashed onto his. She kissed him with a wild, frantic need, and he sure wasn't foolish enough to let her go. His hands curled around her hips as he pulled her closer, as he caged her against him. He thrust his tongue into her mouth. Tasted and savored. He'd been without Gwen for too many years. So, while he had her, now, he would take every single thing that she had to give.

"I want you," she breathed those words against his mouth. "Right now, Simon. Right. Now."

Like he had to be told twice. She didn't love him, but she wanted him and he'd take that. He'd take *her*. He kissed her again even as he yanked open the snap of her jeans. He jerked down the zipper, and his fingers slid inside, pushing under the silken edge of her panties so that he could touch her sex. Her soft, hot sex. He worked her with his fingers until she was wet and moaning into his mouth.

Her nails bit into his shoulders even as her hips rocked against his hand.

More. He was going to have every single bit of her.

He shoved her jeans and panties down to the floor. She kicked them away, and he knelt before her.

"Simon?" Her hands pressed against his shoulders.

He eased her legs apart more. Brought her forward. Lifted her up just enough—*ah, yes.* He put his mouth on her. His tongue licked between her legs.

"*Simon!*" That was the way he liked for her to say his name. The rough, high cry. The breath of pleasure. She was stretching onto her tip-toes as he held her there, as he licked and tasted. As he savored her.

And as she came against his mouth.

Her body shuddered with her climax. He pulled back to gaze up at her. She was such a thing of fucking beauty when she came. He could stare at her all day long and never get tired.

Her hair had fallen forward, and her eyes locked on him as she looked down at him.

Then he swore her lower lip trembled.

Alarm flared through him. "Baby?"

"I wouldn't have."

His heart thudded into his chest.

"I wouldn't have slammed the stupid door. Because I wanted you—*I always wanted you.*"

His control shattered. He heaved up, lifting her into his arms. He pinned her to the nearest wall and kissed her, hard and deep, and oh, God, this was *Gwen.*

He grabbed for his wallet. Yanked out the lone condom in there and had it on in a blink. She reached for him, her eyes gleaming, her lips red— *his.*

He positioned his cock and drove into her, sinking as far as he could go. And when he was balls deep in her, Simon stilled. He wanted to take this moment and memorize every single detail. The way the gold in her eyes seemed to shine. The way her lips were wet and plump from his mouth. The way their heaving breaths seemed to fill the air. The way her body clamped down on his, so tight, so perfect, her delicate inner muscles clinging to him. The way that—just for an instant—they were one.

And he was complete.

But he couldn't hold back, not with need pounding at him, the wild lust he felt for her. He withdrew and plunged deep, thrusting in a fury as need overtook him. Thrusting and driving toward release. Oblivion. She found it first. Her body tensed. Her lips parted as she screamed his name.

Her climax sent him hurtling into his own. Simon leaned forward and his mouth pressed to her neck. The pleasure burst through him, complete and total, and he emptied into her. Gwen. Not a fantasy, not any longer. She was real. She was his.

And he'd truly love her forever.

***

The beep of his phone woke him later. Simon had carried Gwen to bed and collapsed beside her. He'd only intended to stay there for a little while. He wanted to wait and hear more about Eveline but—

But he'd fallen asleep with Gwen.

The phone beeped again.

Frowning, his hand flew toward the nightstand. He grabbed the phone, seeing that two texts had just come in. Texts from a number that he didn't recognize. Frowning now, he sat up in bed as he tried to get a better look at the images. He clicked the first one to make it bigger and—

Gwen.

Gwen in the body-hugging, black dress she'd worn just the other night when she'd been filming on set. The club scene.

Only...

This wasn't a scene from the movie.

This was Gwen in an alley. Her dark hair slid over her lover as he fucked her up against a dirty wall. This was Gwen...with her co-star. With Austin Quest's face clearly visible as he smiled at her.

"What is it?" Gwen's sleepy voice asked.

He clicked the second picture.

Another shot. Gwen's face was buried in Austin's shoulder. That hair of hers—her long, dark, trademark hair was tumbling down his arm as he pounded into her.

"Is something wrong?" Gwen's fingers touched his shoulder. "Simon?"

Another text came through. No picture this time. Just cold, stark words.

She's playing you. Gwen is fucking him even while she's with you.

Rage tightened every muscle in Simon's body.

Another text appeared.

Just like she was fucking Xavier and you never knew. You can't trust her.

Then...

Leave the bitch.

CHAPTER SIXTEEN

"Simon?" Gwen sat up in bed, pulling the covers to her chest. The glow of the phone lit his face, and his expression appeared absolutely brutal.

His fingers tapped over the phone as he typed in a text.

"What did you just send? What's happening?"

Without a word, he handed her the phone.

She saw the pictures first, and her hand shook so badly that Gwen nearly dropped the phone. "That's not me!" Yes, yes, dammit, it looked like her, but it wasn't. It *wasn't*. Horrified, she looked up at him. "Simon, that's not me!"

He slid from the bed.

Her gaze snapped back to the phone. She read the texts he'd gotten as her stomach twisted. She felt like vomiting right then and there because this wasn't true. It wasn't true and Simon was going to believe—

Her breath left her in a fast rush as she read his response.

I'm going to destroy you. Gwen is mine, and no one comes after her. That was the text he'd sent. She stared back up at him just as he turned on the lamp. He'd jerked on jeans, and they hung loosely on his hips. The light fell on his body, shoving off the hard lines of his muscles, those powerful abs, and the scars that slid across his tanned skin.

Slices that looked like they were from knife attacks. A rough pucker—two of them—that she feared were from gunshot wounds. She'd felt those scars beneath her touch, beneath her mouth, but she'd been afraid to ask about them. She hadn't wanted to hurt him by stirring up the past.

Yet as she looked at him, as she looked at those scars, Gwen had one thought...

Simon is mine, and no one hurts him. Her chin lifted. "That's not me in the pictures. You're the only man I'm with right now. You're the only man I want to be with."

He took the phone from her. "I know. I was with you the night you wore that dress for filming. If I wasn't touching you that night, then I was watching you—every moment. I know it wasn't you."

He called someone. Barked an order to trace a number—she figured it was the number that had just sent him the texts.

Simon lowered the phone. Gazed at her. "You weren't the only one wearing the black dress that night. Your stunt double had on the same thing. And I'm pretty sure that when I saw her leave the set, she had the dress hanging out of her bag. I figured the clothing wasn't supposed to leave the set, but it wasn't my place to say anything to Raven."

OhmyGod. Raven. Gwen scrambled out of the bed.

"The bastard is trying to drive us apart, Gwen. He wants me away from you." Simon shook his head. "That isn't happening. I won't walk away from you again. *Count on it.*"

But she'd already learned that she could count on Simon. Wasn't that the reason she'd gone to him when this whole mess started? Because he was the one man she could count on. The one who'd always have her back.

And...he'd said that he loved her. Those words had poured over her. Through her. *Simon loved her.* He'd come after her. He'd wanted a second chance.

Didn't she want the same thing?

Didn't she just want him?

Because...she still loved him. The feelings she'd had long ago had surged back when they were together again. No, actually, those feelings were stronger now. Deeper. This man was willing to stand by her no matter what happened. He was brave and strong and sexy, and he was *hers.* She wanted to tell him that she loved him. Wanted to ask him what would happen next. Wanted to say they could make this work.

"We have to get down to the police station." His expression was hard and cold. Dangerously deadly.

Hell, he'd just seen supposed pics of her with another man. Probably *not* the most romantic time for her to make a big confession.

His eyes narrowed as he seemed to consider things. "If Eveline is still in custody, she couldn't have sent the texts. And if she didn't do it..."

Gwen's shoulders stiffened. "The stalker is still out there."

"I thought Dale Sanders was just taking orders. And if that's the case, if he was doing the grunt work, then we have to find the bastard who was giving those orders and stop *him*."

***

"You think I'm letting you in the interrogation room?" Layla looked tired. Dark circles lined her eyes, and an angry scratch cut across her cheek. "Seriously? What do you believe happens at this station, Simon? That I just let you and your buddy Eric make the rules here?"

He shoved his phone at Layla.

She blinked, then narrowed her eyes. "Um..."

"My people at Wilde are trying to track the number now. You have Eveline in there because we thought she was the one pulling the strings with Dale Sanders. But this text sure as hell seems to indicate that someone else is playing the game. Give us a few minutes with Eveline, and we can get to the truth." His gaze cut to Gwen.

Jeez, she sure hoped he was right.

"I need to call and check on my partner." Layla pushed the phone back at him after she finished reading the texts. "So maybe I'm just gonna walk away from interrogation for a few minutes. And what you do when I'm not there...I guess that's up to you." She nodded briskly and headed down the hall.

Gwen's shoulders sagged. Step one, down. Now, to get Eveline to actually talk to her.

Simon yanked open the interrogation room door. There was a uniformed cop inside, looking uncomfortable.

"I want my lawyer," Eveline was snapping at the fellow. "I want him now, and I'm not saying another word to *any* cop until he arrives. Why don't you run along and tell your detective boss that fact, huh? And let her know that my lawyer is going to destroy this place. Rip it apart. I will sue Detective Lopez and every cop I can find for—"

"Eveline," Gwen said her name softly but firmly.

Eveline whirled toward her. "Gwen!" She lunged out of the chair and took three quick steps toward her. Her hands flew out and curled around Gwen's shoulders. "I don't know what you've heard, but this is bullshit." She turned her head and glared at the young cop. "*Bullshit.*"

Simon motioned to the cop. "Let Layla know the lady asked for her lawyer."

He nodded, then scrambled out.

Eveline's attention shifted back to Gwen. Her fingers tightened on Gwen's shoulders. "You know I wouldn't hurt you."

She wanted to know that. She wanted to believe that truth because Eveline wasn't just her agent. The other woman was one of Gwen's closest friends.

"I'm not a cop." Simon pulled out a chair at the narrow table. "You said you wouldn't talk to cops, but I'm hoping you'll talk to me."

Eveline's fingers dropped away from Gwen.

Gwen stared at her friend. "Where is your phone, Eveline?"

"I don't know." Her right hand waved vaguely in the air. "The cops took it. I mean, they said I wasn't under arrest or anything, that I was just here to answer questions, but I've been sitting and sitting in here *forever*."

Simon nodded. "Layla likes to keep her perps waiting."

"I'm not a perp!" Eveline's cheeks flushed. "They've had a cop with me every single moment that I've been here! Hell, I'm surprised that guy left just then—"

"Officer Kryer left because he knows me. He knows I won't let a suspect slip away on my watch."

Simon had known that young cop? Did the guy know everyone at the station? Almost seemed that way.

"Gwen, you haven't said anything." Eveline raked her with a stare. "Tell me that you believe me. Tell me that—"

"Dale Sanders was paid with money from one of my accounts. From the *first* account I created after I signed with you."

She saw understanding sink in for Eveline. "Both of our names are on that account."

"Yes. You have access. And..." Gwen's voice trailed away.

Eveline gave her a twisted smile. "And you thought I was the one who was bloodthirsty enough to stage all this? You thought I'd planned these attacks on you to get attention? PR?"

Gwen started to speak—

"No," Simon answered. "I'm the one who thought that. Gwen said it couldn't be you."

Eveline's lower lip trembled. Her eyes seemed to fill with tears, but she blinked them away. "Thank you," she whispered to Gwen.

"Show her the pictures," Gwen said.

Simon pushed the phone across the table. Eveline scooped it up. Frowned as her fingers flew over the screen. "Raven is screwing Austin? Figures. That girl is always hooking up with people on set." A shrug of one shoulder. "And off. I mean, I remember when I caught her with Van—" She stopped, and Gwen realized that Eveline had just read the threat in the text. Eveline's head snapped up. "*Xavier.*" There was fear in that one word.

Holy hell. She knows about Xavier.

Simon rose to his feet. Gwen knew he'd come to the same conclusion.

"The stalker has been talking about Xavier?" Eveline dropped the phone. "Why?"

"Better question," Gwen managed to say. "Just how the hell do you know about him?"

Eveline winced. "You talk in your sleep."

The words didn't quite register.

"*Shit.*" Simon stalked toward Gwen.

Eveline rubbed her temples. "You do! Remember, back when you first got started with films, you didn't have a place to stay? I let you crash at my place, but Gwen, you'd wake up screaming. You were so upset and scared, and I-I could hear the name that you cried out. I did a little research, and I found out about the guy..."

This was unbelievable. "You knew about Xavier Gray. All this time?"

Simon's arm brushed against hers. He'd taken up a position at her side.

Miserably, Eveline nodded. "I-I know that something happened between you. You'd cry out and scream for him to stop." Her hands dropped and fisted. "I figured the bastard had hurt you. There was only one Xavier that popped up in the news stories around Pensacola, so I knew it had to be him. It seemed like the jerk was dead, so I thought—good riddance to him. Let him rot somewhere."

Gwen could only stare at Eveline as shock swept through her. "You never said a word to me."

Eveline straightened to her full height. "Because you wouldn't talk about it in the light of day! You shut down."

Because I was scared. Terrified.

"I tried to get you to go to my shrink, remember? Gave you his card, but you never did. I wanted to help you. I swear, I did. But I didn't know how. So, I thought...just...if you didn't want to talk about it, then maybe *not* mentioning it was helping you."

Gwen turned toward Simon. She felt lost. "I have nightmares."

His expression was tender. "I know, baby."

Because she'd woken him up their first night together. "OhmyGod."

His gaze hardened as he asked, "How often do you have the nightmares? How often do you wake up like you did with me?"

Her throat had gone dry. "It used to be bad. That's why—why I never let most of my lovers stay the night. I didn't want to wake up screaming while someone else was there." Her breath pushed out. "I don't think any other lover—only you—you're the only one who has been with me when I've had the nightmare." But what if she was wrong? What if she'd said something in her sleep and she didn't remember? If Eveline had learned about Xavier, then others could have stumbled on the truth, too. And Gwen had always thought that she'd been so careful.

"I swear, Gwen," Eveline's voice was intense and shaking, "I didn't pay Dale Sanders. I didn't stage this thing, and I have *never* told anyone else about your past." Her gaze darted to the phone on the table. "And I'm not threatening you. I've been here for hours. I didn't send that text. And I sure didn't take pictures of Raven and Austin together. I mean, that's something the paparazzi would do, not me, not—"

"Andy," Gwen murmured.

She felt Simon tense beside her.

Her head turned. "Andy would have taken pictures like that." Her mind was spinning fast. "After you told him to stop following me, maybe he went back to the set. He took those photos, and the killer saw him. The killer attacked."

Someone who'd been at the set. Someone who'd been watching.

A sharp knock sounded at the door. A moment later, Layla swung open the door. "Time's up." She motioned to Simon and Gwen. "You need to both leave. Now."

Gwen turned away from Eveline.

Her agent grabbed her hand. Squeezed. "I didn't hire Dale." Her voice was low. Just for Gwen. "And I never said a word to anyone about your dreams. Please, believe me."

Gwen nodded. The thing was—she did.

She and Simon slipped outside. The young officer headed back in with Eveline while Layla exited with Simon and Gwen. Layla shut the door and glanced at them with one raised eyebrow. "Get what you needed?"

Maybe.

"Her lawyer will be here soon, so I doubt I'll be getting more intel from her." She pointed at Gwen. "Your account. Your money...you know I will have to ask you questions. You're gonna want to get that fancy attorney of yours down here. I'm sure Kendrick will jump at the chance to face-off with me again."

More grilling? "I didn't do it." Now she sounded like Eveline.

Layla nodded. "You didn't. Your agent didn't. Someone else is pulling strings." Her gaze turned cold. "You think I don't know you're holding back on me? That you've *been* holding back? Who is Xavier? Why is the stalker using him to threaten you?"

Simon curled his fingers around Gwen's wrist as he answered, "He's a jackass from our past. He's a man who—"

"He's a man who attacked me and tried to rape me when I was eighteen years old." Saying the words—voicing that pain out loud somehow felt...right. Like she was breaking free of a chain that had held her back for too long. "And he's the man that I think I killed."

Layla stared at her. Just stared. All of the emotion left the detective's face. "All right then." She pointed down the hall. "Interrogation room two." She stepped toward Gwen. "Your lawyer," her voice was low, "get him in there with you. You will need him." She backed away. "And she doesn't need you, Simon. You're not going in there. Until I get this mess sorted out, Gwen Soloman is staying at the station."

He pulled Gwen toward him. "Why?" His green stare held so many raging emotions.

"Because it's time. He's not going to hurt me anymore." He...Xavier. His ghost. And...the stalker. Whoever the hell that bastard was. "I won't let him." The truth was supposed to set a person free, wasn't it?

The interrogation room was waiting.

She might lose her fame. She might lose her job. She might lose everything.

Gwen leaned up and pressed a kiss to Simon's jaw.

But I won't lose him.

And she knew that with certainty. No matter what happened, Simon was going to stand by her.

***

"Did your girlfriend really just confess to murder?" Ben asked.

Simon hurried down the stone steps at the front of the police station. Kendrick had shown up right before he headed for the exit—because there was no way he would have left until Gwen's lawyer arrived. But since he hadn't been allowed in the interrogation room, Simon knew he needed to get busy.

He hadn't expected to find Ben waiting for him on the steps. He'd worried he might have to dodge some reporters, but Ben hadn't been part of the equation.

Luckily, the reporters seemed to have vanished for the night.

Simon frowned at his friend. "How the hell do you know that?"

Ben shrugged. Tried and failed to look casual. "You know that Wilde has contacts everywhere. My brother got a tip, and while he's tied up at the office making phone calls to the agents in Pensacola, he asked me to come down here." A pause. "Because he said you might need a friend you could trust."

He did. "I have to find Raven Charles. She's a stunt double for Gwen, and I think she may have seen our killer."

Ben's eyes widened. "Then why the hell isn't she already at the police station?"

"Because she seems to have vanished. Layla sent uniforms over to her hotel—" After Simon had convinced the detective that the woman needed to be brought in, ASAP. "But she wasn't there. The cops said it looked like Raven had cleared out."

Ben nodded. "I'll help you find her. Let's go."

Simple as that. The guy wasn't part of Wilde, wasn't supposed to be hunting prey, but he was already set to ride shotgun.

"We also need to talk with Austin Quest," Simon added as his voice sharpened.

Ben had already turned to head down the remaining steps, but now he glanced back at Simon. "The actor?"

"Yeah."

"You think Quest is involved in this mess?"

"Sure seems so."

"Man, he was *awesome* in those spy flicks. I am such a fan."

Simon forced his back teeth to unclench. "Get ready for some disappointment."

***

"I'm going to advise you to stay silent," Kendrick said as he leaned in close to Gwen. "The cops have nothing. Why do this?"

"Because as long as I stay silent, then the jerk out there thinks he has power over me."

Sweat dotted his forehead. "At least tell *me* everything first."

He didn't get it. She was pretty much shaking apart. If she didn't do this now, then she might lose her nerve and run.

Before Gwen could hurtle out of the room, Layla appeared. Her heels clicked across the floor, then she pulled out a chair at the table.

"How's your partner?" Gwen blurted.

Layla blinked. Her features softened. "He's going to be okay. The docs have Mac in ICU, but they say he'll pull through."

A sigh of relief slipped from Gwen. "I'm glad."

"Me, too." Layla flattened her hands on the table. "Shall we begin?"

"Ahem." Kendrick cleared his throat. "My client is here voluntarily because she wants to help—"

"When I was eighteen years old, a guy named Xavier Gray knocked me out while I was walking home from work." Gwen's voice was flat and unemotional. Almost as if she was telling a story about someone else. And that was exactly what she was doing. Pretending that it hadn't been her. That she was just acting from a script. Reading the lines. Telling a story. Because if she did it this way, then Gwen wouldn't break into a million pieces. "When I woke up, I was on his boat. We were alone. He was laughing. And he said that he was going to do anything he wanted to me..."

CHAPTER SEVENTEEN

They went to the movie set. The set was supposed to be closed down, so it wasn't exactly a big surprise to find the place deserted. But since Raven was in the wind, Simon had thought that maybe—just maybe—she'd be there.

He checked the trailer that had been assigned to her. Found it empty. The place felt cold.

"What are we looking for?" Ben wanted to know.

Simon rifled through her small closet. The vanity. Even searched under the couch cushions. "Something that will tell us where the hell she's been. Or where the hell she is going."

But there was nothing.

Nothing at all.

Shit.

He whirled around.

"Where do we go next?" Ben asked.

Simon brushed by him. He'd already looked in Austin Quest's dressing room—sure, the place had been locked, but it had been easy enough to get past the flimsy piece of security. He'd found a fridge filled with organic fruit and an oddly big stock pile of garlic, but no sign of Austin.

"I'm checking Gwen's area." Just in case.

Ben hurried behind him. And when they drew close to Gwen's—

The door was ajar.

Shit.

He motioned to Ben, and his friend nodded.

***

"I swam to shore." Her voice still held no emotion as Gwen finished the story. "I thought that maybe Xavier had made it to shore, too, but then a news report came on a few days later, saying he was missing. And..." And there was nothing more to say.

Her lawyer squeezed her hand. Was Kendrick giving her support? Or asking her to stop?

Layla glanced down at the notebook on the table. She'd been making notes while Gwen talked. "His body was never recovered?"

Gwen leaned forward. "I don't...I don't think so."

Beep. Gwen's head turned.

Kendrick had just looked down at his phone. At the text he'd received. A faint smile curled his lips.

Layla cleared her throat. Her gaze met Gwen's. "And you have no evidence to prove the attack on you? You have nothing to verify the claims you've made?"

Her heart squeezed. No, she didn't, she—

"Yes," Kendrick replied smoothly. "Absolutely, we have evidence. We have another woman who saw Gwen get knocked out that night." A quick glance at his phone and then, "Stacy Clair. She saw the attack but didn't speak up because she was also afraid of Xavier Gray."

Stacy Clair? The name was vaguely familiar to Gwen. She and Stacy...yes, they'd both worked together at that beachside restaurant—

"And I have the names of five other women who also say that Xavier Gray assaulted them on his boat. The man had a dark and sadistic pattern, and my client was only defending herself when she acted against him."

What other women?

Kendrick pointed toward the door. "Eric Wilde will be arriving any moment with material on these other witnesses. His team has been down in Pensacola, and they've got the evidence. Evidence that will prove a pattern of abuse. Evidence that will show you my client wasn't the first victim..." A satisfied and slightly cruel smile. "But she was the last."

OhmyGod. Was it true? Seriously? Was that the text he'd just gotten? A note from Eric with proof?

As if on cue, the interrogation room door opened, and Eric stepped inside.

***

Simon pushed against the door, letting it slide open. The smell hit him first—the bitter, coppery scent. And, Jesus, he knew he was going to find a nightmare before he even stepped all the way inside.

"Oh, fuck," Ben whispered from behind him. "Is that blood?"

Blood on the floor. A whole lot of it. Simon rushed forward and saw the woman on the floor. A woman with long, thick, dark hair. A woman who *could* have been Gwen.

But she wasn't. She *wasn't.*

Raven Charles was on the floor, and her body was covered with blood. And she wasn't alone.

Simon had his gun up and out. He'd taken the gun from the locked glove box of his vehicle before he'd stepped foot on set. And now, as he stared at the man who was cradling Raven—cradling her even as a knife waited at the guy's side—Simon realized the end had come.

"Let her go," Simon ordered flatly.

Austin Quest's head whipped up. He gazed blankly at Simon. "Are you the one?"

The one what?

Ben slipped around Simon, inching toward the knife—and Austin.

Simon wanted Austin's attention to stay on him. So, deliberately, he spoke and ordered, "Let Raven go. Put her down and step the fuck back."

Austin blinked and shook his head. Then he peered down at Raven. "She's alive." His body jerked. "I was stopping the blood."

The guy was *covered* in Raven's blood.

"We have to get her to the hospital. We have to help her!" Austin's eyes were wild as his stare darted back to Simon. "We have to—" He stopped, frowned. Seemed so confused. "You *are* the one." And he reached for the knife.

"Fuck," Ben growled.

Yes, fuck, indeed. Locking his jaw, Simon snarled, "This isn't some movie, jackass. That's real blood. That's a real knife, and this—this is a real gun. If you don't put the knife down right now and *get away from her,* then I will shoot you."

But Austin tightened his hold on the knife. "You can't hurt her. I won't let you!" He lunged up and came at Simon.

Simon fired his gun.

***

Layla was talking with Eric. Eric was talking with Kendrick. Their words were spinning around Gwen and she felt like she was stuck in some kind of surreal nightmare.

"No charges are being filed against you. Did you hear me, Gwen? You are free to go. Nothing is happening here. You are clear." Kendrick blew out a breath. "I'm sure the press is going to get wind of all this soon. I'm asking you, though, don't do any interviews, okay? I want to make sure our asses are covered, and you don't get a covered ass by doing a tell-all with the first talking head that comes along."

She blinked.

Layla and Eric were gone. When had they left? They'd been there just a moment before. Yet now she was alone in the interrogation room with Kendrick.

He smiled at her. "You did very well. You held your shit together. You were a concise and clear witness."

Witness?

"Victim," he clarified quickly. "That's what the detective saw. That's how the rest of the world will see you. You're all good now." He gathered his briefcase and headed for the door. "You're one fine actress."

"What?"

He stiffened.

Did he think she'd been lying? "All of that happened to me. Everything I said was true."

He turned toward her. Studied her in silence for a moment as rage bent and twisted, breaking the cold ice that had enclosed her.

Then Kendrick inclined his head. "Sorry. Sometimes, you defend so many monsters that you forget everyone isn't like that. It's easy to see darkness, even when it's not there."

She had plenty of darkness. So did everyone. Darkness was just as important as light in this world. And it didn't make someone *evil*. Gwen swallowed several times and managed to clear her throat. "The cops aren't going to charge me with anything? I mean, I was defending myself, but I didn't report the crime afterwards. I ran. I covered up what I'd done—"

"The Atlanta PD knows a PR nightmare when it sees one. And locking up America's sweetheart when she fought off an attacker is hardly a brilliant move for them."

She could only shake her head.

The faint lines around his mouth deepened. "Layla Lopez is the best cop I've ever met. You really think she's going to let an assault victim get thrown in jail? Not on her watch. She'll work out something where you do a community outreach, where you talk to other victims. She and I will get it smoothed with the DA, and you will be good. Consider that a Kendrick Shaw guarantee."

She was dazed. Pretty numb. But Gwen managed, "Thank you." How was she supposed to repay him? Simon? Eric? Layla?

Kendrick just nodded. "Your assistant is here. One of the cops told me he's been waiting for you near the check-in desk. He can take you back home."

She didn't have a home in Atlanta. She had a safe house, and Van didn't know where that was.

"Please accept my apologies." Kendrick's voice was low and sounded sincere. "My job is to help you, not to make some kind of judgment. If that is what I seemed to be doing, then I was in the wrong. I truly only wanted to help you."

He had. Eric had. Simon had. Layla had. Gwen wasn't running. And the stalker didn't have power any longer.

"Though for the record, I do think you are one hell of an actress." He gave her a brief smile. "Maybe I can even get an autograph for my son. He's a big fan."

She wasn't going to jail. She was about to walk out of the police station as a free woman. Hell, yes, he could have an autograph. He could have a million of them. "Your son can have as many autographs as he wants."

His smile stretched. Seemed to warm his eyes. But before he could speak again, Kendrick's phone rang. He looked down. "Sorry. Another client..." He put the phone to his ear. "No, absolutely not, do not say another word until I get there..." He hurried from the room.

Gwen glanced at her reflection in the one-way mirror. She barely recognized the tired, scared-looking woman staring back at her. *I'm so over the fear.* Screw it.

She marched out of that room and hurried to the front of the station.

"Gwen!" Van ran toward her. He pulled her into a tight, fierce hug. "OhmyGod, I was so worried about you! I heard that Eveline was brought in, that the demolitions guy we used on *The Wrong Alibi* was some kind of psychotic stalker to you—"

She shoved against his arms. "Where did you hear all that?"

Van blinked. "It's...online. Everything is online." His smile came and went. "You're a celebrity. That's what happens. You always make the news. You *are* the news."

A shiver slid down her as she stared up at Van.

"Gwen?" His brow furrowed.

She backed away from him. She needed Simon. Where had he gone? Her gaze flew around the station.

A hand curled around her shoulder, and Gwen jumped.

"Easy." Eric's voice. Eric was standing behind her, looking all solid and intent. "We need to leave, Gwen. The press is lining up out front. The story has leaked online."

"Where's Simon?"

Eric's lips thinned.

Over his shoulder, she saw Layla running through the station. The detective had on her shoulder holster.

"Let's move!" Layla yelled to two of the uniformed cops near her. "We've got a shooting on the movie set!"

"*My* movie set?"

"We need to leave," Eric said again.

Gwen felt rooted to the spot. "Where is Simon?"

"He's okay," Eric assured her. "But he wants me to get you back to the safe house. Let's go, now."

Dazed, she nodded. There was suddenly a whole lot of activity in the station. When Eric started to guide her away from Van, her assistant reached for Gwen's wrist.

"I'll come with you," Van offered at once. "I can keep you company."

"Not right now, buddy," Eric fired back. "I need you to step back."

Van gaped at him. Then he looked at Gwen.

"I'll call you," she promised him. "I'm okay. Really."

His lips pressed together, and he stepped back. But his eyes seemed to harden as he stared at her.

Eric hustled her out of there, and Gwen glanced over her shoulder. Van was still staring after her, and his eyes—eyes that had always looked so friendly and warm to her before—were cold and glaring.

***

"Do you know who I am?" Austin bellowed. He was being shoved toward the back of a patrol car.

"Yeah," Layla assured him, "I know you're the idiot resisting arrest."

Austin tried to head-butt the uniform behind him. *"That dick shot me!"*

"I barely grazed him," Simon muttered to Ben. And he had. A graze on the arm, and the actor had folded. He'd dropped his knife and started screaming for an ambulance.

The ambulance was there, all right. But the EMTs were helping Raven, not Austin.

Austin was headed for the police station—and a long interrogation with Layla.

"He's an asshole," Ben retorted, staring after the guy. "But is he a killer?"

The cops had bagged and tagged the knife. Of course, it would have Austin's prints on it. From the way the scene looked, it sure appeared that Austin had attacked his lover. But there was always more to things than met the eye.

The uniform succeeded in throwing Austin into the patrol car. Layla shook her head and strode toward Simon. He held his breath as she approached. What had happened with Gwen? Where was his Gwen right then?

"You must like trouble." Layla pointed her index finger at him and then at Ben. "Both of you do. Can't you ever just step back and let cops handle this stuff? Let us do—you know—our jobs?"

Ben sprang forward. "If we hadn't been searching here, that woman could have died." His head inclined toward the ambulance. "We found her. We saved her."

Layla sighed. "When Raven Charles is conscious, I'll find out exactly what happened. Until then, I have to deal with the guy screaming about being attacked...by *you*, Simon."

He'd already turned over his weapon. "He was lunging at me with a knife."

"I saw that shit," Ben agreed immediately. "Dude was out of control." He spared Simon a quick glance. "You're right—meeting him in real life was such a disappointment."

It sounded like Layla might be choking. Or growling. Then she snapped, "You both still have to make a statement down at the station. Come on. Let's get this mess going."

"Is Gwen at the station?" Simon asked. He needed to let her know what had happened. Needed to make sure she was okay.

"Eric told me he'd take her to the safe house. And, yeah, I saw all the evidence that Wilde collected."

Some of the tension snaked from him. Eric had been briefing him on the discoveries, but Simon hadn't said anything to Gwen. He hadn't wanted to reveal anything until the other victims were clear on the evidence they had. "No charges for Gwen?" He held his breath.

"She's safe," Layla assured him.

The patrol car's blue lights flashed on.

"But you're the one who just shot a man. So, let's get to the station and figure this mess out."

CHAPTER EIGHTEEN

"I didn't use the knife on her!" Austin Quest slammed his fist down on the table. His perfect hair stuck up all over his head, and his face flushed a dark red. "I got there and Raven was already like that! I tried to help her! I put pressure on the wound."

Layla sat on the opposite side of the narrow table. "Why didn't you call for help?"

"Good fucking question," Ben muttered. They were on the other side of the one-way mirror, watching the interrogation. Breaking the rules, yes, because that was what they did.

Some of the cops at the station had owed Simon a few favors, so they'd looked the other way. For the moment.

"I didn't have time to call for help!" Again, Austin's fist hit the table.

Ben whistled. "Someone has an anger issue."

Yeah, someone sure did.

"I was going to call for help, but then that jackass with the gun showed up." Austin looked down at his injured arm. "He'd better be in a jail cell."

Layla shifted her weight forward in her chair. "According to eye witness testimony, you lunged up with a knife and tried to stab Simon Forrest."

"Well, yes, but I thought he was going to hurt me! I thought he was the one who'd texted me. The one who'd released those photos of me and Raven to the media." He sniffed. "Shit, like I needed that publicity! Now everyone will think I've got some sick thing for Gwen. And I mean, I don't. I just, you know, it helped me to get in character to screw a woman who looked like her."

Simon's back teeth ground together.

"Oh, he's a straight-up dick." Ben was definite. "You should've done more than just graze him with the bullet."

Damn straight.

"I got a text. Look—check my phone! One of those uniforms took it from me. The text said I had to get to set. Had to get to Gwen's room, and I was supposed to pay the guy money. Money so he wouldn't release any other pictures. I thought—when that psycho arrived with the gun—I thought he was the one who'd sent the text! I was freaking out!"

"He's still freaking out," Ben noted. "Not the least bit calm."

No, he wasn't. But...

Austin's story was easy enough to check out. They just needed the guy's phone.

Layla was already leaving the room. He knew she was going to talk with the uniform who'd taken the phone. Simon rushed to meet her. A few minutes later, sure enough, they read the texts. Texts that had come from the *same* number the stalker had used when he sent the photos to Simon.

A burner phone, at least that was what the Wilde techs suspected. They were trying to geo-locate it right then, using cell towers in their search. It was only a matter of time until they found the phone.

"Looks like he was telling the truth," Layla murmured.

"Yeah." Didn't mean Simon liked the sonofabitch, though. "But why was Raven there?" Had the perp lured her there, too?

"We'll find out." Layla's gaze was hard and focused. "She might've even gotten a look at his face. She could identify him for us."

Simon nodded. "We just have to wait for her to wake up."

***

She had a Wilde agent stationed outside of the safe house. An agent who was there to keep her safe. When Eric had dropped her off, he'd assured Gwen that the place had top of the line security. She figured he'd installed the security so it had to be good.

But as Gwen sat inside the safe house, her fear didn't lessen. In fact, it got worse. The longer she was there, the worse it became.

Her phone rang, the quick peal of sound making her jump. Swearing, Gwen grabbed for the phone.

Eveline. Her agent's smiling face showed on the screen. Gwen swiped her finger over the screen and put the phone to her ear. "Eveline?"

"I lied to you."

Her heart seemed to squeeze in her chest.

"I-I'm sorry, Gwen."

"What did you lie about?"

Silence.

"What is it, Eveline?"

"I did tell someone else." Her voice was stilted. "I should have mentioned it sooner, but he's so harmless."

Gwen could barely breathe.

"I mean...he was checking your mail—he was the one who was taking away the crazy letters. I only wanted him to watch out for you. You know, in case anyone ever wrote to you about Xavier Gray."

Now her heart was doing a double-time rhythm. "You told Van about Xavier?"

Van had access to Gwen's accounts. He had access to every single detail of her life.

He'd known about Xavier.

"I told him to let me know if anyone ever mentioned the name Xavier in a note. I just wanted to protect you, Gwen. That's all I ever wanted. I'm sorry," Eveline said again. She hung up.

Shit. *Shit.*

A knock sounded at the door.

Gwen frowned as she jumped to her feet. Was that Simon? God, she hoped so. She had to tell him about Eveline's call. Gwen shoved her phone into her pocket as she rushed forward. But she didn't just yank open the door. Gwen put her eye to the peephole.

Not Simon. *Van.* Standing on the other side of the door. Looking calm and normal. *And standing right there.*

As she watched him, he lifted his hand and knocked again.

Gwen's breath sawed out. He shouldn't be there. No way. How had he found her? How had he gotten past the agent outside? And after what Eveline had just said—

"Gwen?" Van's strained voice reached her easily. He looked normal—so normal—standing there in his stylish clothes with his hair carefully tousled. "Gwen, I know you're in there. We need to talk. Open the door."

Hell, no. Every instinct she had screamed for her not to move.

But then...

Then she saw the knife. A knife that was pressed right to his throat. And Gwen realized that Van really wasn't so calm and collected.

"Gwen!" The blade gleamed under the overhead light. "If you don't open the door, she's going to kill me. Right here."

Gwen was frozen.

Until a long rivulet of blood slid down Van's throat.

***

Simon opened the interrogation room door.
Austin glanced up and blanched. "Hell—*you!*"
He gave Austin a cold smile. "Yeah, me."

Austin leapt to his feet. "Don't shoot me again!"

"Don't be a dick and I won't." He marched forward. "You like to pretend you're fucking *my* Gwen?"

"Oh, no, see, it's not like that! I'm a method actor, man, method!"

Simon growled. It would be so much fun to drive his fist into the "method" actor's face.

Austin seemed to get that. He backed up another step. "And you know, um, it wasn't even my idea. Raven is the one who came up with it. I wasn't even into that—I mean, not at first—"

Not at first?

"But she told me—um, just recently—that it would help me to get in the scene more. She came to me the other day, right after we'd filmed that club scene where Gwen and I were supposed to get intel. She came back to the set with the wig and wearing that tight-ass, little black dress. Raven told me it would help me get in character. So, you know, it was hot, and I—"

In a lightning fast move, Simon caught the guy by the back of his neck. He slammed Austin's face into the table.

Austin screamed.

Layla came running. So did several cops. They gaped.

Simon shrugged. "He tripped." He looked back at Austin. Blood poured from the actor's nose. "Didn't you?"

Fear had made Austin's eyes bulge. "Yes."

To be clear..."*Raven* is the one who wanted to dress up like Gwen?"

"Y-yes...I mean, she's almost exactly like her, you know? Oh, wait, shit, don't—" He scrambled back. "I mean, no one is just like Gwen. There's only one Gwen. Only one. But without her, Raven is a good stand-in—*oh, fuck me!*" He lifted his hands to cover his face.

Simon didn't attack. Not then. Because the guy's words had just made a cold sort of sense to Simon.

There *was* only one Gwen. And maybe someone was tired of Gwen being the big star. Maybe someone was tired of her being the one. Someone who wanted Gwen to get out of the way.

The idea settled uncomfortably inside of him, and Simon shot out of the interrogation room, shoving past the cops even as he yanked out his phone and called her. He had to talk with Gwen. Right then.

***

Gwen yanked open the door even as her phone pealed, vibrating in her pocket. "Let him go!"

The knife cut deeper into his throat. More blood trickled down. "I'm so sorry," Van gasped. "She's fucking crazy, and I didn't—"

The knife sliced across his throat. Gwen screamed because there was blood, too much of it. She grabbed for Van—

Even as his attacker shoved Van's body on top of her.

Gwen slipped and fell, with Van slamming down on top of her. The coppery scent of blood filled the air, and Gwen was pretty sure she heard the crack of her phone. The pealing rings stopped as Gwen grunted at the impact of Van's body on top of her.

"He's such a dumbass." Raven's voice was annoyed. "I mean, why can't the guy just do what I want without being such a giant dick about it?"

Gwen shoved Van to the side. His hand was over his throat, and he stared at her with terrified eyes. He mouthed...*I'm sorry*.

"Yeah, he should be sorry." Raven stepped over Van's body and leaned down toward Gwen. She put the knife under Gwen's chin.

Gwen barely breathed.

"I had to fuck him to get the good intel on you. And he is a seriously bad fuck. But, hey, it was worth it. I mean, I knew he'd spill your secrets. He was the one closest to you, wasn't he? He *had* to know your secrets. He told me about Xavier. Gave me the number for your old bank account. Told me everything I needed so I could set my plan in motion." She smiled. "I got tired, you see. Tired of taking all the risks while *you* got the rewards. Hell, put a wig on me, and I'm you, right? So why do I need to stay in the shadows? Why couldn't I come into the light?"

She was in the light. Gwen could see her so clearly—and the mad fury was bright in Raven's eyes. "I-I thought you were in the hospital."

Laughter. "I was. But I slipped out. Don't worry. I'll manage to get back before anyone even notices I'm gone. The wound wasn't bad. Looked a lot worse than it was. After all, I know how to take a hit."

This wasn't happening. She *liked* Raven.

"I had to tie up my loose ends. Had to make sure I had the perfect alibi. I'll be the victim in this piece. The poor, wounded victim who will somehow rise from the ashes and become the star I was always meant to be." Her gaze cut to Van. Blood had soaked his hand. "He's gonna die. He'll bleed out right here. And as for you, Gwen..." Her wild stare turned back to Gwen. "I had wanted to take your money before I got rid of you. That cold million should have come to me, but too late now."

"I can get you the money if—"

"Too late!" Her smile was wild and cruel. "Time for your final act. People will wonder—was *she* a victim? Or the killer? Because, see, I have the perfect end for you. You are gonna love it so hard. It's an end that was inspired by your buddy Xavier."

She loved nothing about this nightmare. "Xavier was never my friend."

"Whatever. I don't give a shit what he was to you. He disappeared. No one ever saw him again. *That's* what I got from the news articles I found on him. A big old disappearing act. And I'm going to make you vanish, too. You'll disappear tonight, and the press can wonder. People can spin stories about you being the villain or about you being the tragic victim. But either way, you'll be long gone. *I'll* be the one living your life."

She was staring at one crazy bitch. "I *liked* you."

Raven blinked. "Well, I like you, too. That's why it will be easy for me to take over your life. I'll be the star. I'll even get Eveline to be my agent. It's all going to be so easy. Heck, I'm already screwing your co-star. It's like I'm already living your life."

No, it wasn't. It wasn't a thing like that.

"Everything has been planned. The cops have no clue what's going on." Raven was smug. Proud. "I was there when they went for Dale. I'd tied the idiot up in his rental, and I knew he'd call out for them. He'd lure them in. I was hoping I'd take one or two of them out, but...hey, guess they got lucky."

Lucky? "Why would you want to kill cops?"

Raven blinked and looked at Gwen as if she was crazy. "High body counts always sell more tickets."

What? "This isn't a movie!"

Raven's lips trembled, then flattened. "Get up, Gwen." Raven's voice hardened. "I'm not killing you here. I told you, I'm going to make you disappear."

Gwen slowly rose as the knife nicked her throat. She tried to figure out the best moment to attack—

Raven laughed at her. "You actually think you can take me? Not happening. You're a piece of fluff. I'm ex-MMA. I can knock you out in my sleep."

But she hadn't knocked out Gwen. *Because she wants me awake. It's harder to move an unconscious body.* So Gwen just had to figure this out. Figure out the perfect time to attack.

Raven grabbed her, yanking Gwen close, and looping one arm around Gwen's neck. Raven's other hand shoved the blade against Gwen's right side. "We're heading out. Got a ride waiting. Van's ride."

A Wilde agent was supposed to be outside. He could help her. Gwen just had to stay calm. Help was waiting.

But when she got outside, she saw the slumped figure of a man on the sidewalk. She tried to leap toward him.

Raven tightened her hold and shoved the tip of the blade into Gwen's side.

Gwen cried out at the stab of pain.

"He's unconscious, not dead. Never even saw me coming. Security, my ass." She hauled Gwen toward the sidewalk. "Come on. We're getting the hell out of here."

Gwen stumbled with her to the waiting car. A small, four-door. Raven popped the trunk. "Get your ass in there."

Gwen stared into the darkness of the trunk. No interior lights glowed in there—had Raven turned them off? It looked like a gaping hole. "Don't do this."

"Screw you." In a fast move, Raven yanked up the knife and slammed the handle into the side of Gwen's head. The blow was hard and brutal and Gwen fell—even as Raven pushed her into the trunk. Gwen tried to turn and jump out, but Raven had already sealed her inside. The trunk closed in a flash, and darkness filled the cramped space.

Gwen's breath heaved in and out. She was so freaking scared. She was...

Her hand slid down to her pocket. She fumbled and pulled out the phone she'd shoved inside right before Van had appeared at her door. Her fingers flew over the now cracked screen. When she touched the screen, light immediately spilled from her phone.

And she sent a text. A fast and furious text because she was not going to disappear. Hell, *no*.

Raven wasn't getting her life.

CHAPTER NINETEEN

Raven took me.

Simon was running down the police station's front steps when that text came through from Gwen. He stopped. Staggered. And ignored the flurry of reporters around him. Word had spread that Austin Quest was in custody, and every tabloid and internet reporter in the area had swarmed. Simon ignored them all as he stared down at his phone.

In a dark car. Van at safe house. Hurt.

He typed back, frantic. *You're hurt? I'm coming—I'm coming for you—*

His phone vibrated with another text. *Van is hurt. She's going to make me disappear.*

The fuck she was. His fingers flew over the phone. *Keep your phone turned on. I'll find you.*

Fear nearly strangled him. Raven had done this?

Again, his phone vibrated. *If I disappear, know...I love you.*

What? His fingers flew fast. *You aren't disappearing. I'm coming for you.*

Nothing.

Gwen?

No response.
Gwen?

***

Her stupid phone wasn't working. The cracked screen was still lit up. She could see Simon's messages to her, but the phone wasn't responding any longer when she touched the screen. *Dammit.* Okay, fine, she could handle this. The car was rolling, moving fast, bumping along a rough road. Simon was going to find her. If her phone was on, then he could trace her, couldn't he?

And since the phone was providing her with plenty of light...

Gwen angled the phone toward the back of the car. There was supposed to be a trunk release lever back there. She'd done a scene like this in a movie once. There should have been a glowing T-handle release lever for the trunk. Except...

There wasn't one. Her frantic fingers flew around the back, and she found rough, cut wires.

The bitch cut the release lever. Because Raven had her plans. Her insane plans to take over Gwen's life.

Too bad—Gwen had plans, too. *To live my own damn life, thank you very much.* She heaved her body around and lifted her feet toward the backseat. Raven was driving. So, if Gwen could manage to kick her way into the backseat, she could attack Raven from behind. She could have the advantage.

She kicked at the seat. Again and again. And at first, nothing happened.

So she kicked harder. She lifted up her hips as she pounded with her feet. Over and over. She wasn't stopping. This was her life on the line. She was going to save herself. She was getting her ass out of there.

And one of the rear seats finally shoved forward.

Gwen cried out in relief. She twisted around and crawled through that opening, her upper body going in the back seat.

"What in the hell are you doing?" Raven shrieked.

Staying alive. What did it look like she was doing? *Fighting* for her life. Gwen dragged herself forward.

Raven's right hand flew back at her, the knife swiping toward Gwen. The blade sliced her arm, but Gwen didn't care. She heaved into the backseat. The car was going hell fast, but she still thrust open the back door. She'd jump out. It would hurt, but she'd survive.

"No!" Raven screamed. "You're not getting away! You're not doing this! *No!*"

Raven was coming at her. Trying to lunge into the backseat. Only the crazy bitch was supposed to be *driving!*

"The car!" Gwen yelled. "Watch the road!"

But it was too late.

The car swerved. Gwen tried to jump out from the back door but Raven was clawing at her. The scream of metal filled Gwen's ears. Glass shattered. Broke. The vehicle began rolling as it left the road. Tumbling over and over. The knife stabbed her. Or was it broken glass? Was glass cutting her? The world was going crazy, and Gwen just wanted one thing. Just one thing—

Simon.

The car slammed hard into something. A tree? The ground?

More metal screamed. More metal crunched. And something hard shoved into Gwen's side, burning deep and trapping her in the car...with the woman who wanted her dead.

***

Simon raced to the scene. Wilde had traced Gwen's phone. It had been on until two minutes ago. *Two minutes.*

Why had the phone turned off?

"She's okay." Ben was beside him.

Eric drove the SUV that tailed them. They were all going in hot to the scene.

"She's going to be okay, man," Ben added, but his voice sounded strained.

She had to be okay.

The cops had gone to the safe house. Van had still been alive, but bleeding like a bastard. He hadn't been able to talk, but he'd scribbled some note to Layla—something about low jacking Gwen's phone with an app so that he could track her. Then he'd just written *Sorry*. Over and over again.

If that prick lived and Gwen didn't...if *anything* happened to Gwen, Simon would make absolutely sure that Van was *sorry* for the rest of his miserable life. And it would be miserable. Miserable and painful. Every. Single. Second.

"Okay, um, we're coming up on the area where her phone gave off its last—"

Simon slammed on the brakes.

"*Jesus!*" Ben's right hand slammed into the dashboard. "Warn somebody when you are about to—"

Simon was already running from the vehicle. He could see the area where the guard-rail had been ripped apart and when he hurtled past that railing, the moon shone down on the wreckage below.

A dark vehicle, smashed and twisted. Steam rising from the crumpled hood. "Gwen!" Simon bellowed her name as he rushed for the vehicle. She had to be inside. She had to be okay.

Broken glass crunched beneath his feet. One of the vehicle's back doors hung open and the interior light from the car flickered—on, off, on—

He saw her in the backseat. A slumped figure with long, dark hair that covered her face. *Oh, God.* "Gwen!" He lunged toward her.

And she leapt up at him, screaming.

Only it wasn't his Gwen.

It was Raven. Wearing another fucking wig and coming at him with her knife. She flew toward him and the blade sliced across his chest. She laughed and yanked the knife up, ready to come at him again—

He whipped up his gun as he took two steps back, moving out of her range. After the cops had taken his main weapon, Simon had made damn sure to keep his backup close. "Don't fucking think about it."

Blood pumped down his chest. The wound stung like hell, but he ignored it. A little blood and pain didn't matter. Only Gwen mattered.

Raven smiled at him. She crawled from the wreckage. Raven threw the wig behind her, but kept a grip on the knife. "I used this to kill her."

Gwen.

"I shoved it into her heart. She's gone. I'm the star now." Blood dripped from the blade. "Knew you'd be a problem. Have to get rid of you, too. Could tell by the way you looked at her. You were obsessed. Like so many others." Glass crunched beneath her feet.

"I'm not obsessed."

Mocking laughter. She gestured with the knife. "Yes, you are. You're—"

"I'm in love with Gwen. Just like I have been since I was nineteen years old." He kept a rock-steady grip on the gun. "Tell me where she is, or I'll start shooting."

More laughter. Laughter with a wicked, wild edge. "Shoot and I'll never tell. *Never tell, never tell!*"

Okay, she was crazy.

Like he hadn't already figured that shit out.

"She's going to disappear," Raven promised. "Just like Xavier disappeared. Gwen is gone, gone, gone, and you won't see her again. You won't ever see—"

"I'll start by shooting you in the leg. The right, then the left. Then when you're on the ground and screaming in pain, I'll take a gut shot. That way, you'll bleed out slowly. You'll suffer and bleed and you'll *beg* to tell me everything I want to know."

Simon heard footsteps rush behind him and knew that Ben and Eric were closing in.

Raven gaped at him. Then she shook her head. "You won't. You're one of the *good* guys. You won't do that, not to me. You don't have it in you, you don't—"

"You don't know me," he cut through her words with a snarl. "And you don't know what I will do for Gwen." Gwen could be hurt. She could need medical attention. She could be *dying*. He didn't have time to waste. "Tell me where she is, or I will start shooting."

"No!" Raven roared at him. "You don't get to save her! She doesn't get to keep it all! She doesn't get *everything!*" And she jumped straight at Simon. "I'll take you from her! I'll take *you!*"

"*Simon?*" Gwen's broken cry. It came from the darkness.

Raven's knife stabbed toward him.

He didn't fire his gun. He didn't have to. He sidestepped her attack. She was wild and frantic and her body twisted—

He kicked the knife out of her hand. She screamed and lunged—

He put the gun right to her forehead. "Don't move a muscle."

Her breath heaved in and out.

"No one will take me from Gwen," he promised softly. "I'm hers, forever."

Eric and Ben rushed toward them. Eric grabbed Raven. She struggled against him, but he just held her tighter.

A siren shrieked in the distance.

"You got her?" Simon demanded of Eric.

"Go!" Eric shouted.

Like Simon had to be told twice. Gwen hadn't called out again, and the silence was scaring the ever-loving-hell out of him. Her cry had come from behind the car, and he raced over there, nearly falling in his haste. And when he rounded the remains of the wreckage...

Gwen was on the ground. Her hands were clasped to her side.

And there was blood. Even in the darkness, he could see the blood.

He fell to his knees beside her. "Baby?"

"I...got out." Her voice was weaker.

Simon's hands rose to her side. Pressed to the wound. *So much blood.* "Get an ambulance!" Simon yelled at Eric and Ben. "*She needs help!*"

Raven started laughing. He hated her laughter. "*Gone, gone, gone!*" Raven chanted.

"Shut her up!" Simon shouted. Gwen's blood was pumping through his fingers.

"I...got out of the car, but something...cut me..."

It was a whole lot more than a cut. "You're going to be absolutely fine." He scooped her into his arms. One hand curled so it could keep pressing over her wound as he held her.

She let out a low, pain-filled moan.

Oh, Jesus. *Jesus.* "Baby, you're going to be okay. We'll get you stitched up and you're going to be okay." He said those same words over and over as he ran back up to the top of the hill. As he began running toward the ambulance that was coming at him with its lights flashing. He couldn't think clearly. Couldn't act clearly.

All he could do was run and hold tight to Gwen.

And then the EMTs were there. Cops were swarming him. Hard hands yanked her away from him and put Gwen in the back of the ambulance. Under that stark, bright light, he saw the dark red of her blood. Saw the paleness of her skin.

"*Gwen, don't leave me!*" He bounded into the ambulance with her. Grabbed her hand. "*Please, baby, stay with me.* Stay with me!"

Her head turned toward him. Her lips tried to curve. "You...found me."

An EMT ripped open her shirt.

Simon brought Gwen's hand to his mouth. Pressed a desperate kiss to her hand. "I love you. I love you, Gwen. *I love you.*"

"Love, you...too..."

Her eyelids were closing, and Simon was *losing* it. Gwen was in pain. Gwen was bleeding. Gwen was weak.

Don't leave, sweetheart. God, just don't leave me!

CHAPTER TWENTY

"Get. The. Fuck. Out. Of. Here."

The low, lethal words pulled Gwen from sleep. Her eyes fluttered open as she glanced around. *A hospital.* She was in a hospital bed and the room was filled with flowers. Roses. Daisies. Tulips. Giant *Get-Well* balloons.

"If I see your fool ass here again, I'll kick the hell out of you."

Ah...that angry voice was wonderfully familiar to Gwen. A smile curled her lips. Everything was okay.

"Her pain is not your lead story. You're not going to get some money-shot of Gwen in her hospital room. Try again, and I will break you."

There was the sound of footsteps frantically running away. Gwen pushed up in the bed, wincing a bit at the stab of pain, right before the hospital door opened.

Simon stood there, holding roses in his hand.

For a moment, he simply stared at her. Raw emotion flashed across his face. Emotion that made her tremble because no one had ever looked at her with such pure love before.

Only Simon.

"You're up," he rasped.

Gwen nodded.

He slipped into the room. Shut the door behind him. Gripped the roses a little too tightly. One petal fell to the floor.

"Jerk paparazzi was trying to get inside. Don't worry." He took a few slow, almost hesitant steps toward the bed. "I have extra guards out there. You're safe."

He was there. Yes, she was safe.

"The doctors say you'll be fine." He was at the side of the bed now. She could see the line of stubble on his jaw. The dark shadows under his eyes. "I've been in here with you. Just left because—"

"You thought I needed more flowers?" Gwen tried to tease.

He swallowed. "No." He put the flowers down on the bedside table. "I wanted to make sure you were safe so I checked the security myself. I almost lost you last night. That shit can't happen again. Not ever."

Gwen reached for his hand. "I'm not going anywhere."

His hand turned over, and his fingers twined with hers. "Neither am I. I'm right where I want to be." His gaze held hers. "With you. I love you, Gwen. I always will."

She was not going to cry. Would not. "I love you."

Simon's smile was absolutely beautiful. She loved the way it lit up his eyes. She just loved him. All of him.

"You need to kiss me," Gwen told him. Her voice was all husky and weak. "Because I have to know this isn't just a dream."

"Sweetheart, you are my dream. The only dream I've ever had." He leaned toward her. Softly, tenderly, his lips pressed to hers. "And I will love you until I take my last breath."

Those pesky tears were stinging her eyes, but she blinked them away. She kissed him. Once, twice.

The nightmare was over. They were safe. She had Simon, and he was all that she needed. Her hand reached up and pressed to his chest. But...was that some kind of bandage beneath his shirt? Gwen sucked in a sharp breath.

"It's okay," Simon reassured her instantly. "Barely just scrapes. Her knife didn't do any serious damage to me."

I want to kill her. Raven had used her knife on Simon?

He eased away, just enough so that he could stare into her eyes. "Raven is in custody. She was behind it all, Gwen. She used Van to hack into your bank account. She transferred the money to Dale. Got him to build the bombs for her. And then she got rid of him."

"Is Van...alive?" Because she knew Raven had wanted to eliminate him, too.

Simon nodded. "Right down the hall. He's the one who told Raven about Xavier. That's how she got the idea to use him as a threat to you. This was never about him. This wasn't about some stalker wanting pictures of you or even wanting your money. Raven played that game—it was all a trick.

She wanted to set this stuff up so that when you vanished..."

"Everyone would think the stalker got me." Villain or victim—wasn't that what Raven had said? Maybe some people would have thought that Gwen faked everything. And others would have thought Gwen had been abducted by the man stalking her.

"She wanted your life," he said, voice thick. "Raven was willing to do anything in order to take it."

But Raven hadn't taken her life. Gwen had survived. And Simon was right there. Telling her that he loved her. They had a second chance. They just had to take it.

Their fingers were still locked together. His touch made her feel better. Stronger. "What happens next?" Gwen asked.

"Raven goes to prison. And she doesn't get out."

"Hell, yes." A pause. "What happens between us?"

Another kiss. Even more tender than the last. "Anything you want, baby. *Anything you want.*"

They could make this work. They'd survived Raven's craziness. They could survive anything. They could do it. They could get their chance at a happy ending.

She'd fight like hell for that chance.

***

One week later...

A knock sounded at her hotel room door. Gwen was back in the presidential suite—only this time, at a different hotel. She'd gotten out of the hospital and the studio had insisted on moving her into a posh location and sending around-the-clock nursing care to her.

She didn't need nursing care.

She didn't need the fancy suite.

She needed Simon.

When she heard the knock at the door, she hurried forward, barely noticing the sting of pain in her side. The stitches would come out soon. She'd be back to normal.

No, better than normal. *Because I've got Simon.*

She gave a quick glance through the peephole and then opened the door.

He was there. Holding more roses. The man was about to drown her in flowers.

"Simon!" Gwen smiled—

He stiffened.

And a very, very bad feeling settled in the pit of her stomach. He wasn't reaching for her. He was just standing there, holding tightly to the flowers.

Her hands dropped to her sides. She'd wanted to go to his place when she left the hospital. But *he'd* agreed with the studio and said that she should go to the suite. Why? Why had he done that? Didn't he want her with him?

"We need to talk."

Oh, jeez. Not the words she wanted to hear. No one ever wanted to hear *those* four words.

Simon cleared his throat. "I made a mistake."

Her skin felt icy.

"When I left you all those years ago, I made the worst mistake of my life. I loved you then, and leaving you—being without you for so long—it was like I had a hole in my heart. In my very soul."

Gwen shook her head.

"I'm sorry, sweetheart. I'm so sorry that I wasn't there when you needed me. And I swear, if you give me the chance, I *will* be there in the future. I will be there for you always." He offered the flowers to her.

Her shaking fingers took them.

And Simon lowered to one knee in front of her. "I want another chance."

She'd had this fantasy. In her head, she'd slammed the door on him. Walked away. But...

No...no, that wasn't the way she'd really wanted the fantasy to end.

He reached into his pocket and pulled out a small, black box. "I will do anything to prove myself to you." Simon opened the box. "Gwen, will you please marry me?"

Okay, the ring hadn't been part of her original fantasy. But it was sure working for her right then. "Why...why didn't you want me to go back to your place?" The question just came out.

His brow furrowed, then cleared. "Because I didn't want bad memories for you. Andy's car exploded there. I didn't want you going back, thinking about that night. We don't need bad memories. I can get a new place. I can go *anywhere,* as long as I have you. We can get a home together. Or, hell, screw that, *you're* my home, Gwen. The only home I want. When I'm with you, I'm happy and complete and I—"

"Yes." She dropped the roses and yanked him up. Pulled him against her. "*Yes.*"

Simon kissed her. It was pretty much one of the best kisses of her life. Sensual and deep and toe-curling, and it just made her want more.

So much more.

Like...a lifetime more.

A lifetime with the man she loved. Kissing and laughing and making love and having a family and being *happy*. Being free. The past was over. She wasn't letting it pull her down any longer.

Not when she had such a bright future waiting.

Not when she had Simon waiting.

Because Simon Forrest belonged to her. He always had.

He always would.

"Yes," Gwen whispered against his mouth.

Reality was way better than her fantasy.

THE END

A NOTE FROM THE AUTHOR

Thank you for reading GUARDING GWEN! I am so glad that you got to know Gwen and Simon. They were a fun couple to write—Gwen was my first actress heroine, and Simon might just be my favorite sexy bodyguard.

If you'd like to stay updated on my releases and sales, please join my newsletter list.

https://cynthiaeden.com/newsletter/

Again, thank you for reading GUARDING GWEN.

Best,
Cynthia Eden
cynthiaeden.com

ABOUT THE AUTHOR

Cynthia Eden is a *New York Times, USA Today, Digital Book World*, and *IndieReader* best-seller.

Cynthia writes sexy tales of contemporary romance, romantic suspense, and paranormal romance. Since she began writing full-time in 2005, Cynthia has written over one hundred novels and novellas.

Cynthia lives along the Alabama Gulf Coast. She loves romance novels, horror movies, and chocolate.

For More Information

- *cynthiaeden.com*
- *facebook.com/cynthiaedenfanpage*

HER OTHER WORKS

Wilde Ways

- Protecting Piper (Book 1)
- Guarding Gwen (Book 2)
- Before Ben (Book 3)
- The Heart You Break (Book 4)
- Fighting For Her (Book 5)
- Ghost Of A Chance (Book 6)
- Crossing The Line (Book 7)
- Counting On Cole (Book 8)
- Chase After Me (Book 9)
- Say I Do (Book 10)

Dark Sins

- Don't Trust A Killer (Book 1)
- Don't Love A Liar (Book 2)

Lazarus Rising

- Never Let Go (Book One)
- Keep Me Close (Book Two)
- Stay With Me (Book Three)
- Run To Me (Book Four)
- Lie Close To Me (Book Five)
- Hold On Tight (Book Six)

- Lazarus Rising Volume One (Books 1 to 3)
- Lazarus Rising Volume Two (Books 4 to 6)

Dark Obsession Series

- Watch Me (Book 1)
- Want Me (Book 2)
- Need Me (Book 3)
- Beware Of Me (Book 4)
- Only For Me (Books 1 to 4)

Mine Series

- Mine To Take (Book 1)
- Mine To Keep (Book 2)
- Mine To Hold (Book 3)
- Mine To Crave (Book 4)
- Mine To Have (Book 5)
- Mine To Protect (Book 6)
- Mine Box Set Volume 1 (Books 1-3)
- Mine Box Set Volume 2 (Books 4-6)

Bad Things

- The Devil In Disguise (Book 1)
- On The Prowl (Book 2)
- Undead Or Alive (Book 3)
- Broken Angel (Book 4)
- Heart Of Stone (Book 5)
- Tempted By Fate (Book 6)
- Wicked And Wild (Book 7)
- Saint Or Sinner (Book 8)
- Bad Things Volume One (Books 1 to 3)
- Bad Things Volume Two (Books 4 to 6)

- Bad Things Deluxe Box Set (Books 1 to 6)

Bite Series

- Forbidden Bite (Bite Book 1)
- Mating Bite (Bite Book 2)

Blood and Moonlight Series

- Bite The Dust (Book 1)
- Better Off Undead (Book 2)
- Bitter Blood (Book 3)
- Blood and Moonlight (The Complete Series)

Purgatory Series

- The Wolf Within (Book 1)
- Marked By The Vampire (Book 2)
- Charming The Beast (Book 3)
- Deal with the Devil (Book 4)
- The Beasts Inside (Books 1 to 4)

Bound Series

- Bound By Blood (Book 1)
- Bound In Darkness (Book 2)
- Bound In Sin (Book 3)
- Bound By The Night (Book 4)
- Bound in Death (Book 5)
- Forever Bound (Books 1 to 4)

Other Romantic Suspense

- Never Gonna Happen
- One Hot Holiday
- Secret Admirer
- First Taste of Darkness

- Sinful Secrets
- Until Death
- Christmas With A Spy

Made in the USA
Coppell, TX
30 December 2024

43731011R00177